Ten Tales
of Adventure

[See page 4

So thinking, he drew his sword and tried to set his back against the door

Ten Tales of Adventure

chosen and edited by
Roger Lancelyn Green

with colour frontispiece
and line drawings by
Philip Gough

London: J. M. Dent & Sons Ltd
New York: E. P. Dutton & Co. Inc.

ROGER LANCELYN GREEN *was born on 2nd November 1918 at Norwich, but has spent most of his life at Poulton-Lancelyn in Cheshire, where his ancestors have been Lords of the Manor for thirty generations. He spent most of his childhood at home, owing to ill health, but in 1937 entered Merton College, Oxford, where he took an honours degree in English Language and Literature, followed by the post-graduate degree of Bachelor of Letters, and later was Deputy Librarian of the college for five years. He has also been a professional actor, an antiquarian bookseller, a schoolmaster and a Research Fellow at Liverpool University for short periods. Since 1950 he has lived at Poulton-Lancelyn and devoted most of his time to writing.*

Besides scholarly works on Andrew Lang, Lewis Carroll, A. E. W. Mason, J. M. Barrie and others, he has written many books for young readers. These include adventure stories such as 'The Theft of the Golden Cat' (1955), fairytale fantasies such as 'The Land of the Lord High Tiger' (1958), and romances set in Greece of the legendary period such as 'Mystery at Mycenae' (1957) and 'the Luck of Troy' (1961). But he is best known for his retelling of the old myths and legends, from 'King Arthur' (1953) and 'Robin Hood' (1956) to 'Heroes of Greece and Troy' (1960) and 'Myths of the Norsemen' (1962). He has visited Egypt once and Greece many times, and has written about them for young readers, telling of their history as well as of their legends— his own favourites being 'Old Greek Fairy Tales' (1958), his adventure story set in ancient Greece, Scandinavia and Britain 'The Land Beyond the North' (1958), 'Ancient Egypt' (1963) aud 'The book of Dragons' (1970).

Included in this series are 'A Book of Myths' (1965), 'Ten Tales of Detection' (1967), 'The Tale of Ancient Israel' (1969), and 'Thirteen Uncanny Tales' (1969).

DENT 0 460 05093 1
DUTTON 0-525-40875-4

Acknowledgements

The compiler and publishers are grateful to the following for permission to include copyright material:

The Executors of the Estate of H. Rider Haggard for 'Magepa the Buck' from *Smith and the Pharaohs* by H. Rider Haggard; the Executors of the Estate of Stanley Weyman for 'The King's Stratagem' from *In King's Byways* by Stanley Weyman; the Trustees of the Estate of Sir Arthur Conan Doyle, John Murray (Publishers) Ltd and the Estate of Sir Arthur Conan Doyle for 'How the Brigadier Saved an Army' from *Adventures of Gerard* by Sir Arthur Conan Doyle; Mrs Bambridge, the Macmillan Companies, Doubleday & Company Inc. for 'Red Dog' from *The Second Jungle Book* by Rudyard Kipling; Trinity College, Oxford, for 'The Cruise of the *Willing Mind*' from *Ensign Knightley and other stories* by A. E. W. Mason; the Estate of the late Baroness Orczy, and Cassell & Co. Ltd for 'A Question of Passports' from *League of the Scarlet Pimpernel* by Baroness Orczy; the Tweedsmuir Trustees and Blackwood and Sons for 'The Lemnian' from *The Moon Endureth* by John Buchan; and the Estate of Anthony Hope for 'The Sin of the Bishop of Modenstein' from *The Heart of Princess Osra* by Anthony Hope.

Sources

'The Sire de Malétroit's Door' by Robert Louis Stevenson (1850–1894) appeared originally in the magazine *Temple Bar* for January 1878 before being collected in *The New Arabian Nights* in 1882. Sir Henry Rider Haggard (1856–1925) told his first adventure story in the person of Allan Quatermain, *King Solomon's Mines* in 1885; his short story 'Magepa the Buck' first appeared in *Pears' Christmas Annual* in 1912 and was collected in *Smith and the Pharaohs, and Other Stories* (1920). 'The King's Stratagem' by Stanley John Weyman (1855–1928) is from his collection of historical tales *In Kings' Byways* (1902) but had been published in *The Strand Magazine* for April 1891. 'How the Brigadier saved an Army' by Sir Arthur Conan Doyle (1859–1930) also appeared in *The Strand Magazine*, in November 1902, before being collected in *The Adventures of Gerard* the following year. 'Red Dog', the last but one of the Mowgli stories by Rudyard Kipling (1865–1936) was first published under the title of 'Good Hunting!' in *The Pall Mall Gazette* 29th and 30th July 1895 and collected in *The Second Jungle Book* a few months later. Sir Anthony Hope Hawkins (1863–1933), who wrote as 'Anthony Hope', included 'The Sin of the Bishop of Modenstein' in *The Heart of Princess Osra* (1896), which was serialized in *The Idler* during the previous year. 'Captain Pink' by Andrew Lang (1844–1912) is reprinted here for the first time since its original appearance in *The Pall Mall Magazine* for May 1904. 'The Cruise of the *Willing Mind*', by Alfred Edward Woodley Mason (1865–1948) appeared on 1st December 1900 in *The Illustrated London News* and was collected the following year in *Ensign Knightley, and Other Stories*. 'A Question of Passports' by Baroness Orczy (1865–1947) comes from her collection of short stories *The League of the Scarlet Pimpernel* (1919); and 'The Lemnian' by John Buchan (1875–1940) after appearing in *Blackwood's Magazine* was collected in *The Moon Endureth* (1912).

R. L. G.

Contents

Illustrations

Colour

So, thinking, he drew his sword and tried to set his back against the door *frontispiece*

Black and White

Introduction

'Dost never dream of adventures, Morrice? A life brimful of them, and a quick death at the end?' cries a character in *The Courtship of Morrice Buckler* (1896), A. E. W. Mason's first tale of adventure—and that dream was the inspiration of all the stories in this book.

The earliest of them was written nearly a hundred years ago, and the latest well over fifty: for the 'Age of the Storytellers' was an age of peace and high civilization, before the days of world wars and the bombing of civilians, in the Golden Age between the last of the highwaymen and the first of the hijackers.

With peace and tranquillity all about them, readers longed for more books of excitement and adventure than ever before or since, and writers sought for it chiefly in the past, since in the present adventure and danger were hard to find, except in distant places still remote and romantic before the days of television and air travel.

The authors who wrote the stories in this selection are some of the most skilful guides into the lands of adventure that have ever undertaken to transport us there. Most of them wrote longer books, some of which may be found in the same series as these shorter Tales of Adventure, but I have tried to choose stories which not only do full justice to their powers of enchantment, but also represent the kind of story they were best at writing and to introduce characters or scenes about which they wrote at greater length elsewhere, or for which they are particularly famous.

Robert Louis Stevenson, the earliest and one of the greatest, is best known for *Treasure Island*. He wrote no other tales of pirates, but his stories set in more definite historical periods and backgrounds, such as *Kidnapped*, and *Catriona* and *The Black Arrow*, are almost as well loved as the adventures of Jim Hawkins and Long John Silver. One of his earliest, 'The Sire de Malétroit's Door', first published in 1878, is also one of the most perfect of romantic adventures, and needs no historical knowledge to enjoy simply for its excitement and for its charming and unexpected love story.

Another love story, but with a difference, is set in an historical period too, but in a country that you will not find in the ordinary history books. Princess Osra was an Elphberg, the ruling family of Ruritania, the land whose capital is Strelsau and whose most interesting historical monument is the Castle of Zenda. The story of how the Englishman Rudolf Rassendyll rescued the Prisoner of Zenda—a later King of Ruritania—and won the love of Princess Flavia is perhaps the most famous and satisfying of all adventure stories. The Bishop of Modenstein did not win his princess either, for in both cases duty came before inclination— and he, as a bishop in the Roman Catholic Church, was vowed to live a single life and could not go seeking a wife. But he was a Hentzau—and so, as one would expect, he was as ready for dare-devilry and dashing adventure as a more famous member of his family in later years, whose final adventures Anthony Hope chronicled in *Rupert of Hentzau*.

Other writers may not have invented countries for their stories of adventure, but they did invent characters to have the adven-tures—or adventures for real historical characters to have, quite unrecorded by historians.

Andrew Lang, who is best remembered now for his fairy tales, both the invented ones set in another country of the imagination such as *Prince Prigio* who became King of Pantouflia, and for his retellings of the old fairy tales of the world in the Fairy Books of many colours, wished even more to be remembered for his historical romances. He did not succeed quite as well as most of the authors in this book, though the Jacobite romance, *Parson Kelly*, which he and A. E. W. Mason wrote together, is unde-servedly forgotten. But one of his shorter stories, 'Captain Pink', shows his love of adventure and his great knowledge of Jacobite intrigues. As a serious historian Lang wrote a life of Bonnie Prince Charlie and several volumes of 'Historical Mysteries' most of which took place in the Jacobite period and most of which he was able to solve—so one cannot be quite sure that he did not have some real bit of secret history in the background of 'Captain Pink' as he certainly did in *Parson Kelly*. The background of the story is true enough and was one of the most romantic adventures in history: 'Bonnie Prince Charlie' had landed in Scotland in 1745 with nine followers and was now marching into England at the head of an army to make his father, 'James III', no longer 'the King over the water' but the king indeed—and send George II across the sea. Bad luck attended Prince Charles, and many of his supporters allowed private feuds to prevent them from giving the support that might have brought his cause to victory. Perhaps the adventure of Captain Pink also played its part in the downfall of the last of the Stuarts—in spite of all that Kate could do: and *she* was a Wogan, and it was her Uncle Charles who had rescued Princess Clementina from prison in Innsbruck with only three companions, and brought her to become the wife of the 'Old Pretender', James III, and mother of the 'Young Pretender', Prince Charlie.

The rescue of Clementina formed the plot of one of A. E. W. Mason's earlier and most famous historical romances. He is best remembered now for his story of contemporary adventure, *The Four Feathers*, and for the doings of his great French detective, Inspector Hanaud, *At the Villa Rose* and in several other cases. To show that adventures as exciting as any in historical times take place every day, the story included here, 'The Cruise of the *Willing Mind*', tells of a contemporary sea adventure—and Mason himself 'served before the mast' on a sailing ship in the North Sea for one cruise at least before writing this story—to earn a Master Mariner's certificate and later own a yacht, before becoming one of the most successful secret agents off the coast of Spain in the First World War.

Another writer of adventure stories who had himself taken part in exciting adventures was Rider Haggard. Though he did not actually fight in the Zulu War of 1879 (had the volunteer regiment which he had joined taken part in the Battle of Isandhlwana, Haggard would probably not have survived to tell the tale), he had many adventures and narrow escapes during his years in South Africa at the time of the Zulu War and the First Boer War. He also had many friends, some of them Zulus, from whom he heard first-hand stories out of Zulu and Boer history which later formed a uniquely authentic background to his great historical romances such as *Nada the Lily* and *Marie* and *Child of Storm*. Haggard's most popular character, Allan Quatermain, the hero of

King Solomon's Mines and many of his South African stories, was, as he once wrote, 'only myself set in a variety of imagined situations, thinking my thoughts and looking at life through my eyes'. And so we have here an incident in Allan's adventurous career, the story of 'Magepa the Buck'—perhaps based on a real event that one of Haggard's Zulu friends told to him, and certainly based on the heroic Zulu character which he had such excellent opportunities of observing.

Sir Arthur Conan Doyle also lived an adventurous life, or at least was ready for any adventure that was going. As a young man he worked as ship's doctor on several voyages, including one to the edge of the Arctic regions, and he wrote histories both of the Great Boer War and the First World War often based on personal observations on the battlefields. He is, of course, best known for the creation of Sherlock Holmes, the most famous detective of fact or fiction; but he was always better pleased when readers and critics praised his historical stories, which he considered to be his real contribution to literature. How successful *The White Company* and *The Refugees* really are depends very much on individual taste, but there is no doubt that he created a character second only to Holmes in his Brigadier Gerard—the superbly conceited and self-centred French officer of Napoleon's army who yet proves himself again and again not merely a reckless adventurer but a truly brave and heroic soldier.

Besides the seventeen adventures of Brigadier Gerard, Doyle wrote two historical romances about the Napoleonic Wars, and achieved not merely historical accuracy in his background but a vivid glimpse into the world where these things happened: one of the most important achievements of the successful historical novelist.

An even more meticulous historian who wrote romances as thrilling as any was Stanley Weyman whose special interest was also in French history—but of an earlier period than that of Napoleon. His most famous books such as *The House of the Wolf* and *Under the Red Robe* present many of the most exciting episodes in French history, from the Massacre on St Bartholomew's Eve in 1572 to the early years of Louis XIV a century later. One of the most romantic characters from the earlier part of this period, Henry of Navarre, is the hero of 'The King's Stratagem'—a story which is but one among the many included in *From the Memoirs of a Minister of France* and *In Kings' Byways* which show Weyman at his very best.

Yet another period in French history supplied Baroness Orczy with unlimited material for her ten full-length romances and two collections of short stories about the Scarlet Pimpernel whose mission in life was to rescue victims doomed in the French Revolution of 1789 to die beneath the cruel blade of 'Madame la Guillotine'.

Exciting though Baroness Orczy's stories are, she was a less good writer than any of the storytellers so far mentioned. Yet she was able to invent one of the few characters in fiction whom everyone knows by name. Very few reach this unexpected eminence, and they are an oddly mixed selection: over the last hundred years perhaps only Sherlock Holmes, Peter Pan, the Scarlet Pimpernel and Tarzan of the Apes have achieved it. Perhaps James Bond among the moderns will take his place as the greatest of secret agents; but maybe he will hold that position no longer than such a once-famous predecessor as Richard Hannay of *The Thirty-Nine Steps*.

John Buchan wrote other kinds of stories as well as the thrilling adventures of Hannay and his friends. He himself considered that his own best books were his historical romances such as *Midwinter* and *Witch Wood*, and among his shorter tales 'The Lemnian' was one that pleased him most. In it we go farther back in history than any other tale in the present collection—back to the days when Xerxes, the great King of Persia, was trying to conquer the known world, and was turned back from adding Europe to his Empire by the various peoples of Greece who for once gave up quarrelling among themselves and united to defeat an army ten times greater than their own. At Thermopylae the little band of Spartans under Leonidas was betrayed by a traitor who showed the Persians a secret path over the mountains. Leonidas and his Spartans were overcome and died bravely, scorning to yield or flee. Xerxes marched his armies down to Athens and destroyed the city; but the united forces of the Hellenes—Athenians, Spartans and the rest—defeated his fleet at Salamis and his army at Plataea, and the Persians never again dared to invade Greece.

An even greater writer of short stories than Buchan, Rudyard

Kipling, also tried his hand at historical adventures in *Puck of Pook's Hill* and *Rewards and Fairies*. But the best known of all the characters whom he created was Mowgli, the Indian boy who was brought up by the wolves and became Master of the Jungle. And so, as a change from history, we have one of Mowgli's most memorable adventures, when he saved his jungle from an invasion of a different kind—the terrible Red Dogs, the Dholes of the Deccan. Indeed Mowgli holds such a special place in the affections of so many readers that no book of tales by the great storytellers of the last hundred years would be complete without one of his exploits.

ROGER LANCELYN GREEN

Robert Louis Stevenson

The Sire de Malétroit's Door

Denis de Beaulieu was not yet two-and-twenty, but he counted himself a grown man, and a very accomplished cavalier into the bargain. Lads were early formed in that rough, warfaring epoch; and when one has been in a pitched battle and a dozen raids, has killed one's man in an honourable fashion, and knows a thing or two of strategy and mankind, a certain swagger in the gait is surely to be pardoned. He had put up his horse with due care, and supped with due deliberation; and then, in a very agreeable frame of mind, went out to pay a visit in the grey of the evening. It was not a very wise proceeding on the young man's part. He would have done better to remain beside the fire or go decently to bed. For the town was full of the troops of Burgundy and England under a mixed command; and though Denis was there on safe-conduct, his safe-conduct was like to serve him little on a chance encounter.

It was September 1429; the weather had fallen sharp; a flighty piping wind, laden with showers, beat about the township; and the dead leaves ran riot along the streets. Here and there a window was already lighted up; and the noise of men-at-arms making merry over supper within, came forth in fits and was swallowed up and carried away by the wind. The night fell swiftly; the flag of England, fluttering on the spire top, grew ever fainter and fainter against the flying clouds—a black speck like a swallow in the tumultuous, leaden chaos of the sky. As the night fell the wind rose and began to hoot under archways and roar amid the tree tops in the valley below the town.

Denis de Beaulieu walked fast and was soon knocking at his

friend's door; but though he promised himself to stay only a little
while and make an early return, his welcome was so pleasant, and
he found so much to delay him, that it was already long past
midnight before he said goodbye upon the threshold. The wind
had fallen again in the meanwhile; the night was as black as the
grave; not a star, nor a glimmer of moonshine, slipped through
the canopy of cloud. Denis was ill-acquainted with the intricate
lanes of Château Landon; even by daylight he had found some
trouble in picking his way; and in this absolute darkness he soon
lost it altogether. He was certain of one thing only—to keep
mounting the hill; for his friend's house lay at the lower end, or
tail, of Château Landon, while the inn was up at the head, under
the great church spire. With this clue to go upon he stumbled
and groped forward, now breathing more freely in open places
where there was a good slice of sky overhead, now feeling along
the wall in stifling closes. It is an eerie and mysterious position
to be thus submerged in opaque blackness in an almost unknown
town. The silence is terrifying in its possibilities. The touch of
cold window bars to the exploring hand startles the man like the
touch of a toad; the inequalities of the pavement shake his heart
into his mouth; a piece of denser darkness threatens an ambuscade
or a chasm in the pathway; and where the air is brighter, the
houses put on strange and bewildering appearances, as if to lead
him farther from his way. For Denis, who had to regain his inn
without attracting notice, there was real danger as well as mere
discomfort in the walk; and he went warily and boldly at once,
and at every corner paused to make an observation.

He had been for some time threading a lane so narrow that
he could touch a wall with either hand, when it began to open
out and go sharply downward. Plainly this lay no longer in the
direction of the inn; but the hope of a little more light tempted
him forward to reconnoitre. The lane ended in a terrace with a
bartisan wall, which gave an outlook between high houses, as
out of an embrasure, into the valley lying dark and formless
several hundred feet below. Denis looked down, and could
discern a few tree tops waving and a single speck of brightness
where the river ran across a weir. The weather was clearing up,
and the sky had lightened, so as to show the outline of the
heavier clouds and the dark margin of the hills. By the uncertain

2

glimmer, the house on his left hand should be a place of some pretensions; it was surmounted by several pinnacles and turret tops; the round stern of a chapel, with a fringe of flying buttresses, projected boldly from the main block; and the door was sheltered under a deep porch carved with figures and overhung by two long gargoyles. The windows of the chapel gleamed through their intricate tracery with a light as of many tapers, and threw out the buttresses and the peaked roof in a more intense blackness against the sky. It was plainly the hotel of some great family of the neighbourhood; and as it reminded Denis of a town house of his own at Bourges, he stood for some time gazing up at it and mentally gauging the skill of the architects and the consideration of the two families.

There seemed to be no issue to the terrace but the lane by which he had reached it; he could only retrace his steps, but he had gained some notion of his whereabouts, and hoped by this means to hit the main thoroughfare and speedily regain the inn. He was reckoning without that chapter of accidents which was to make this night memorable above all others in his career; for he had not gone back above a hundred yards before he saw a light coming to meet him, and heard loud voices speaking together in the echoing narrows of the lane. It was a party of men-at-arms going the night-round with torches. Denis assured himself that they had all been making free with the wine-bowl, and were in no mood to be particular about safe-conducts or the niceties of chivalrous war. It was as like as not that they would kill him like a dog and leave him where he fell. The situation was inspiriting, but nervous. Their own torches would conceal him from sight, he reflected; and he hoped that they would drown the noise of his footsteps with their own empty voices. If he were but fleet and silent, he might evade their notice altogether.

Unfortunately, as he turned to beat a retreat, his foot rolled upon a pebble; he fell against the wall with an ejaculation, and his sword rang loudly on the stones. Two or three voices demanded who went there—some in French, some in English; but Denis made no reply, and ran the faster down the lane. Once upon the terrace, he paused to look back. They still kept calling after him, and just then began to double the pace in pursuit, with a considerable clank of armour, and great tossing of the torch-light to and fro in the narrow jaws of the passage.

Denis cast a look around and darted into the porch. There he might escape observation, or—if that were too much to expect—was in a capital posture whether for parley or defence. So thinking, he drew his sword and tried to set his back against the door. To his surprise, it yielded behind his weight; and though he turned in a moment, continued to swing back on oiled and noiseless hinges, until it stood wide open on a black interior. When things fall out opportunely for the person concerned, he is not apt to be critical about the how or why, his own immediate personal convenience seeming a sufficient reason for the strangest oddities and revolutions in our sublunary things; and so Denis, without a moment's hesitation, stepped within and partly closed the door behind him to conceal his place of refuge. Nothing was further from his thoughts than to close it altogether; but for some inexplicable reason—perhaps by a spring or a weight—the ponderous mass of oak whipped itself out of his fingers and clanked to, with a formidable rumble and a noise like the falling of an automatic bar.

The round, at that very moment, debouched upon the terrace and proceeded to summon him with shouts and curses. He heard them ferreting in the dark corners, the stock of a lance even rattled along the outer surface of the door behind which he stood; but these gentlemen were in too high a humour to be long delayed, and soon made off down a corkscrew pathway which had escaped Denis's observation, and passed out of sight and hearing along the battlements of the town.

Denis breathed again. He gave them a few minutes' grace for fear of accidents, and then groped about for some means of opening the door and slipping forth again. The inner surface was quite smooth, not a handle, not a moulding, not a projection of any sort. He got his fingernails round the edges and pulled, but the mass was immovable. He shook it; it was as firm as a rock. Denis de Beaulieu frowned and gave vent to a little noise-less whistle. What ailed the door? he wondered. Why was it open? How came it to shut so easily and so effectually after him? There was something obscure and underhand about all this that was little to the young man's fancy. It looked like a snare; and yet who would suppose a snare in such a quiet by-street and in a house of so prosperous and even noble an exterior? And yet—snare or no snare, intentionally or unintentionally—here he was, prettily trapped; and for the life of him he could see no way out of it again. The darkness began to weigh upon him. He gave ear; all was silent without, but within and close by he seemed to catch a faint sighing, a faint sobbing rustle, a little stealthy creak—as though many persons were at his side, holding themselves quite still, and governing even their respiration with the extreme of slyness. The idea went to his vitals with a shock, and he faced about suddenly as if to defend his life. Then, for the first time, he became aware of a light about the level of his eyes and at some distance in the interior of the house—a vertical thread of light, widening towards the bottom, such as might escape between two wings of arras over a doorway. To see anything was a relief to Denis; it was like a piece of solid ground to a man labouring in a morass; his mind seized upon it with avidity; and he stood staring at it and trying to piece together some logical conception of his surroundings. Plainly there was a flight of steps ascending from his own level to that of this illuminated doorway; and indeed he thought he could make out another thread of light, as fine as a needle, and as faint as phosphorescence, which might very well be reflected along the polished wood of a handrail. Since he had begun to suspect that he was not alone, his heart had continued to beat with smothering violence, and an intolerable desire for action of any sort had possessed itself of his spirit. He was in deadly peril, he believed. What could be more natural than to mount the staircase, lift the curtain, and confront his difficulty at once? At least he would be dealing with something tangible; at least he would be no longer in the dark. He stepped slowly forward with outstretched hand, until his foot struck the bottom step; then he rapidly scaled the stairs, stood for a moment to compose his expression, lifted the arras, and went in.

He found himself in a large apartment of polished stone. There were three doors; one on each of three sides; all similarly curtained with tapestry. The fourth side was occupied by two large windows and a great stone chimney-piece, carved with the arms of the Malétroits. Denis recognized the bearings, and was

Robert Louis Stevenson

gratified to find himself in such good hands. The room was strongly illuminated; but it contained little furniture except a heavy table and a chair or two, the hearth was innocent of fire, and the pavement was but sparsely strewn with rushes clearly many days old.

On a high chair beside the chimney, and directly facing Denis as he entered, sat a little old gentleman in a fur tippet. He sat with his legs crossed and his hands folded, and a cup of spiced wine stood by his elbow on a bracket on the wall. His countenance had a strongly masculine cast; not properly human, but such as we see in the bull, the goat, or the domestic boar; something equivocal and wheedling, something greedy, brutal, and dangerous. The upper lip was inordinately full, as though swollen by a blow or a toothache; and the smile, the peaked eyebrows, and the small, strong eyes were quaintly and almost comically evil in expression. Beautiful white hair hung straight all round his head, like a saint's, and fell in a single curl upon the tippet. His beard and moustache were the pink of venerable sweetness. Age, probably in consequence of inordinate precautions, had left no mark upon his hands; and the Malétroit hand was famous. It would be difficult to imagine anything at once so fleshy and so delicate in design; the tapered, sensual fingers were like those of one of Leonardo's women; the fork of the thumb made a dimpled protuberance when closed; the nails were perfectly shaped, and of a dead, surprising whiteness. It rendered his aspect tenfold more redoubtable, that a man with hands like these should keep them devoutly folded in his lap like a virgin martyr—that a man with so intense and startling an expression of face should sit patiently on his seat and contemplate people with an unwinking stare, like a god, or a god's statue. His quiescence seemed ironical and treacherous, it fitted so poorly with his looks.

Such was Alain, Sire de Malétroit.

Denis and he looked silently at each other for a second or two.

'Pray step in,' said the Sire de Malétroit. 'I have been expecting you all the evening.'

He had not arisen, but he accompanied his words with a smile and a slight but courteous inclination of the head. Partly from the smile, partly from the strange musical murmur with which the Sire prefaced his observation, Denis felt a strong shudder

6

of disgust go through his marrow. And what with disgust and honest confusion of mind, he could scarcely get words together in reply.

'I fear,' he said, 'that this is a double accident. I am not the person you suppose me. It seems you were looking for a visit; but for my part, nothing was further from my thoughts—nothing could be more contrary to my wishes—than this intrusion.'

'Well, well,' replied the old gentleman indulgently, 'here you are, which is the main point. Seat yourself, my friend, and put yourself entirely at your ease. We shall arrange our little affairs presently.'

Denis perceived that the matter was still complicated with some misconception, and he hastened to continue his explanation.

'Your door . . .' he began.

'About my door?' asked the other, raising his peaked eyebrows. 'A little piece of ingenuity.' And he shrugged his shoulders. 'A hospitable fancy! By your own account, you were not desirous of making my acquaintance. We old people look for such reluctance now and then; and when it touches our honour, we cast about until we find some way of overcoming it. You arrive uninvited, but believe me, very welcome.'

'You persist in error, sir,' said Denis. 'There can be no question between you and me. I am a stranger in this countryside. My name is Denis, damoiseau de Beaulieu. If you see me in your house, it is only——'

'My young friend,' interrupted the other, 'you will permit me to have my own ideas on that subject. They probably differ from yours at the present moment,' he added, with a leer, 'but time will show which of us is in the right.'

Denis was convinced he had to do with a lunatic. He seated himself with a shrug, content to wait the upshot; and a pause ensued, during which he thought he could distinguish a hurried gabbling as of prayer from behind the arras immediately opposite him. Sometimes there seemed to be but one person engaged, sometimes two; and the vehemence of the voice, low as it was, seemed to indicate either great haste or an agony of spirit. It occurred to him that this piece of tapestry covered the entrance to the chapel he had noticed from without.

The old gentleman meanwhile surveyed Denis from head to

foot with a smile, and from time to time emitted little noises like a bird or a mouse, which seemed to indicate a high degree of satisfaction. This state of matters became rapidly insupportable; and Denis to put an end to it, remarked politely that the wind had gone down.

The old gentleman fell into a fit of silent laughter, so prolonged and violent that he became quite red in the face. Denis got upon his feet at once, and put on his hat with a flourish.

'Sir,' he said, 'if you are in your wits, you have affronted me grossly. If you are out of them, I flatter myself I can find better employment for my brains than to talk with lunatics. My conscience is clear; you have made a fool of me from the first moment; you have refused to hear my explanations; and now there is no power under God will make me stay here any longer; and if I cannot make my way out in a more decent fashion, I will hack your door in pieces with my sword.'

The Sire de Malétroit raised his right hand and wagged it at Denis with the fore and little fingers extended.

'My dear nephew,' he said, 'sit down.'

'Nephew!' retorted Denis, 'you lie in your throat'; and he snapped his fingers in his face.

'Sit down, you rogue!' cried the old gentleman, in a sudden harsh voice, like the barking of a dog. 'Do you fancy,' he went on, 'that when I had made my little contrivance for the door I had stopped short with that? If you prefer to be bound hand and foot till your bones ache, rise and try to go away. If you choose to remain a free young buck, agreeably conversing with an old gentleman—why, sit where you are in peace, and God be with you.'

'Do you mean I am a prisoner?' demanded Denis.

'I state the facts,' replied the other. 'I would rather leave the conclusion to yourself.'

Denis sat down again. Externally he managed to keep pretty calm; but within, he was now boiling with anger, now chilled with apprehension. He no longer felt convinced that he was dealing with a madman. And if the old gentleman was sane, what, in God's name, had he to look for? What absurd or tragical adventure had befallen him? What countenance was he to assume?

While he was thus unpleasantly reflecting, the arras that overhung the chapel door was raised, and a tall priest in his robes

8

came forth and, giving a long, keen stare at Denis, said something in an undertone to the Sire de Malétroit.

'She is in a better frame of spirit?' asked the latter.

'She is more resigned, messire,' replied the priest.

'Now the Lord help her, she is hard to please!' sneered the old gentleman. 'A likely stripling—not ill-born—and of her own choosing, too? Why, what more would the jade have?'

'The situation is not usual for a young damsel,' said the other, 'and somewhat trying to her blushes.'

'She should have thought of that before she began the dance. It was none of my choosing, God knows that: but since she is in it, by our Lady, she shall carry it to the end.' And then addressing Denis, 'Monsieur de Beaulieu,' he asked, 'may I present you to my niece? She has been waiting your arrival, I may say, with even greater impatience than myself.'

Denis had resigned himself with a good grace—all he desired was to know the worst of it as speedily as possible; so he rose at once, and bowed in acquiescence. The Sire de Malétroit followed his example and limped, with the assistance of the chaplain's arm, towards the chapel door. The priest pulled aside the arras, and all three entered. The building had considerable architectural pretensions. A light groining sprang from six stout columns, and hung down in two rich pendants from the centre of the vault. The place terminated behind the altar in a round end, embossed and honeycombed with a superfluity of ornament in relief, and pierced by many little windows shaped like stars, trefoils, or wheels. These windows were imperfectly glazed, so that the night air circulated freely in the chapel. The tapers, of which there must have been half a hundred burning on the altar, were unmercifully blown about; and the light went through many different phases of brilliancy and semi-eclipse. On the steps in front of the altar knelt a young girl richly attired as a bride. A chill settled over Denis as he observed her costume; he fought with desperate energy against the conclusion that was thrust upon his mind; it could not—it should not—be as he feared.

'Blanche,' said the Sire, in his most flute-like tones, 'I have brought a friend to see you, my little girl; turn round and give him your pretty hand. It is good to be devout; but it is necessary to be polite, my niece.'

9

The girl rose to her feet and turned towards the newcomers. She moved all of a piece; and shame and exhaustion were expressed in every line of her fresh young body; and she held her head down and kept her eyes upon the pavement, as she came slowly forward. In the course of her advance, her eyes fell upon Denis de Beaulieu's feet—feet of which he was justly vain, be it remarked, and wore in the most elegant accoutrement even while travelling. She paused—started, as if his yellow boots had conveyed some shocking meaning—and glanced suddenly up into the wearer's countenance. Their eyes met; shame gave place to horror and terror in her looks; the blood left her lips; with a piercing scream she covered her face with her hands and sank upon the chapel floor.

'That is not the man!' she cried. 'My uncle, that is not the man!'

The Sire de Malétroit chirped agreeably. 'Of course not,' he said; 'I expected as much. It was so unfortunate you could not remember his name.'

'Indeed,' she cried, 'indeed, I have never seen this person till this moment—I have never so much as set eyes upon him— I never wish to see him again. Sir,' she said, turning to Denis, 'if you are a gentleman, you will bear me out. Have I ever seen you—have you ever seen me—before this accursed hour!'

'To speak for myself, I have never had that pleasure,' answered the young man. 'This is the first time, messire, that I have met with your engaging niece.'

The old gentleman shrugged his shoulders.

'I am distressed to hear it,' he said. 'But it is never too late to begin. I had little more acquaintance with my own late lady ere I married her; which proves,' he added with a grimace, 'that these impromptu marriages may often produce an excellent understanding in the long run. As the bridegroom is to have a voice in the matter, I will give him two hours to make up for lost time before we proceed with the ceremony.' And he turned towards the door, followed by the clergyman.

The girl was on her feet in a moment. 'My uncle, you cannot be in earnest,' she said. 'I declare before God I will stab myself rather than be forced on that young man. The heart rises at it; God forbids such marriages; you dishonour your white hair.

Oh, my uncle, pity me! There is not a woman in all the world but would prefer death to such a nuptial. Is it possible,' she added, faltering, 'is it possible that you do not believe me—that you still think this'—and she pointed at Denis with a tremor of anger and contempt—'that you still think *this* to be the man?'

'Frankly,' said the old gentleman, pausing on the threshold, 'I do. But let me explain to you once for all, Blanche de Malétroit, my way of thinking about this affair. When you took it into your head to dishonour my family and the name that I have borne, in peace and war, for more than three-score years, you forfeited, not only the right to question my designs, but that of looking me in the face. If your father had been alive, he would have spat on you and turned you out of doors. His was the hand of iron. You may bless your God you have only to deal with the hand of velvet, mademoiselle. It was my duty to get you married without delay. Out of pure goodwill, I have tried to find your own gallant for you. And I believe I have succeeded. But before God and all the holy angels, Blanche de Malétroit, if I have not, I care not one jack-straw. So let me recommend you to be polite to our young friend; for upon my word, your next groom may be less appetizing.'

And with that he went out, with the chaplain at his heels; and the arras fell behind the pair.

The girl turned upon Denis with flashing eyes.

'And what, sir,' she demanded, 'may be the meaning of all this?'

'God knows,' returned Denis gloomily. 'I am a prisoner in this house, which seems full of mad people. More I know not, and nothing do I understand.'

'And how came you here?' she asked.

He told her as briefly as he could. 'For the rest,' he added, 'perhaps you will follow my example, and tell me the answer to all these riddles, and what, in God's name, is like to be the end of it.'

She stood silent for a little, and he could see her lips tremble and her tearless eyes burn with a feverish lustre. Then she pressed her forehead in both hands.

'Alas, how my head aches!' she said wearily—'to say nothing of my poor heart! But it is due to you to know my story, unmaidenly as it must seem. I am called Blanche de Malétroit; I have been without father or mother for—oh! for as long as I can recollect, and indeed I have been most unhappy all my life. Three months ago a young captain began to stand near me every day in church. I could see that I pleased him; I am much to blame, but I was so glad that anyone should love me; and when he passed me a letter, I took it home with me and read it with great pleasure. Since that time he has written many. He was so anxious to speak with me, poor fellow! and kept asking me to leave the door open some evening that we might have two words upon the stair. For he knew how much my uncle trusted me.' She gave something like a sob at that, and it was a moment before she could go on. 'My uncle is a hard man, but he is very shrewd,' she said at last. 'He has performed many feats in war, and was a great person at court, and much trusted by Queen Isabeau in old days. How he came to suspect me I cannot tell; but it is hard to keep anything from his knowledge; and this morning, as we came from mass, he took my hand in his, forced it open, and read my little billet, walking by my side all the while. When he had finished, he gave it back to me with great politeness. It contained another request to have the door left open; and this has been the ruin of us all. My uncle kept me strictly in my room until evening, and then ordered me to dress myself as you see me—a hard mockery for a young girl, do you not think so? I suppose, when he could not prevail with me to tell him the young captain's name, he must have laid a trap for him: into which you have fallen in the anger of God. I looked for much confusion; for how could I tell whether he was willing to take me for his wife on these sharp terms? He might have been trifling with me from the first; or I might have made myself too cheap in his eyes. But truly I had not looked for such a shameful punishment as this! I could not think that God would let a girl be so disgraced before a young man. And now I have told you all; and I can scarcely hope that you will not despise me.'

Denis made her a respectful inclination.

'Madam,' he said, 'you have honoured me by your confidence. It remains for me to prove that I am not unworthy of the honour. Is Messire de Malétroit at hand?'

'I believe he is writing in the salle without,' she answered.

'May I lead you thither, madam?' asked Denis, offering his hand with his most courtly bearing.

She accepted it; and the pair passed out of the chapel, Blanche in a very drooping and shamefast condition, but Denis strutting and ruffling in the consciousness of a mission, and the boyish certainty of accomplishing it with honour.

The Sire de Malétroit rose to meet them with an ironical obeisance.

'Sir,' said Denis, with the grandest possible air, 'I believe I am to have some say in the matter of this marriage; and let me tell you at once, I will be no party to forcing the inclination of this young lady. Had it been freely offered to me, I should have been proud to accept her hand, for I perceive she is as good as she is beautiful; but as things are, I have now the honour, messire, of refusing.'

Blanche looked at him with gratitude in her eyes; but the old gentleman only smiled and smiled, until his smile grew positively sickening to Denis.

'I am afraid,' he said, 'Monsieur de Beaulieu, that you do not perfectly understand the choice I have to offer you. Follow me, I beseech you, to this window.' And he led the way to one of the large windows which stood open on the night. 'You observe,' he went on, 'there is an iron ring in the upper masonry, and reeved through that a very efficacious rope. Now, mark my words; if you should find your disinclination to my niece's person insurmountable, I shall have you hanged out of this window before sunrise. I shall proceed to such an extremity with the greatest regret, you may believe me. For it is not at all your death that I desire, but my niece's establishment in life. At the same time, it must come to that if you prove obstinate. Your family, Monsieur de Beaulieu, is very well in its way; but if you sprang from Charlemagne, you should not refuse the hand of a Malétroit with impunity—not if she had been as common as the Paris road—not if she were as hideous as the gargoyle over my door. Neither my niece nor you, nor my own private feelings, move me at all in this matter. The honour of my house has been compromised; I believe you to be the guilty person; at least you are now in the secret; and you can hardly wonder if I request you to wipe out the stain. If you will not, your blood be on your

own head! It will be no great satisfaction to me to have your
interesting relics kicking their heels in the breeze below my
windows; but half a loaf is better than no bread, and if I cannot
cure the dishonour, I shall at least stop the scandal.'

There was a pause.

'I believe there are other ways of settling such imbroglios
among gentlemen,' said Denis. 'You wear a sword, and I hear
you have used it with distinction.'

The Sire de Malétroit made a signal to the chaplain, who
crossed the room with long silent strides and raised the arras
over the third of the three doors. It was only a moment before he
let it fall again; but Denis had time to see a dusky passage full of
armed men.

'When I was a little younger, I should have been delighted
to honour you, Monsieur de Beaulieu,' said Sire Alain; 'but
I am now too old. Faithful retainers are the sinews of age, and I
must employ the strength I have. This is one of the hardest
things to swallow as a man grows up in years; but with a little
patience, even this becomes habitual. You and the lady seem
to prefer the salle for what remains of your two hours; and as I
have no desire to cross your preference, I shall resign it to your
use with all the pleasure in the world. No haste!' he added,
holding up his hand, as he saw a dangerous look come into Denis
de Beaulieu's face. 'If your mind revolts against hanging, it
will be time enough two hours hence to throw yourself out of
the window or upon the pikes of my retainers. Two hours of
life are always two hours. A great many things may turn up
in even as little a while as that. And, besides, if I understand
her appearance, my niece has still something to say to you.
You will not disfigure your last hours by a want of politeness
to a lady?'

Denis looked at Blanche, and she made him an imploring
gesture.

It is likely that the old gentleman was hugely pleased at this
symptom of an understanding; for he smiled on both, and added
sweetly: 'If you will give me your word of honour, Monsieur de
Beaulieu, to await my return at the end of the two hours before
attempting anything desperate, I shall withdraw my retainers,
and let you speak in greater privacy with mademoiselle.'

Denis again glanced at the girl, who seemed to beseech him to agree.

'I give you my word of honour,' he said.

Messire de Malétroit bowed, and proceeded to limp about the apartment, clearing his throat the while with that odd musical chirp which had already grown so irritating in the ears of Denis de Beaulieu. He first possessed himself of some papers which lay upon the table; then he went to the mouth of the passage and appeared to give an order to the men behind the arras; and lastly he hobbled out through the door by which Denis had come in, turning upon the threshold to address a last smiling bow to the young couple, and followed by the chaplain with a hand-lamp.

No sooner were they alone than Blanche advanced towards Denis with her hands extended. Her face was flushed and excited, and her eyes shone with tears.

'You shall not die!' she cried, 'you shall marry me after all.'

'You seem to think, madam,' replied Denis, 'that I stand much in fear of death.'

'Oh, no, no,' she said, 'I see you are no poltroon. It is for my own sake—I could not bear to have you slain for such a scruple.'

'I am afraid,' returned Denis, 'that you underrate the difficulty, madam. What you may be too generous to refuse, I may be too proud to accept. In a moment of noble feeling towards me, you forget what you perhaps owe to others.'

He had the decency to keep his eyes upon the floor as he said this, and after he had finished, so as not to spy upon her confusion. She stood silent for a moment, then walked suddenly away, and falling on her uncle's chair, fairly burst out sobbing. Denis was in the acme of embarrassment. He looked round, as if to seek for inspiration, and seeing a stool, plumped down upon it for something to do. There he sat, playing with the guard of his rapier, and wishing himself dead a thousand times over, and buried in the nastiest kitchen-heap in France. His eyes wandered round the apartment, but found nothing to arrest them. There were such wide spaces between the furniture, the light fell so badly and cheerlessly over all, the dark outside air looked in so coldly through the windows, that he thought he had never seen a church so vast, nor a tomb so melancholy. The regular sobs of Blanche de Malétroit measured out the time like the ticking of a clock. He read the device upon the shield over and over again, until his eyes became obscured; he stared into shadowy corners until he imagined they were swarming with horrible animals; and every now and again he awoke with a start, to remember that his last two hours were running, and death was on the march.

Oftener and oftener, as the time went on, did his glance settle on the girl herself. Her face was bowed forward and covered with her hands, and she was shaken at intervals by the convulsive hiccup of grief. Even thus she was not an unpleasant object to dwell upon, so plump and yet so fine, with a warm brown skin, and the most beautiful hair, Denis thought, in the whole world of womankind. Her hands were like her uncle's; but they were more in place at the end of her young arms, and looked infinitely soft and caressing. He remembered how her blue eyes had shone upon him, full of anger, pity, and innocence. And the more he dwelt on her perfections, the uglier death looked, and the more deeply was he smitten with penitence at her continued tears. Now he felt that no man could have the courage to leave a world which contained so beautiful a creature; and now he would have given forty minutes of his last hour to have unsaid his cruel speech.

Suddenly a hoarse and ragged peal of cockcrow rose to their ears from the dark valley below the windows, and this shattering noise in the silence of all around was like a light in a dark place, and shook them both out of their reflections.

'Alas, can I do nothing to help you?' she said, looking up.

'Madam,' replied Denis, with a fine irrelevancy, 'if I have said anything to wound you, believe me, it was for your own sake and not for mine.'

She thanked him with a tearful look.

'I feel your position cruelly,' he went on. 'The world has been bitter hard on you. Your uncle is a disgrace to mankind. Believe me, madam, there is no young gentleman in all France but would be glad of my opportunity to die in doing you a momentary service.'

'I know already that you can be very brave and generous,' she answered. 'What I *want* to know is whether I can serve you —now or afterwards,' she added, with a quaver.

'Most certainly,' he answered, with a smile. 'Let me sit beside you as if I were a friend, instead of a foolish intruder; try to forget how awkwardly we are placed to one another; make my last moments go pleasantly; and you will do me the chief service possible.'

'You are very gallant,' she added, with a yet deeper sadness ... 'very gallant ... and it somehow pains me. But draw nearer, if you please; and if you find anything to say to me, you will at least make certain of a very friendly listener. Ah! Monsieur de Beaulieu,' she broke forth—'ah! Monsieur de Beaulieu, how can I look you in the face?' And she fell to weeping again with a renewed effusion.

'Madam,' said Denis, taking her hand in both of his, 'reflect on the little time I have before me, and the great bitterness into which I am cast by the sight of your distress. Spare me, in my last moments, the spectacle of what I cannot cure even with the sacrifice of my life.'

'I am very selfish,' answered Blanche. 'I will be braver, Monsieur de Beaulieu, for your sake. But think if I can do you no kindness in the future—if you have no friends to whom I could carry your adieux. Charge me as heavily as you can; every burden will lighten, by so little, the invaluable gratitude I owe you. Put it in my power to do something more for you than weep.'

'My mother is married again, and has a young family to care for. My brother Guichard will inherit my fiefs; and if I am not in error, that will content him amply for my death. Life is a little vapour that passeth away, as we are told by those in holy orders. When a man is in a fair way and sees all life open in front of him, he seems to himself to make a very important figure in the world. His horse whinnies to him; the trumpets blow and the girls look out of windows as he rides into town before his company; he receives many assurances of trust and regard—sometimes by express in a letter—sometimes face to face, with persons of great consequence falling on his neck. It is not wonderful if his head is turned for a time. But once he is dead, were he as brave as Hercules or as wise as Solomon, he is soon forgotten. It is not ten years since my father fell, with many other knights around him, in a very fierce encounter, and I do not think that anyone of them, nor so much as the name of the fight, is now remembered. No, no, madam, the nearer you come to it, you see that death is a dark and dusty corner, where a man gets into his tomb and has the door shut after him till the Judgment Day. I have few friends just now, and once I am dead I shall have none.'

'Ah, Monsieur de Beaulieu!' she exclaimed, 'you forget Blanche de Malétroit.'

'You have a sweet nature, madam, and you are pleased to estimate a little service far beyond its worth.'

'It is not that,' she answered. 'You mistake me if you think I am so easily touched by my own concerns. I say so, because you are the noblest man I have ever met; because I recognize in you a spirit that would have made even a common person famous in the land.'

'And yet here I die in a mousetrap—with no more noise about it than my own squeaking,' answered he.

A look of pain crossed her face, and she was silent for a little while. Then a light came into her eyes, and with a smile she spoke again.

'I cannot have my champion think meanly of himself. Anyone who gives his life for another will be met in Paradise by all the heralds and angels of the Lord God. And you have no such cause to hang your head. For . . . pray, do you think me beautiful?' she asked, with a deep flush.

'Indeed, madam, I do,' he said.

'I am glad of that,' she answered heartily. 'Do you think there are many men in France who have been asked in marriage by a beautiful maiden—with her own lips—and who have refused her to her face? I know you men would half despise such a triumph; but, believe me, we women know more of what is precious in love. There is nothing that should set a person higher in his own esteem; and we women would prize nothing more dearly.'

'You are very good,' he said; 'but you cannot make me forget that I was asked in pity and not for love.'

'I am not so sure of that,' she replied, holding down her head. 'Hear me to an end, Monsieur de Beaulieu. I know how you must despise me; I feel you are right to do so; I am too poor a creature to occupy one thought of your mind, although, alas! you must die for me this morning. But when I asked you to marry me, indeed, and indeed, it was because I respected and admired you, and loved you with my whole soul, from the very moment that you took my part against my uncle. If you had seen yourself, and how noble you looked, you would pity rather than despise me. And now,' she went on, hurriedly checking him with her hand, 'although I have laid aside all reserve and told you so much, remember that I know your sentiments towards me already. I would not, believe me, being nobly born, weary you with importunities into consent. I too have a pride of my own: and I declare before the holy mother of God, if you should now go back from your word already given, I would no more marry you than I would marry my uncle's groom.'

Denis smiled a little bitterly.

'It is a small love,' he said, 'that shies at a little pride.'

She made no answer, although she probably had her own thoughts.

'Come hither to the window,' he said, with a sigh. 'Here is the dawn.'

And indeed the dawn was already beginning. The hollow of the sky was full of essential daylight, colourless and clean; and the valley underneath was flooded with a grey reflection. A few thin vapours clung in the coves of the forest or lay along the winding course of the river. The scene disengaged a surprising effect of stillness, which was hardly interrupted when the cocks began once more to crow among the steadings. Perhaps the same fellow who had made so horrid a clangour in the darkness not half an hour before, now sent up the merriest cheer to greet the coming day. A little wind went bustling and eddying among the tree tops underneath the windows. And still the daylight kept flooding insensibly out of the east, which was soon to grow incandescent and cast up that red-hot cannon-ball, the rising sun.

Denis looked out over all this with a bit of a shiver. He had taken her hand, and retained it in his almost unconsciously.

'Has the day begun already?' she said; and then, illogically enough: 'the night has been so long! Alas! what shall we say to my uncle when he returns?'

'What you will,' said Denis, and he pressed her fingers in his.

She was silent.

'Blanche,' he said, with a swift, uncertain, passionate utterance, 'you have seen whether I fear death. You must know well enough that I would as gladly leap out of that window into the empty air as lay a finger on you without your free and full consent. But if you care for me at all do not let me lose my life in a misapprehension; for I love you better than the whole world; and though I will die for you blithely, it would be like all the joys of Paradise to live on and spend my life in your service.'

As he stopped speaking, a bell began to ring loudly in the interior of the house; and a clatter of armour in the corridor showed that the retainers were returning to their post, and the two hours were at an end.

'After all that you have heard?' she whispered, leaning towards him with her lips and eyes.

'I have heard nothing,' he replied.

'The captain's name was Fiorimond de Champdivers,' she said in his ear.

'I did not hear it,' he answered, taking her supple body in his arms and covering her wet face with kisses.

A melodious chirping was audible behind, followed by a beautiful chuckle, and the voice of Messire de Malétroit wished his new nephew a good morning.

H Rider Haggard

Magepa the Buck

In a preface to the story of the early life of the late Allan Quatermain, known in Africa as Macumazahn, which has recently been published under the name of 'Marie,' Mr Curtis, the brother of Sir Henry Curtis, tells of how he found a number of manuscripts that were left by Mr Quatermain in his house in Yorkshire. Of these 'Marie' was one, but in addition to it and sundry other completed stories, I, the Editor to whom it was directed that these manuscripts should be handed for publication, have found a quantity of unclassified notes and papers.

One of these notes—it is contained in a book, much soiled and worn, that evidently its owner had carried about with him for years—reminds me of a conversation I had with Mr Quatermain long ago when I was his guest in Yorkshire. The note itself is short; I think that he must have jotted it down within an hour or two of the event to which it refers. It runs thus:

'I wonder whether in the "Land Beyond" any recognition is granted for acts of great courage and unselfish devotion—a kind of spiritual Victoria Cross. If so I think it ought to be accorded to that poor old savage, Magepa, at least it would be if I had any voice in the matter. Upon my word he has made me feel proud of humanity. And yet he was nothing but a "nigger," as so many call the Kaffirs.'

For a while I, the Editor, wondered to what this entry could allude. Then of a sudden it all came back to me. I saw myself, as a young man, seated in the hall of Quatermain's house one evening after dinner. With me were Sir Henry Curtis and Captain Good. We were smoking, and the conversation had turned upon deeds of heroism. Each of us detailed such acts as he could remember which had made the most impression on him. When we had finished, old Allan said:

'With your leave I'll tell you a story of what I think was one of the bravest things I ever saw. It happened at the beginning of the Zulu war, when the troops were marching into Zululand. Now at that time, as you know, I was turning an honest penny transport-riding for Government, or rather for the military authorities. I hired them three wagons with the necessary voorloopers and drivers, sixteen good salted oxen to each wagon, and myself in charge of the lot. They paid me—well, never mind how much— I am rather ashamed to mention the amount. I asked a good price for my wagons, or rather for the hire of them, of a very well satisfied young gentleman in uniform who had been exactly three weeks in the country, and, to my surprise, got it. But when I went to those in command and warned them what would happen if they persisted in their way of advance, then in their pride they would not listen to the old hunter and transport-rider, but politely bowed me out. If they had, there would have been no Isandhlwana disaster.'

He brooded awhile, for, as I knew, this was a sore subject with him, one of which he would rarely talk. Although he escaped himself, Quatermain had lost friends on that fatal field. He went on:

To return to old Magepa. I had known him for many years. The first time we met was in the battle of the Tugela. I was fighting for the king's son, Umbelazi the Handsome, in the ranks of the Amawombe regiment—I mean to write all that story, for it should not be lost.[1] Well, as I have told you before, the Amawombe were wiped out; of the three thousand or so of them I think only about fifty remained alive after they had annihilated the three of Cetewayo's regiments that set upon them. But Magepa was one who survived.

I met him afterwards at old King Panda's kraal and recognized him as having fought by my side. Whilst I was talking with him the Prince Cetewayo came by; to me he was civil enough, for he

[1] For this story see the book named *Child of Storm*, by H. Rider Haggard.

knew how I chanced to be in the battle, but he glared at Magepa, and said:

'Why, Macumazahn, is not this man one of the dogs with which you tried to bite me by the Tugela not long ago? He must be a cunning dog also, one who can run fast, for how comes it that he lives to snarl when so many will never bark again? *Ow!* if I had my way I would find a strip of hide to fit his neck.'

'Not so,' I answered; 'he has the king's peace and he is a brave man—braver than I am, anyway, Prince, seeing that I ran from the ranks of the Amawombe, while he stood where he was.'

'You mean that your horse ran, Macumazahn. Well, since you like this dog, I will not hurt him'; and with a shrug he went his way.

'Yet soon or late he will hurt me,' said Magepa, when the Prince had gone. 'U'Cetewayo has a memory long as the shadow thrown by a tree at sunset. Moreover, as he knows well, it is true that I ran, Macumazahn, though not till all was finished and I could do no more by standing still. You remember how, after we had eaten up the first of Cetewayo's regiments, the second charged us and we ate that up also. Well, in that fight I got a tap on the head from a kerry. It struck me on my man's ring which I had just put on, for I think I was the youngest soldier in that regiment of veterans. The ring saved me; still, for a while I lost my mind and lay like one dead. When I found it again the fight was over and Cetewayo's people were searching for our wounded that they might kill them. Presently they found me and saw that there was no hurt on me.

'"Here is one who shams dead like a stink-cat," said a big fellow, lifting his spear.

'Then it was that I sprang up and ran, I who was but just married and desired to live. He struck at me, but I jumped over the spear, and the others that they threw missed me. Then they began to hunt me, but, Macumazahn, I, who am named "The Buck" because I am swifter of foot than any man in Zululand, outpaced them all and got away safe.'

'Well done, Magepa,' I said. 'Still, remember the saying of your people, "At last the strong swimmer goes with the stream and the swift runner is run down."'

'I know it, Macumazahn,' he answered, with a nod, 'and perhaps in a day to come I shall know it better.'

I took little heed of his words at the time, but more than thirty years afterwards I remembered them.

Such was my first acquaintance with Magepa. Now, friends, I will tell you how it was renewed at the time of the Zulu war.

As you know, I was attached to the centre column that advanced into Zululand by Rorke's Drift on the Buffalo River. Before war was declared, or at any rate before the advance began, while it might have been and many thought it would be averted, I was employed transport-riding goods to the little Rorke's Drift station, that which became so famous afterwards, and incidentally in collecting what information I could of Cetewayo's intentions. Hearing that there was a kraal a mile or so the other side of the river, of which the people were said to be very friendly to the English, I determined to visit it. You may think this was rash, but I was so well known in Zululand, where for many years, by special leave of the king, I was allowed to go whither I would quite unmolested, that I felt no fear for myself so long as I went alone.

Accordingly one evening I crossed the drift and headed for a kloof in which I was told the kraal stood. Ten minutes' ride brought me in sight of it. It was not a large kraal; there may have been six or eight huts and a cattle enclosure surrounded by the usual fence. The situation, however, was very pretty, a knoll of rising ground backed by the wooded slopes of the kloof. As I approached I saw women and children running to the kraal to hide, and when I reached the gateway for some time no one would come out to meet me. At length a small boy appeared who informed me that the kraal was 'empty as a gourd.'

'Quite so,' I answered; 'still, go and tell the headman that Macumazahn wishes to speak with him.'

The boy departed, and presently I saw a face that seemed familiar to me peeping round the gateway. After a careful inspection its owner emerged.

He was a tall, thin man of indefinite age, perhaps between sixty and seventy, with a finely-cut face, a little grey beard, kind eyes and very well shaped hands and feet, the fingers, which twitched incessantly, being remarkably long.

'Greeting, Macumazahn,' he said. 'I see you do not remember

me. Well, think of the battle of the Tugela, and of the last stand of the Amawombe, and of a certain talk at the kraal of our Father-who-is-dead' (that is, King Panda), 'and of how he who sits in his place' (he meant Cetewayo) 'told you that if he had his way he would find a hide rope to fit the neck of a certain one.'

'Ah!' I said, 'I know you now; you are Magepa the Buck. So the Runner has not yet been run down.'

'No, Macumazahn, not yet; but there is still time. I think that many swift feet will be at work ere long.'

'How have you prospered?' I asked him.

'Well enough, Macumazahn, in all ways except one. I have three wives, but my children have been few and are dead, except one daughter, who is married and lives with me, for her husband, too, is dead. He was killed by a buffalo, and she has not yet married again. But enter and see.'

So I went in and saw Magepa's wives, old women all of them. Also, at his bidding, his daughter, whose name was Gita, brought me some *maas*, or curdled milk, to drink. She was a well-formed woman, very like her father, but sad-faced, perhaps with a pre-science of evil to come. Clinging to her finger was a beautiful boy of something under two years of age, who, when he saw Magepa, ran to him and threw his little arms about his legs. The old man lifted the child and kissed him tenderly, saying:

'It is well that this toddler and I should love one another, Macumazahn, seeing that he is the last of my race. All the other children here are those of the people who have come to live in my shadow.'

'Where are their fathers?' I asked, patting the little boy (who, his mother told me, was named Sinala) upon the cheek, an attention that he resented.

'They have been called away on duty,' answered Magepa shortly; and I changed the subject.

Then we began to talk about old times, and I asked him if he had any oxen to sell, saying that this was my reason for visiting his kraal.

'Nay, Macumazahn,' he answered, in a meaning voice. 'This year all the cattle are the king's.'

I nodded and replied that, as it was so, I had better be going; whereon, as I half expected, Magepa announced that he would

see me safe to the drift. So I bade farewell to the wives and the
widowed daughter, and we started.

As soon as we were clear of the kraal Magepa began to open
his heart to me.

'Macumazahn,' he said, looking up at me earnestly, for I was
mounted and he walked beside my horse, 'there is to be war.
Cetewayo will not consent to the demands of the great White
Chief from the Cape'—he meant Sir Bartle Frere. 'He will fight
with the English; only he will let them begin the fighting. He
will draw them on into Zululand and then overwhelm them with
his *impis* and stamp them flat, and eat them up; and I, who love
the English, am very sorry. Yes, it makes my heart bleed. If it
were the Boers now, I should be glad, for we Zulus hate the
Boers; but the English we do not hate; even Cetewayo likes them;
still he will eat them up if they attack him.'

'Indeed,' I answered; and then, as in duty bound, I proceeded
to get what I could out of him, and that was not a little. Of course,
however, I did not swallow it all, since I suspected that Magepa
was feeding me with news that he had been ordered to dis-
seminate.

Presently we came to the mouth of the kloof in which the kraal
stood, and here, for greater convenience of conversation, we
halted, for I thought it as well that we should not be seen in close
talk on the open plain beyond. The path here, I should add, ran
past a clump of green bushes; I remember they bore a white
flower that smelt sweet, and were backed by some tall grass,
elephant-grass I think it was, among which grew mimosa trees.

'Magepa,' I said, 'if in truth there is to be fighting, why don't
you move over the river one night with your people and cattle,
and get into Natal?'

'I would if I could, Macumazahn, who have no stomach for
this war against the English. But there I should not be safe, since
presently the king will come into Natal too, or send thirty thousand assegais as his messengers. Then what will happen to those
who have left him?'

'Oh, if you think that,' I answered, 'you had better stay where
you are.'

'Also, Macumazahn, the husbands of those women at my kraal
have been called up to their regiments, and if their wives fled to

the English they would be killed. Again, the king has sent for nearly all our cattle, "to keep it safe." He fears lest we Border Zulus might join our people in Natal, and that is why he is keeping our cattle "safe".'

'Life is more than cattle, Magepa. At least you might come.'

'What! And leave my people to be killed? Macumazahn, you did not use to talk so. Still, hearken. Macumazahn, will you do me a service? I will pay you well for it. I would get my daughter Gita and my little grandson Sinala into safety. If I and my wives are wiped out it does not matter, for we are old. But her I would save, and the boy I would save, so that one may live who will remember my name. Now, if I were to send them across the drift, say at the dawn, not tomorrow, and not the next day, but the day after, would you receive them into your wagon and deliver them safe to some place in Natal? I have money hidden, fifty pieces of gold, and you may take half of these and also half of the cattle if ever I live to get them back out of the keeping of the king.'

'Never mind about the money, and we will speak of the cattle afterwards,' I said. 'I understand that you wish to send your daughter and your little grandson out of danger, and I think you wise, very wise. When once the advance begins, if there is an advance, who knows what may happen? War is a rough game, Magepa. It is not the custom of you black people to spare women and children, and there will be Zulus fighting on our side as well as on yours; do you understand?'

'*Ow!* I understand, Macumazahn. I have known the face of war and seen many a little one like my grandson Sinala assegaied upon his mother's back.'

'Very good. But if I do this for you, you must do something for me. Say, Magepa, does Cetewayo *really* mean to fight, and if so, how? Oh yes, I know all you have been telling me, but I want not words, but truth from the heart.'

'You ask secrets,' said the old fellow, peering about him into the gathering gloom. 'Still, "a spear for a spear and a shield for a shield," as our saying runs. I have spoken no lie. The king *does* mean to fight, not because he wants to, but because the regiments swear that they will wash their assegais, they who have never seen blood since that battle of the Tugela in which we two played a part; and if he will not suffer it, well, there are more of his race!

27

Also he means to fight thus,' and he gave me some very useful information; that is, information which would have been useful if those in authority had deigned to pay any attention to it when I passed it on.

Just as he finished speaking I thought that I heard a sound in the dense green bush behind us. It reminded me of the noise a man makes when he tries to stifle a cough, and frightened me. For if we had been overheard by a spy, Magepa was as good as dead, and the sooner I was across the river the better.

'What's that?' I asked.

'A bush buck, Macumazahn. There are lots of them about here.'

Not being satisfied, though it is true that buck do cough like this, I turned my horse to the bush, seeking an opening. Thereon something crashed away and vanished into the long grass. In those shadows, of course, I could not see what it was, but such light as remained glinted on what might have been the polished tip of the horn of an antelope or—an assegai.

'I told you it was a buck, Macumazahn,' said Magepa. 'Still, if you smell danger, let us come away from the bush, though the orders are that no white man is to be touched as yet.'

Then, while we walked on towards the ford, he set out with great detail, as Kaffirs do, the exact arrangements that he proposed to make for the handing over of his daughter and her child into my care. I remember that I asked him why he would not send her on the following morning, instead of two mornings later. He answered because he expected an outpost of scouts from one of the regiments at his kraal that night, who would probably remain there over the morrow and perhaps longer. While they were in the place it would be difficult for him to send away Gita and her son without exciting suspicion.

Near the drift we parted, and I returned to our provisional camp and wrote a beautiful report of all that I had learned, of which report I may add, no one took the slightest notice.

I think it was the morning before that whereon I had arranged to meet Gita and the little boy at the drift that just about dawn I went down to the river for a wash. Having taken my dip I climbed on to a flat rock to dress myself, and looked at the billows of beautiful, pearly mist which hid the face of the water, and considered—I almost said listened to—the great silence, for as yet no live thing was stirring.

Ah! if I had known of the hideous sights and sounds that were destined to be heard ere long in this same haunt of perfect peace! Indeed, at that moment there came a kind of hint or premonition of them, since suddenly through the utter quiet broke the blood-curdling wail of a woman. It was followed by other wails and shouts, distant and yet distinct. Then the silence fell again.

Now, thought I to myself, that noise might very well have come from old Magepa's kraal; luckily, however, sounds are deceptive in mist.

Well, the end of it was that I waited there till the sun rose. The first thing on which its bright beams struck was a mighty column of smoke rising to heaven from where Magepa's kraal had stood!

I went back to my wagons very sad, so sad that I could scarcely eat my breakfast. While I walked I wondered hard whether the light had glinted upon the tip of a buck's horn in that patch of green bush with the sweet-smelling white flowers a night or two ago. Or had it perchance fallen upon the point of the assegai of some spy who was watching my movements! In that event yonder column of smoke and the horrible cries which preceded it were easy to explain. For had not Magepa and I talked secrets together, and in Zulu.

On the following morning at the dawn I attended at the drift in the faint hope that Gita and her boy might arrive there as arranged. But nobody came, which was not wonderful, seeing that Gita lay dead, stabbed through and through, as I saw afterwards (she made a good fight for the child), and that her spirit had gone to wherever go the souls of the brave-hearted, be they white or black. Only on the farther bank of the river I saw some Zulu scouts who seemed to know my errand, for they called to me, asking mockingly where was the pretty woman I had come to meet?

After that I tried to put the matter out of my head, which indeed was full enough of other things, since now definite orders had arrived as to the advance, and with these many troops and officers.

It was just then that the Zulus began to fire across the river at such of our people as they saw upon the bank. At these they took aim, and, as a result, hit nobody. A raw Kaffir with a rifle, in my experience, is only dangerous when he aims at nothing, for then the bullet looks after itself, and may catch you. To put a stop to this nuisance a regiment of the friendly natives—there may have been several hundred of them—was directed to cross the river and clear the kloofs and rocks of the Zulu skirmishers who were hidden among them. I watched them go off in fine style.

Towards evening someone told me that our *impi*, as he grandiloquently called it, was returning victorious. Having at the moment nothing else to do, I walked down to the river at a point where the water was deep and the banks were high. Here I climbed to the top of a pile of boulders, whence with my field-glasses I could sweep a great extent of plain which stretched away on the Zululand side till at length it merged into hills and bush.

Presently I saw some of our natives marching homewards in a scattered and disorganised fashion, but evidently very proud of themselves, for they were waving their assegais and singing scraps of war-songs. A few minutes later, a mile or more away, I caught sight of a man running.

Watching him through the glasses I noted three things: first, that he was tall; secondly, that he ran with extraordinary swiftness; and, thirdly, that he had something tied upon his back. It was evident, further, that he had good reason to run, since he was being hunted by a number of our Kaffirs, of whom more and more continually joined in the chase. From every side they poured down upon him, trying to cut him off and kill him, for as they got nearer I could see the assegais which they threw at him flash in the sunlight.

Very soon I understood that the man was running with a definite object and to a definite point; he was trying to reach the river. I thought the sight very pitiful, this one poor creature being hunted to death by so many. Also I wondered why he did not free himself from the bundle on his back, and came to the conclusion that he must be a witch-doctor, and that the bundle contained his precious charms or medicines.

This was while he was yet a long way off, but when he came nearer, within three or four hundred yards, of a sudden I caught the outline of his face against a good background, and knew it for that of Magepa.

. . . he was being hunted by a number of our Kaffirs

'My God!' I said to myself, 'it is old Magepa the Buck, and the bundle in the mat will be his grandson, Sinala!'

Yes, even then I felt certain that he was carrying the child upon his back.

What was I to do? It was impossible for me to cross the river at that place, and long before I could get round by the ford all would be finished. I stood up on my rock and shouted to those brutes of Kaffirs to let the man alone. They were so excited that they did not hear my words; at least, they swore afterwards that they thought I was encouraging them to hunt him down.

But Magepa heard me. At that moment he seemed to be failing, but the sight of me appeared to give him fresh strength. He gathered himself together and leapt forward at a really surprising speed. Now the river was not more than three hundred yards away from him, and for the first two hundred of these he quite out-distanced his pursuers, although they were most of them young men and comparatively fresh. Then once more his strength began to fail.

Watching through the glasses I could see that his mouth was wide open, and that there was red foam upon his lips. The burden on his back was dragging him down. Once he lifted his hands as though to loose it; then with a wild gesture let them fall again.

Two of the pursuers who had outpaced the others crept up to him—lank, lean men of not more than thirty years of age. They had stabbing spears in their hands, such as are used at close quarters, and these of course they did not throw. One of them gained a little on the other.

Now Magepa was not more than fifty yards from the bank with the first hunter about ten paces behind him and coming up rapidly. Magepa glanced over his shoulder and saw, then put out his last strength. For forty yards he went like an arrow, running straight away from his pursuers, until he was within a few feet of the bank, when he stumbled and fell.

'He's done,' I said, and, upon my word, if I had a rifle in my hand I think I would have stopped one or both of those blood-hounds and taken the consequences.

But, no! Just as the first man lifted his broad spear to stab him through the back on which the bundle lay, Magepa leapt up and wheeled round to take the thrust in his chest. Evidently he did not wish to be speared in the back—for a certain reason. He took it sure enough, for the assegai was wrenched out of the hand of the striker. Still, as he was reeling backwards, it did not go through Magepa, or perhaps it hit a bone. He drew out the spear and threw it at the man, wounding him. Then he staggered on, back and back, to the edge of the little cliff.

It was reached at last. With a cry of 'Help me, Macumazahn!' Magepa turned, and before the other man could spear him, leapt straight into deep water. He rose. Yes, the brave old fellow rose and struck out for the other bank, leaving a little line of red behind him.

I rushed, or rather sprang and rolled down to the edge of the stream, to where a point of shingle ran out into the water. Along this I clambered, and beyond it up to my middle. Now Magepa was being swept past me. I caught his outstretched hand and pulled him ashore.

'The boy!' he gasped; 'the boy! Is he dead?'

I severed the lashings of the mat that had cut right into the old fellow's shoulders. Inside of it was little Sinala, spluttering out water, but very evidently alive and unhurt, for presently he set up a yell.

'No,' I said, 'he lives, and will live.'

'Then all is well, Macumazahn.' (*A pause.*). 'It *was* a spy in the bush, not a buck. He overheard our talk. The king's slayers came. Gita held the door of the hut while I took the child, cut a hole through the straw with my assegai, and crept out at the back. She was full of spears before she died, but I got away with the boy. Till your Kaffirs found me I lay hid in the bush, hoping to escape to Natal. Then I ran for the river, and saw you on the further bank. *I* might have got away, but that child is heavy.' (*A pause.*) 'Give him food, Macumazahn, he must be hungry.' (*A pause.*) 'Farewell. That was a good saying of yours—the swift runner is outrun at last. Ah! yet I did not run in vain.' (*Another pause, the last.*) Then he lifted himself upon one arm and with the other saluted, first the boy Sinala and next me, muttering, 'Remember your promise, Macumazahn.'

'That is how Magepa the Buck died. I never saw any one carrying weight who could run quite so well as he,' and Quatermain turned his head away as though the memory of this incident affected him somewhat.

'What became of the child Sinala?' I asked presently.

'Oh, I sent him to an institution in Natal, and afterwards was able to get some of his property back for him. I believe that he is being trained as an interpreter.'

Stanley Weyman

The King's Stratagem

In the days when Henry the Fourth of France was as yet King of
Navarre only, and in that little kingdom of hills and woods which
occupies the south-western corner of the larger country, was
with difficulty supporting the Huguenot cause against the French
court and the Catholic League—in the days when every little
moated town, from the Dordogne to the Pyrenees, was a bone of
contention between the young king and the crafty queen-mother,
Catherine de Medicis, a conference between these warring person-
ages took place in the picturesque town of La Réole. And great
was the fame of it.

La Réole still rises grey, time-worn, and half-ruined on a lofty
cliff above the broad green waters of the Garonne, forty odd
miles from Bordeaux. It is a small place now, but in the days of
which we are speaking it was important, strongly fortified, and
guarded by a castle which looked down on some hundreds of
red-tiled roofs, rising in terraces from the river. As the meeting-
place of the two sovereigns it was for the time as gay as Paris
itself. Catherine had brought with her a bevy of fair maids of
honour, and trusted more perhaps in the effect of their charms
than in her own diplomacy. But the peaceful appearance of the
town was as delusive as the smooth bosom of the Gironde; for
even while every other house in its streets rang with music and
silvery laughter, each party was ready to fly to arms at a word if
it saw that any advantage could be gained thereby.

On an evening shortly before the end of the conference two
men were seated at play in a room, the deep-embrasured window
of which looked down from a considerable height upon the river.

The hour was late; below them the town lay silent. Outside, the moonlight fell bright and pure on sleeping fields, on vineyards, and dark far-spreading woods. Within the room a silver lamp suspended from the ceiling threw light upon the table, but left the farther parts of the chamber in shadow. The walls were hung with faded tapestry, and on a low bedstead in one corner lay a handsome cloak, a sword, and one of the clumsy pistols of the period. Across a high-backed chair lay another cloak and sword, and on the window seat, beside a pair of saddle-bags, were strewn half a dozen trifles such as soldiers carried from camp to camp—a silver comfit-box, a jewelled dagger, a mask, a velvet cap.

The faces of the players, as they bent over the cards, were in shadow. One—a slight, dark man of middle height, with a weak chin—and a mouth that would have equally betrayed its weakness had it not been shaded by a dark moustache—seemed, from the occasional oaths which he let drop, to be losing heavily. Yet his opponent a stouter and darker man, with a sword-cut across his left temple, and the swaggering air that has at all times marked the professional soldier, showed no signs of triumph or elation. On the contrary, though he kept silence, or spoke only a formal word or two, there was a gleam of anxiety and suppressed excitement in his eyes; and more than once he looked keenly at his companion, as if to judge of his feelings or to learn whether the time had come for some experiment which he meditated. But for this, an observer looking in through the window would have taken the two for that common conjunction—the hawk and the pigeon.

At last the younger player threw down his cards, with an exclamation.

'You have the luck of the evil one,' he said, bitterly. 'How much is that?'

'Two thousand crowns,' the other replied without emotion. 'You will play no more?'

'No! I wish to Heaven I had never played at all!' was the answer. As he spoke the loser rose, and moving to the window stood looking out. For a few moments the elder man remained in his seat, gazing furtively at him; at length he too rose, and, stepping softly to his companion, he touched him on the shoulder. 'Your pardon a moment, M. le Vicomte,' he said. 'Am I right in concluding that the loss of this sum will inconvenience you?'

'A thousand fiends!' the young gamester exclaimed, turning on him wrathfully. 'Is there any man whom the loss of two thousand crowns would not inconvenience? As for me——'

'For you,' the other continued smoothly, filling up the pause, 'shall I be wrong in supposing that it means something like ruin?'

'Well, sir, and if it does?' the young man retorted, and he drew himself up, his cheek a shade paler with passion. 'Depend upon it you shall be paid. Do not be afraid of that!'

'Gently, gently, my friend,' the winner answered, his patience in strong contrast to the other's violence. 'I had no intention of insulting you, believe me. Those who play with the Vicomte de Noirterre are not wont to doubt his honour. I spoke only in your own interest. It has occurred to me, Vicomte, that the matter may be arranged at less cost to yourself.'

'How?' was the curt question.

'May I speak freely?' The Vicomte shrugged his shoulders, and the other, taking silence for consent, proceeded: 'You, Vicomte, are governor of Lusigny for the King of Navarre; I, of Créance, for the King of France. Our towns lie but three leagues apart. Could I by any chance, say on one of these fine nights, make myself master of Lusigny, it would be worth more than two thousand crowns to me. Do you understand?'

'No,' the young man answered slowly, 'I do not.'

'Think over what I have said, then,' was the brief answer.

For a full minute there was silence in the room. The Vicomte gazed from the window with knitted brows and compressed lips, while his companion, seated near at hand, leant back in his chair, with an air of affected carefulness. Outside, the rattle of arms and hum of voices told that the watch were passing through the street. The church bell rang one o'clock. Suddenly the Vicomte burst into a forced laugh, and, turning, took up his cloak and sword. 'The trap was well laid, M. le Capitaine,' he said almost jovially; 'but I am still sober enough to take care of myself—and of Lusigny. I wish you good night. You shall have your money, do not fear.'

'Still, I am afraid it will cost you dearly,' the Captain answered, as he rose and moved towards the door to open it for his guest. And then, when his hand was already on the latch, he paused.

'My lord,' he said, 'what do you say to this, then? I will stake the two thousand crowns you have lost to me, and another thousand to boot—against your town. Oh, no one can hear us. If you win you go off a free man with my thousand. If you lose, you put me in possession—one of these fine nights. Now, that is an offer. What do you say to it? A single hand to decide.'

The younger man's face reddened. He turned; his eyes sought the table and the cards; he stood irresolute. The temptation came at an unfortunate moment; a moment when the excitement of play had given way to depression, and he saw nothing outside the door, on the latch of which his hand was laid, but the bleak reality of ruin. The temptation to return, the thought that by a single hand he might set himself right with the world was too much for him. Slowly—he came back to the table. 'Confound you!' he said passionately. 'I think you are the devil himself!'

'Don't talk child's talk!' the other answered coldly, drawing back as his victim advanced. 'If you do not like the offer you need not take it.'

But the young man was a born gambler, and his fingers had already closed on the cards. Picking them up idly he dropped them once, twice, thrice on the table, his eyes gleaming with the play-fever. 'If I win?' he said doubtfully. 'What then? Let us have it quite clearly.'

'You carry away a thousand crowns,' the Captain answered quietly. 'If you lose you contrive to leave one of the gates of Lusigny open for me before next full moon. That is all.'

'And what if I lose, and do not pay the forfeit?' the Vicomte asked, laughing weakly.

'I trust to your honour,' the Captain answered. And, strange as it may seem, he knew his man. The young noble of the day might betray his cause and his trust, but the debt of honour incurred at play was binding on him.

'Well,' said the Vicomte, with a deep breath, 'I agree. Who is to deal?'

'As you will,' the Captain replied, masking under an appearance of indifference an excitement which darkened his cheek, and caused the pulse in the old wound on his face to beat furiously.

'Then do you deal,' said the Vicomte.

'With your permission,' the Captain assented. And gathering

the cards he dealt with them a practised hand, and pushed his opponent's six across to him.

The young man took up the hand and, as he sorted it, and looked from it to his companion's face, he repressed a groan with difficulty. The moonlight shining through the casement fell in silvery sheen on a few feet of the floor. With the light something of the silence and coolness of the night entered also, and appealed to him. For a few seconds he hesitated. He made even as if he would have replaced the hand on the table. But he had gone too far to retrace his steps with honour. It was too late, and with a muttered word, which his dry lips refused to articulate, he played the first card.

He took that trick and the next; they were secure.

'And now?' said the Captain who knew well where the pinch came. 'What next?'

The Vicomte compressed his lips. Two courses were open to him. By adopting one he could almost for certain win one more trick. By the other he might just possibly win two tricks. He was a gamester, he adopted the latter course. In half a minute it was over. He had lost.

The winner nodded gravely. 'The luck is with me still,' he said, keeping his eyes on the table that the light of triumph which had leapt into them might not be seen. 'When do you go back to your command, Vicomte?'

The unhappy man sat, as one stunned, his eyes on the painted cards which had cost him so dearly. 'The day after tomorrow,' he muttered at last, striving to collect himself.

'Then shall we say—the following evening?' the Captain asked, courteously.

The young man shivered. 'As you will,' he muttered.

'We quite understand one another,' continued the winner, eyeing his man watchfully, and speaking with more urgency. 'I may depend on you, M. le Vicomte, I presume—to keep your word?'

'The Noirterres have never been wanting to their word,' the young nobleman answered stung into passing passion. 'If I live I will put Lusigny into your hands, M. le Capitaine. Afterwards I will do my best to recover it—in another way.'

'I shall be most happy to meet you in that way,' replied the Captain, bowing lightly. And in one more minute, the door of his lodging had closed on the other; and he was alone—alone with his triumph, his ambition, his hopes for the future—alone with the greatness to which his capture of Lusigny was to be the first step. He would enjoy that greatness not a whit the less because fortune had hitherto dealt out to him more blows than caresses, and he was still at forty, after a score of years of roughest service, the governor of a paltry country town.

Meanwhile, in the darkness of the narrow streets, the Vicomte was making his way to his lodgings in a state of despair difficult to describe, impossible to exaggerate. Chilled, sobered, and affrighted he looked back and saw how he had thrown for all and lost all, how he had saved the dregs of his fortune at the expense of his loyalty, how he had seen a way of escape—and lost it for ever! No wonder that as he trudged through the mud and darkness of the sleeping town his breath came quickly and his chest heaved, and he looked from side to side as a hunted animal might look, uttering great sighs. Ah, if he could have retraced the last three hours! If he could have undone that he had done!

In a fever, he entered his lodging, and securing the door behind him stumbled up the stone stairs and entered his room. The impulse to confide his misfortunes to some one was so strong upon him that he was glad to see a dark form half sitting, half lying in a chair before the dying embers of a wood fire. In those days a man's natural confidant was his valet, the follower, half friend, half servant, who had been born on his estate, who lay on a pallet at the foot of his bed, who carried his *billets-doux* and held his cloak at the duello, who rode near his stirrup in fight and nursed him in illness, who not seldom advised him in the choice of a wife, and lied in support of his suit.

The young Vicomte flung his cloak over a chair. 'Get up, you rascal!' he cried impatiently. 'You pig, you dog!' he continued, with increasing anger. 'Sleeping there as though your master were not ruined by that scoundrel of a Breton! Bah!' he added, gazing bitterly at his follower, 'you are of the *canaille*, and have neither honour to lose nor a town to betray!'

The sleeping man moved in his chair but did not awake. The Vicomte, his patience exhausted, snatched the bonnet from his head, and threw it on the ground. 'Will you listen?' he said. 'Or go, if you choose look for another master. I am ruined! Do you hear? Ruined, Gil! I have lost all—money, land, Lusigny itself—at the cards!'

The man, roused at last, stooped with a sleepy movement, and picking up his hat dusted it with his hand, then rose with a yawn to his feet.

'I am afraid, Vicomte,' he said, in tones that, quiet as they were, sounded like thunder in the young man's astonished and bewildered ears, 'I am afraid that if you have lost Lusigny—you have lost something which was not yours to lose!'

As he spoke he struck the embers with his boot, and the fire, blazing up, shone on his face. The Vicomte saw, with stupor, that the man before him was not Gil at all—was indeed the last person in the world to whom he should have betrayed himself. The astute smiling eyes, the aquiline nose, the high forehead, and projecting chin, which the short beard and moustache scarcely concealed, were only too well known to him. He stepped back with a cry of despair. 'Sir!' he said, and then his tongue failed him. His arms dropped by his sides. He stood silent, pale, convicted, his chin on his breast. The man to whom he had confessed his treachery was the master whom he had agreed to betray.

'I had suspected something of this,' Henry of Navarre continued, after a lengthy pause, and with a tinge of irony in his tone. 'Rosny told me that that old fox, the Captain of Créance, was affecting your company somewhat too much, M. le Vicomte, and I find, that, as usual, his suspicions were well-founded. What with a gentleman who shall be nameless, who has bartered a ford and a castle for the favour of Mademoiselle de Luynes, and yourself, and another I know of—I am blest with some faithful followers, it seems! For shame! for shame, sir!' he continued, seating himself with dignity in the chair from which he had risen, but turning it so that he confronted his host, 'have you nothing to say for yourself?'

The young noble stood with bowed head, his face white. This was ruin, indeed, absolute irremediable ruin. 'Sir,' he said at last, 'your Majesty has a right to my life, not to my honour.'

'Your honour!' Henry exclaimed, biting contempt in his tone.

The young man started, and for a second his cheek flamed under the well-deserved reproach; but he recovered himself. 'My debt to your Majesty,' he said, 'I am willing to pay.'

'Since pay you must,' Henry muttered softly.

'But I claim to pay also my debt to the Captain of Créance.'

The King of Navarre stared. 'Oh,' he said. 'So you would have me take your worthless life, and give up Lusigny?'

'I am in your hands, sire.'

'Pish, sir!' Henry replied in angry astonishment. 'You talk like a child. Such an offer, M. de Noirterre, is folly, and you know it. Now listen to me. It was lucky for you that I came in tonight, intending to question you. Your madness is known to me only, and I am willing to overlook it. Do you hear? I am willing to pardon. Cheer up, therefore, and be a man. You are young; I forgive you. This shall be between you and me only,' the young prince continued, his eyes softening as the other's head sank lower, 'and you need think no more of it until the day when I shall say to you, "Now, M. de Noirterre, for Navarre and for Henry, strike!"'

He rose as the last words passed his lips, and held out his hand. The Vicomte fell on one knee, and kissed it reverently, then sprang to his feet again. 'Sire,' he said, his eyes shining, 'you have punished me heavily, more heavily than was needful. There is only one way in which I can show my gratitude, and that is by ridding you of a servant who can never again look your enemies in the face.'

'What new folly is this?' Henry asked sternly. 'Do you not understand that I have forgiven you?'

'Therefore I cannot give up Lusigny to the enemy, and I must acquit myself of my debt to the Captain of Créance in the only way which remains,' the young man replied firmly. 'Death is not so hard that I would not meet it twice over rather than again betray my trust.'

'This is midsummer madness!' said the King, hotly.

'Possibly,' replied the Vicomte, without emotion; 'yet of a kind to which your Grace is not altogether a stranger.'

The words appealed to that love of the fanciful and the chivalrous which formed part of the young King's nature, and was one cause alike of his weakness and his strength. In its more extravagant flights it gave opportunity after opportunity to his enemies, in its nobler and saner expressions it won victories which all his astuteness and diplomacy could not have compassed. He stood now, looking with half-hidden admiration at the man whom two minutes before he had despised.

'I think you are in jest,' he said presently and with some scorn.

'No, sir,' the young man answered, gravely. 'In my country they have a proverb about us. "The Noirterres," say they, "have ever been bad players but good payers." I will not be the first to be worse than my name!'

He spoke with so quiet a determination that the King was staggered, and for a minute or two paced the room in silence, inwardly reviling the obstinacy of this weak-kneed supporter, yet unable to withhold his admiration from it. At length he stopped, with a low exclamation.

'Wait!' he cried. 'I have it! *Ventre Saint Gris*, man, I have it!' His eyes sparkled, and, with a gentle laugh, he hit the table a sounding blow. 'Ha! ha! I have it!' he repeated gaily.

The young noble gazed at him in surprise, half suspicious, half incredulous. But when Henry in low, rapid tones had expounded his plan, the young man's face underwent a change. Hope and life sprang into it. The blood flew to his cheeks. His whole aspect softened. In a moment he was on his knee, mumbling the prince's hand, his eyes moist with gratitude. Nor was that all; the two talked long, the murmur of their voices broken more than once by the ripple of laughter. When they at length separated, and Henry, his face hidden by the folds of his cloak, had stolen to his lodgings, where, no doubt, more than one watcher was awaiting him with a mind full of anxious fears, the Vicomte threw open his window and looked out on the night. The moon had set, but the stars still shone peacefully in the dark canopy above. He remembered his throat choking with silent emotion, that he was looking towards his home—the round towers among the walnut woods of Navarre which had been in his family since the days of St Louis, and which he had so lightly risked. And he registered a vow in his heart that of all Henry's servants he would henceforth be the most faithful.

Meanwhile the Captain of Créance was enjoying the sweets of his coming triumph. He did not look out into the night, it is true —he was over old for sentiment—but pacing up and down the room he planned and calculated, considering how he might make the most of his success. He was still comparatively young. He had years of strength before him. He would rise high and higher. He would not easily be satisfied. The times were troubled, opportunities were many, fools not few; bold men with brains and hands were rare.

At the same time he knew that he could be sure of nothing until Lusigny was actually in his possession; and he spent the next few days in painful suspense. But no hitch occurred nor seemed likely. The Vicomte made him the necessary communications; and men in his own pay informed him of dispositions ordered by the governor of Lusigny which left him in no doubt that the loser intended to pay his debt.

It was, therefore, with a heart already gay with anticipation that the Captain rode out of Créance two hours before midnight on an evening eight days later. The night was dark, but he knew his road well. He had with him a powerful force, composed in part of thirty of his own garrison, bold hardy fellows, and in part of sixscore horsemen, lent him by the governor of Montauban. As the Vicomte had undertaken to withdraw, under some pretence or other, one-half of his command and to have one of the gates opened by a trusty hand, the Captain foresaw no difficulty. He trotted along in excellent spirits, now stopping to scan with approval the dark line of his troopers, now to bid them muffle the jingle of their swords and corselets that nevertheless rang sweet music in his ears. He looked for an easy victory; but it was not any slight misadventure that would rob him of his prey. If necessary he would fight and fight hard. Still, as his company wound along the river side or passed into the black shadow of the oak grove, which stands a mile to the east of Lusigny, he did not expect that there would be much fighting.

Treachery alone, he thought, could thwart him; and of treachery there was no sign. The troopers had scarcely halted under the last clump of trees before a figure detached itself from one of the largest trunks, and advanced to the Captain's rein. The Captain saw with surprise that it was the Vicomte himself. For a second he thought that something had gone wrong but the young noble's first words reassured him. 'It is arranged,' M. de Noirterre whispered, as the Captain bent down to him. 'I have kept my word, and I think that there will be no resistance. The planks for crossing the moat lie opposite the gate. Knock thrice at the latter,

44

and it will be opened. There are not fifty armed men in the place.'

'Good!' the Captain answered, in the same cautious tone. 'But you——'

'I am believed to be elsewhere, and must be gone. I have far to ride tonight. Farewell.'

'Till we meet again,' the Captain answered; and without more ado he saw his ally glide away and disappear in the darkness. A cautious word set the troop in motion, and a very few minutes saw them standing on the edge of the moat, the outline of the gateway tower looming above them, a shade darker than the wrack of clouds which overhead raced silently across the sky. A moment of suspense while one and another shivered—for there is that in a night attack which touches the nerves of the stoutest—and the planks were found, and as quietly as possible laid across the moat. This was so skilfully done that it evoked no challenge, and the Captain crossing quickly with a few picked men, stood in the twinkling of an eye under the shadow of the gateway. Still no sound was heard, save the hurried breathing of those at his elbow, the stealthy tread of others crossing, the persistent voices of the frogs in the water beneath. Cautiously he knocked three times and waited. The third rap had scarcely sounded before the gate rolled silently open, and he sprang in, followed by his men.

So far so good. A glance at the empty street and the porter's pale face told him at once that the Vicomte had kept his word. But he was too old a soldier to take anything for granted, and forming up his men as quickly as they entered, he allowed no one to advance until all were inside, and then, his trumpet sounding a wild note of defiance, two-thirds of his force sprang forward in a compact body while the other third remained to hold the gate. In a moment the town awoke to find itself in the hands of the enemy.

As the Vicomte had promised, there was no resistance. In the small keep a score of men did indeed run to arms, but only to lay their weapons down without striking a blow when they became aware of the force opposed to them. Their leader, sullenly acquiescing, gave up his sword and the keys of the town to the victorious Captain; who, as he sat his horse in the middle of the market-place, giving his orders and sending off riders with the news, already saw himself in fancy Governor of Angouleme and Knight of the Holy Ghost.

A cautious word set the troop in motion

As the red light of the torches fell on steel caps and polished hauberks, on the serried ranks of pikemen, and the circle of white-faced townsfolks, the picturesque old square looked doubly picturesque and he who sat in the midst, its master, doubly a hero. Every five minutes, with a clatter of iron on the rough pavement and a shower of sparks, a horseman sprang away to tell the news at Montauban or Cahors; and every time that this occurred, the Captain, astride on his charger, felt a new sense of power and triumph.

Suddenly the low murmur of voices about him was broken by a new sound, the distant beat of hoofs, not departing but arriving, and coming each moment nearer. It was but the tramp of a single horse, but there was something in the sound which made the Captain prick his ears, and secured for the arriving messenger a speedy passage through the crowd. Even at the last the man did not spare his horse, but spurred through the ranks to the Captain's very side, and then and then only sprang to the ground. His face was pale, his eyes were bloodshot. His right arm was bound up in blood-stained cloths. With an oath of amazement, the Captain recognized the officer whom he had left in charge of Créance, and he thundered, 'What is this? What is it?'

'They have got Créance!' the man gasped, reeling as he spoke. 'They have got—Créance!'

'Who?' the Captain shrieked, his face purple with rage.

'The little man of Béarn! The King of Navarre! He assaulted it five hundred strong an hour after you left, and had the gate down before we could fire a dozen shots. We did what we could, but we were but one to seven. I swear, Captain, that we did all we could. Look at this!'

Almost black in the face, the Captain swore another oath. It was not only that he saw governorship and honours vanish like Will-o'-the-wisps, but that he saw even more quickly that he had made himself the laughing-stock of a kingdom! And that was the truth. To this day, among the stories which the southern French love to tell of the prowess and astuteness of their great Henry, there is none more frequently told, none more frequently made the subject of mirth, than that of the famous exchange of Créance for Lusigny; the tradition of the move by which, between dawn and sunrise, without warning, without a word, he gave his opponents mate.

47

Sir Arthur Conan Doyle

How the Brigadier Saved an Army

I have told you, my friends, how we held the English shut up for six months, from October, 1810, to March, 1811, within their lines of Torres Vedras. It was during this time that I hunted the fox in their company, and showed them that amidst all their sportsmen there was not one who could outride a Hussar of Conflans. When I galloped back into the French lines with the blood of the creature still moist upon my blade, the outposts who had seen what I had done raised a frenzied cry in my honour, whilst these English hunters still yelled behind me, so that I had the applause of both armies. It made the tears rise to my eyes to feel that I had won the admiration of so many brave men. These English are generous foes. That very evening there came a packet under a white flag addressed. 'To the Hussar officer who cut down the fox.' Within I found the fox itself in two pieces, as I had left it. There was a note also, short, but hearty as the English fashion is, to say that as I had slaughtered the fox it only remained for me to eat it. They could not know that it was not our French custom to eat foxes, and it showed their desire that he who had won the honours of the chase should also partake of the game. It is not for a Frenchman to be outdone in politeness, and so I returned it to these brave hunters, and begged them to accept it as a side-dish for their next *dejeuner de la chasse*. It is thus that chivalrous opponents make war.

I had brought back with me from my ride a clear plan of the English lines, and this I laid before Massena that very evening.

I had hoped that it would lead him to attack, but all the marshals were at each other's throats, snapping and growling like so many hungry hounds. Ney hated Massena, and Massena hated Junot, and Soult hated them all. For this reason nothing was done. In the meantime food grew more and more scarce, and our beautiful cavalry was ruined for want of fodder. With the end of the winter we had swept the whole country bare, and nothing remained for us to eat, although we sent our forage parties far and wide. It was clear even to the bravest of us that the time had come to retreat. I was myself forced to admit it.

But retreat was not so easy. Not only were the troops weak and exhausted from want of supplies, but the enemy had been much encouraged by our long inaction. Of Wellington we had no great fear. We had found him to be brave and cautious, but with little enterprise. Besides, in that barren country his pursuit could not be rapid. But on our flanks and in our rear there had gathered great numbers of Portuguese militia, of armed peasants, and of guerillas. These people had kept a safe distance all the winter, but now that our horses were foundered they were as thick as flies all round our outposts, and no man's life was worth a sou when once he fell into their hands. I could name a dozen officers of my own acquaintance who were cut off during that time, and the luckiest was he who received a ball from behind a rock through his head or his heart. There were some whose deaths were so terrible that no report of them was ever allowed to reach their relatives. So frequent were these tragedies, and so much did they impress the imagination of the men, that it became very difficult to induce them to leave the camp. There was one especial scoundrel, a guerilla chief named Manuelo, "The Smiler," whose exploits filled our men with horror. He was a large, fat man of jovial aspect, and he lurked with a fierce gang among the mountains which lay upon our left flank. A volume might be written of this fellow's cruelties and brutalities, but he was certainly a man of power, for he organised his brigands in a manner which made it almost impossible for us to get through his country. This he did by imposing a severe discipline upon them and enforcing it by cruel penalties, a policy by which he made them formidable, but which had some unexpected results, as I will show you in my story. Had he not flogged his own lieutenant—but you will hear of that when the time comes.

There were many difficulties in connection with a retreat, but

49

it was very evident that there was no other possible course, and so Massena began to quickly pass his baggage and his sick from Torres Novas, which was his headquarters, to Coimbra, the first strong post on his line of communications. He could not do this unperceived, however, and at once the guerillas came swarming closer and closer upon our flanks. One of our divisions, that of Clausel, with a brigade of Montbrun's cavalry, was far to the south of the Tagus, and it become very necessary to let them know that we were about to retreat, for otherwise they would be left unsupported in the very heart of the enemy's country. I remember wondering how Massena would accomplish this, for simple couriers could not get through, and small parties would be certainly destroyed. In some way an order to fall back must be conveyed to these men, or France would be the weaker by fourteen thousand men. Little did I think that it was I, Colonel Gerard, who was to have the honour of a deed which might have formed the crowning glory of any other man's life, and which stands high among those exploits which have made my own so famous.

At that time I was serving on Massena's staff, and he had two other aides-de-camp, who were also very brave and intelligent officers. The name of one was Cortex and of the other Duplessis. They were senior to me in age, but junior in every other respect. Cortex was a small, dark man, very quick and eager. He was a fine soldier, but he was ruined by his conceit. To take him at his own valuation, he was the first man in the army. Duplessis was a Gascon, like myself, and he was a very fine fellow, as all Gascon gentlemen are. We took it in turn, day about, to do duty, and it was Cortex who was in attendance upon the morning of which I speak. I saw him at breakfast, but afterwards neither he nor his horse was to be seen. All day Massena was in his usual gloom, and he spent much of his time staring with his telescope at the English lines and at the shipping in the Tagus. He said nothing of the mission upon which he had sent our comrade, and it was not for us to ask him any questions.

That night, about twelve o'clock, I was standing outside the Marshal's headquarters when he came out and stood motionless for half an hour, his arms folded upon his breast, staring through the darkness towards the east. So rigid and intent was he that you might have believed the muffled figure and the cocked hat to have been the statue of the man. What he was looking for I could not imagine; but at last he gave a bitter curse, and, turning on his heel, he went back into the house, banging the door behind him.

Next day the second aide-de-camp, Duplessis, had an interview with Massena in the morning, after which neither he nor his horse was seen again. That night, as I sat in the ante-room, the Marshal passed me, and I observed him through the window standing and staring to the east exactly as he had done before. For fully half an hour he remained there, a black shadow in the gloom. Then he strode in, the door banged, and I heard his spurs and his scabbard jingling and clanking through the passage. At the best he was a savage old man, but when he was crossed I had almost as soon face the Emperor himself. I heard him that night cursing and stamping above my head, but he did not send for me, and I knew him too well to go unsought.

Next morning it was my turn, for I was the only aide-de-camp left. I was his favourite aide-de-camp. His heart went out always to a smart soldier. I declare that I think there were tears in his black eyes when he sent for me that morning.

'Gerard!' said he. 'Come here!'

With a friendly gesture he took me by the sleeve and he led me to the open window which faced the east. Beneath us was the infantry camp, and beyond that the lines of the cavalry with the long rows of picketed horses. We could see the French outposts, and then a stretch of open country, intersected by vineyards. A range of hills lay beyond, with one well-marked peak towering above them. Round the base of these hills was a broad belt of forest. A single road ran white and clear, dipping and rising until it passed through a gap in the hills.

'This,' said Massena, pointing to the mountain, 'is the Sierra de Merodal. Do you perceive anything upon the top?'

I answered that I did not.

'Now?' he asked, and he handed me his field-glass.

With its aid I perceived a small mound or cairn upon the crest.

'What you see,' said the Marshal, 'is a pile of logs which was placed there as a beacon. We laid it when the country was in our hands, and now, although we no longer hold it, the beacon remains undisturbed. Gerard, that beacon must be lit tonight. France needs it, the Emperor needs it, the army needs it. Two of your comrades have gone to light it, but neither has made his way to the summit. Today it is your turn, and I pray that you may have better luck.'

It is not for a soldier to ask the reason for his orders, and so I was about to hurry from the room, but the Marshal laid his hand upon my shoulder and held me.

'You shall know all, and so learn how high is the cause for which you risk your life,' said he. 'Fifty miles to the south of us, on the other side of the Tagus, is the army of General Clausel. His camp is situated near a peak named the Sierra d'Ossa. On the summit of this peak is a beacon, and by this beacon he has a picket. It is agreed between us that when at midnight he shall see our signal fire he shall light his own as an answer, and shall then at once fall back upon the main army. If he does not start at once I must go without him. For two days I have endeavoured to send him his message. It must reach him today, or his army will be left behind and destroyed.'

Ah, my friends, how my heart swelled when I heard how high was the task which fortune had assigned to me! If my life were spared, here was one more splendid new leaf for my laurel crown. If, on the other hand, I died, then it would be a death worthy of such a career. I said nothing, but I cannot doubt that all the noble thoughts that were in me shone in my face, for Massena took my hand and wrung it.

'There is the hill and there the beacon,' said he. 'There is only this guerilla and his men between you and it. I cannot detach a large party for the enterprise, and a small one would be seen and destroyed. Therefore to you alone I commit it. Carry it out in your own way, but at twelve o'clock this night let me see the fire upon the hill.'

'If it is not there,' said I, 'then I pray you, Marshal Massena, to see that my effects are sold and the money sent to my mother.' So I raised my hand to my busby and turned upon my heel, my heart glowing at the thought of the great exploit which lay before me.

I sat in my own chamber for some little time considering how I had best take the matter in hand. The fact that neither Cortex nor

Duplessis, who were very zealous and active officers, had succeeded in reaching the summit of the Sierra de Merodal showed that the country was very closely watched by the guerillas. I reckoned out the distance upon a map. There were ten miles of open country to be crossed before reaching the hills. Then came a belt of forest on the lower slopes of the mountain, which may have been three or four miles wide. And then there was the actual peak itself, of no very great height, but without any cover to conceal me. Those were the three stages of my journey.

It seemed to me that once I had reached the shelter of the wood all would be easy, for I could lie concealed within its shadows and climb upwards under the cover of night. From eight till twelve would give me four hours of darkness in which to make the ascent. It was only the first stage, then, which I had seriously to consider.

Over that flat country there lay the inviting white road, and I remembered that my comrades had both taken their horses. That was clearly their ruin, for nothing could be easier than for the brigands to keep watch upon the road, and to lay an ambush for all who passed along it. It would not be difficult for me to ride across country, and I was well horsed at that time, for I had not only Violette and Rataplan, who were two of the finest mounts in the army, but I had the splendid black English hunter which I had taken from Sir Cotton. However, after much thought, I determined to go upon foot, since I should then be in a better state to take advantage of any chance which might offer. As to my dress, I covered my Hussar uniform with a long cloak, and I put a grey forage cap upon my head. You may ask me why I did not dress as a peasant, but I answer that a man of honour has no desire to die the death of a spy. It is one thing to be murdered, and it is another to be justly executed by the laws of war. I would not run the risk of such an end.

In the late afternoon I stole out of the camp and passed through the line of our pickets. Beneath my cloak I had a field-glass and a pocket pistol, as well as my sword. In my pocket were tinder, flint, and steel.

For two or three miles I kept under cover of the vineyards, and made such good progress that my heart was high within me, and I thought to myself that it only needed a man of some brains to take the matter in hand to bring it easily to success. Of course, Cortex and Duplessis galloping down the high road would be easily seen, but the intelligent Gerard lurking among the vines was quite another person. I dare say I had got as far as five miles before I met any check. At that point there is a small winehouse, round which I perceived some carts and a number of people, the first that I had seen. Now that I was well outside the lines I knew that every person was my enemy, so I crouched lower while I stole along to a point from which I could get a better view of what was going on. I then perceived that these people were peasants, who were loading two waggons with empty wine-casks. I failed to see how they could either help or hinder me, so I continued upon my way.

But soon I understood that my task was not so simple as had appeared. As the ground rose the vineyards ceased, and I came upon a stretch of open country studded with low hills. Crouching in a ditch I examined them with a glass, and I very soon perceived that there was a watcher upon every one of them, and that these people had a line of pickets and outposts thrown forward exactly like our own. I had heard of the discipline which was practised by this scoundrel whom they called 'The Smiler,' and this, no doubt, was an example of it. Between the hills there was a cordon of sentries, and, though I worked some distance round to the flank, I still found myself faced by the enemy. It was a puzzle what to do. There was so little cover that a rat could hardly cross without being seen. Of course, it would be easy enough to slip through at night, as I had done with the English at Torres Vedras; but I was still far from the mountain, and I could not in that case reach it in time to light the midnight beacon. I lay in my ditch and I made a thousand plans, each more dangerous than the last. And then suddenly I had that flash of light which comes to the brave man who refuses to despair.

You remember I have mentioned that two waggons were loading up with empty casks at the inn. The heads of the oxen were turned to the east, and it was evident that those waggons were going in the direction which I desired. Could I only conceal myself upon one of them, what better and easier way could I find of passing through the lines of the guerillas? So simple and so good was the plan that I could not restrain a cry of delight as it crossed my mind, and I hurried away instantly in the direction of the inn. There, from behind some bushes, I had a good look at what was going on upon the road.

There were three peasants with red montero caps loading the barrels, and they had completed one waggon and the lower tier of the other. A number of empty barrels still lay outside the wine-house waiting to be put on. Fortune was my friend—I have always said that she is a woman and cannot resist a dashing young Hussar. As I watched, the three fellows went into the inn, for the day was hot, and they were thirsty after their labour. Quick as a flash I darted out from my hiding-place, climbed on to the waggon, and crept into one of the empty casks. It had a bottom but no top, and it lay upon its side with the open end inwards. There I crouched like a dog in its kennel, my knees drawn up to my chin; for the barrels were not very large and I am a well-grown man. As I lay there out came the three peasants again, and presently I heard a crash upon the top of me, which told that I had another barrel above me. They piled them upon the cart until I could not imagine how I was ever to get out again. However, it is time to think of crossing the Vistula when you are over the Rhine, and I had no doubt that if chance and my own wits had carried me so far they would carry me farther.

Soon, when the waggon was full, they set forth upon their way, and I within my barrel chuckled at every step, for it was carrying me whither I wished to go. We travelled slowly, and the peasants walked beside the waggons. This I knew, because I heard their voices close to me. They seemed to me to be very merry fellows, for they laughed heartily as they went. What the joke was I could not understand. Though I speak their language fairly well I could not hear anything comic in the scraps of their conversation which met my ear.

I reckoned that at the rate of walking of a team of oxen we covered about two miles an hour. Therefore, when I was sure that two and a half hours had passed—such hours, my friends, cramped, suffocated, and nearly poisoned with the fumes of the lees—when they had passed, I was sure that the dangerous open country was behind us, and that we were upon the edge of the forest and the mountain. So now I had to turn my mind upon how I was to get out of my barrel. I had thought of several ways, and was balancing one against the other, when the question was decided for me in a very simple but unexpected manner.

The waggon stopped suddenly with a jerk, and I heard a number of gruff voices in excited talk. 'Where, where?' cried one. 'On our cart,' said another. 'Who is he?' said a third. 'A French officer; I saw his cap and his boots.' They all roared with laughter. 'I was looking out of the window of the *posada* and I saw him spring into the cask like a toreador with a Seville bull at his heels.' 'Which cask, then?' 'It was this one,' said the fellow, and, sure enough, his fist struck the wood beside my head.

What a situation, my friends, for a man of my standing! I blush now, after forty years, when I think of it. To be trussed like a fowl and to listen helplessly to the rude laughter of these boors—to know, too, that my mission had come to an ignominious and even ridiculous end. I would have blessed the man who would have sent a bullet through the cask and freed me from my misery.

I heard the crashing of the barrels as they hurled them off the waggon, and then a couple of bearded faces and the muzzles of two guns looked in at me. They seized me by the sleeves of my coat, and they dragged me out into the daylight. A strange figure I must have looked as I stood blinking and gaping in the blinding sunlight. My body was bent like a cripple's, for I could not straighten my stiff joints, and half my coat was as red as an English soldier's from the lees in which I had lain. They laughed and laughed, these dogs, and as I tried to express by my bearing and gestures the contempt in which I held them, their laughter grew all the louder. But even in these hard circumstances I bore myself like the man I am, and as I cast my eye slowly round I did not find that any of the laughers were very ready to face it.

That one glance round was enough to tell me exactly how I was situated. I had been betrayed by these peasants into the hands of an outpost of guerilias. There were eight of them, savage-looking, hairy creatures, with cotton handkerchiefs under their sombreros, and many-buttoned jackets with coloured sashes round the waist. Each had a gun and one or two pistols stuck in his girdle. The leader, a great bearded ruffian, held his gun against my ear while the others searched my pockets, taking from me my overcoat, my pistol, my glass, my sword, and, worst of all, my flint and steel and tinder. Come what might I was ruined, for I had no longer the means of lighting the beacon even if I should reach it.

Eight of them, my friends, with three peasants, and I unarmed! Was Etienne Gerard in despair? Did he lose his wits? Ah, you know me too well; but they did not know me yet, these dogs of brigands. Never have I made so supreme and astounding an effort as at this very instant when all seemed lost. Yet you might guess many times before you would hit upon the device by which I escaped them. Listen and I will tell you.

They had dragged me from the waggon when they searched me, and I stood, still twisted and warped, in the midst of them. But the stiffness was wearing off, and already my mind was very actively looking out for some method of breaking away. It was a narrow pass in which the brigands had their outpost. It was bounded on the one hand by a steep mountain side. On the other the ground fell away in a very long slope, which ended in a bushy valley many hundreds of feet below. These fellows, you understand, were hardy mountaineers, who could travel either up hill or down very much quicker than I. They wore abarcas, or shoes of skin, tied on like sandals, which gave them a foothold everywhere. A less resolute man would have despaired. But in an instant I saw and used the strange chance which Fortune had placed in my way. On the very edge of the slope was one of the wine-barrels. I moved slowly towards it, and then with a tiger spring I dived into it feet foremost, and with a roll of my body I tipped it over the side of the hill.

Shall I ever forget that dreadful journey—how I bounded and crashed and whizzed down that terrible slope? I had dug in my knees and elbows, bunching my body into a compact bundle so as to steady it; but my head projected from the end, and it was a marvel that I did not dash out my brains. There were long, smooth slopes and then came steeper scarps where the barrel ceased to roll, and sprang into the air like a goat, coming down with a rattle and crash which jarred every bone in my body. How the wind whistled in my ears, and my head turned and turned until I was sick and giddy and nearly senseless! Then, with a swish and a great rasping and crackling of branches, I reached the bushes which I had seen so far below me. Through them I broke my way, down a slope beyond, and deep into another patch of under-wood, where striking a sapling my barrel flew to pieces. From amid a heap of staves and hoops I crawled out, my body aching in every inch of it, but my heart singing loudly with joy and my spirit high within me, for I knew how great was the feat which I had accomplished, and I already seemed to see the beacon blazing on the hill.

A horrible nausea had seized me from the tossing which I had undergone, and I felt as I did upon the ocean when first I experienced those movements of which the English have taken so perfidious an advantage. I had to sit for a few moments with my head upon my hands beside the ruins of my barrel. But there was no time for rest. Already I heard shouts above me which told that my pursuers were descending the hill. I dashed into the thickest part of the underwood, and I ran and ran until I was utterly exhausted. Then I lay panting and listened with all my ears, but no sound came to them. I had shaken off my enemies.

When I had recovered my breath I travelled swiftly on, and waded knee-deep through several brooks, for it came into my head that they might follow me with dogs. On gaining a clear place and looking round me, I found to my delight that in spite of my adventures I had not been much out of my way. Above me towered the peak of Merodal, with its bare and bold summit shooting out of the groves of dwarf oaks which shrouded its flanks. These groves were the continuation of the cover under which I found myself, and it seemed to me that I had nothing to fear now until I reached the other side of the forest. At the same time I knew that every man's hand was against me, that I was unarmed, and that there were many people about me. I saw no one, but several times I heard shrill whistles, and once the sound of a gun in the distance.

It was hard work pushing one's way through the bushes, and so I was glad when I came to the larger trees and found a path which led between them. Of course, I was too wise to walk upon it, but I kept near it and followed its course. I had gone some distance, and had, as I imagined, nearly reached the limit of the wood, when a strange, moaning sound fell upon my ears. At first I thought it was the cry of some animals, but then there came words, of which I only caught the French exclamation, 'Mon Dieu!' With great caution I advanced in the direction from which the sound proceeded, and this is what I saw.

On a couch of dried leaves there was stretched a man dressed in the same grey uniform which I wore myself. He was evidently horribly wounded, for he held a cloth to his breast which was crimson with his blood. A pool had formed all round his couch, and he lay in a haze of flies, whose buzzing and droning would certainly have called my attention if his groans had not come to my ear. I lay for a moment, fearing some trap, and then, my pity and loyalty rising above all other feelings, I ran forward and knelt by his side. He turned a haggard face upon me, and it was Duplessis, the man who had gone before me. It needed but one glance at his sunken cheeks and glazing eyes to tell me that he was dying.

'Gerard!' said he; 'Gerard!'

I could but look my sympathy, but he, though the life was ebbing swiftly out of him, still kept his duty before him, like the gallant gentleman he was.

'The beacon, Gerard! You will light it?'

'Have you flint and steel?'

'It is here.'

'Then I will light it tonight.'

'I die happy to hear you say so. They shot me, Gerard. But you will tell the Marshal that I did my best.'

'And Cortex?'

'He was less fortunate. He fell into their hands and died horribly. If you see that you cannot get away, Gerard, put a bullet into your own heart. Don't die as Cortex did.'

I could see that his breath was failing, and I bent low to catch his words.

'Can you tell me anything which can help me in my task?' I asked.

'Yes, yes; De Pombal. He will help you. Trust De Pombal.' With the words his head fell back and he was dead.

'Trust De Pombal. It is good advice.' To my amazement a man was standing at the very side of me. So absorbed had I been in my comrade's words and intent on his advice that he had crept up without my observing him. Now I sprang to my feet and faced him. He was a tall, dark fellow, black-haired, black-eyed, black-bearded, with a long, sad face. In his hand he had a wine-bottle and over his shoulder was slung one of the trebucos, or blunderbusses, which these fellows bear. He made no effort to unsling it, and I understood that this was the man to whom my dead friend had commended me.

'Alas, he is gone!' said he, bending over Duplessis. 'He fled into the wood after he was shot, but I was fortunate enough to find where he had fallen and to make his last hours more easy. This couch was my making, and I had brought this wine to slake his thirst.'

'Sir,' said I, 'in the name of France I thank you. I am but a colonel of light cavalry, but I am Etienne Gerard, and the name stands for something in the French army. May I ask——'

'Yes, sir, I am Aloysius de Pombal, younger brother of the famous nobleman of that name. At present I am the first lieu-tenant in the band of the guerilla chief who is usually known as Manuelo, "The Smiler."'

My word, I clapped my hand to the place where my pistol should have been, but the man only smiled at the gesture.

'I am his first lieutenant, but I am also his deadly enemy,' said he. He slipped off his jacket and pulled up his shirt as he spoke. 'Look at this!' he cried, and he turned upon me a back which was all scored and lacerated with red and purple weals. 'This is what "The Smiler" has done to me, a man with the noblest blood of Portugal in my veins. What I will do to "The Smiler" you have still to see.'

There was such fury in his eyes and in the grin of his white teeth that I could no longer doubt his truth, with that clotted and oozing back to corroborate his words.

'I have ten men sworn to stand by me,' said he. 'In a few days I hope to join your army, when I have done my work here. In the meanwhile——' A strange change came over his face, and he suddenly slung his musket to the front: 'Hold up your hands, you French hound!' he yelled. 'Up with them, or I blow your head off!'

You start, my friends! You stare! Think, then, how I stared and started at this sudden ending of our talk. There was the black muzzle, and there the dark, angry eyes behind it. What could I

'*Hold up your hands, you French hound!*' *he yelled*

do? I was helpless. I raised my hands in the air. At the same
moment voices sounded from all parts of the wood, there were
crying and calling and rushing of many feet. A swarm of dreadful
figures broke through the green bushes, a dozen hands seized me,
and I, poor, luckless, frenzied I, was a prisoner once more. Thank
God, there was no pistol which I could have plucked from my belt
and snapped at my own head. Had I been armed at that moment
I should not be sitting here in this café and telling you these old-
world tales.

With grimy, hairy hands clutching me on every side I was led
along the pathway through the wood, the villain De Pombal
giving directions to my captors. Four of the brigands carried up
the dead body of Duplessis. The shadows of evening were already
falling when we cleared the forest and came out upon the moun-
tainside. Up this I was driven until we reached the headquarters
of the guerillas, which lay in a cleft close to the summit of the
mountain. There was the beacon which had cost me so much, a
square stack of wood, immediately above our heads. Below were
two or three huts which had belonged, no doubt, to goatherds,
and which were now used to shelter these rascals. Into one of these
I was cast, bound and helpless, and the dead body of my poor
comrade was laid beside me.

I was lying there with the one thought still consuming me,
how to wait a few hours and to get at that pile of faggots above
my head, when the door of my prison opened and a man entered.
Had my hands been free I should have flown at his throat, for it
was none other than De Pombal. A couple of brigands were at
his heels, but he ordered them back and closed the door behind
him.

'You villain!' said I.

'Hush!' he cried. 'Speak low, for I do not know who may be
listening, and my life is at stake. I have some words to say to you,
Colonel Gerard; I wish well to you, as I did to your dead companion. As I spoke to you beside his body I saw that we were
surrounded, and that your capture was unavoidable. I should
have shared your fate had I hesitated. I instantly captured you
myself, so as to preserve the confidence of the band. Your own
sense will tell you that there was nothing else for me to do. I do
not know now whether I can save you, but at least I will try.'

This was a new light upon the situation. I told him that I could not tell how far he spoke the truth, but that I would judge him by his actions.

'I ask nothing better,' said he. 'A word of advice to you! The chief will see you now. Speak him fair, or he will have you sawn between two planks. Contradict nothing he says. Give him such information he wants. It is your only chance. If you can gain time something may come in our favour. Now, I have no more time. Come at once, or suspicion may be awakened.' He helped me to rise and then, opening the door, he dragged me out very roughly, and with the aid of the fellows outside he brutally pushed and thrust me to the place where the guerilla chief was seated, with his rude followers gathered round him.

A remarkable man was Manuelo, 'The Smiler.' He was fat and florid and comfortable, with a big, clean-shaven face and a bald head, the very model of a kindly father of a family. As I looked at his honest smile I could scarcely believe that this was, indeed, the infamous ruffian whose name was a horror through the English Army as well as our own. It is well known that Trent, who was a British officer, afterwards had the fellow hanged for his brutalities. He sat upon a boulder and he beamed upon me like one who meets an old acquaintance. I observed, however, that one of his men leaned upon a long saw, and the sight was enough to cure me of all delusions.

'Good evening, Colonel Gerard,' said he. 'We have been highly honoured by General Massena's staff: Major Cortex one day, Colonel Duplessis the next, and now Colonel Gerard. Possibly the Marshal himself may be induced to honour us with a visit. You have seen Duplessis, I understand. Cortex you will find nailed to a tree down yonder. It only remains to be decided how we can best dispose of yourself.'

It was not a cheering speech; but all the time his fat face was wreathed in smiles, and he lisped out his words in the most mincing and amiable fashion. Now, however, he suddenly leaned forward, and I read a very real intensity in his eyes.

'Colonel Gerard,' said he, 'I cannot promise you your life, for it is not our custom, but I can give you an easy death or I can give you a terrible one. Which shall it be?'

'What do you wish me to do in exchange?'

'If you would die easy I ask you to give me truthful answers to the questions which I ask.'

A sudden thought flashed through my mind.

'You wish to kill me,' said I; 'it cannot matter to you how I die. If I answer your questions, will you let me choose the manner of my own death?'

'Yes, I will,' said he, 'so long as it is before midnight tonight.'

'Swear it!' I cried.

'The word of a Portuguese gentleman is sufficient,' said he.

'Not a word will I say until you have sworn it.'

He flushed with anger and his eyes swept round towards the saw. But he understood from my tone that I meant what I said, and that I was not a man to be bullied into submission. He pulled a cross from under his zammara or jacket of black sheepskin.

'I swear it,' said he.

Oh, my joy as I heard the words! What an end—what an end for the first swordsman of France! I could have laughed with delight at the thought.

'Now, your questions!' said I.

'You swear in turn to answer them truly?'

'I do, upon the honour of a gentleman and a soldier.' It was, as you perceive, a terrible thing that I promised, but what was it compared to what I might gain by compliance?

'This is a very fair and a very interesting bargain,' said he, taking a notebook from his pocket. 'Would you kindly turn your gaze towards the French camp?'

Following the direction of his gesture, I turned and looked down upon the camp in the plain beneath us. In spite of the fifteen miles, one could in that clear atmosphere see every detail with the utmost distinctness. There were the long squares of our tents and our huts, with the cavalry lines and the dark patches which marked the ten batteries of artillery. How sad to think of my magnificent regiment waiting down yonder, and to know that they would never see their colonel again! With one squadron of them I could have swept all these cut-throats off the face of the earth. My eager eyes filled with tears as I looked at the corner of the camp where I knew that there were eight hundred men, any-one of whom would have died for his colonel. But my sadness vanished when I saw behind the tents the plumes of smoke which marked the headquarters at Torres Novas. There was Massena, and, please God, at the cost of my life his mission would that night be done. A spasm of pride and exultation filled my breast. I should have liked to have had a voice of thunder that I might call to them, 'Behold it is I, Etienne Gerard, who will die in order to save the army of Clausel!' It was, indeed, sad to think that so noble a deed should be done, and that no one should be there to tell the tale.

'Now,' said the brigand chief, 'you see the camp and you see also the road which leads to Coimbra. It is crowded with your fourgons and your ambulances. Does this mean that Massena is about to retreat?'

One could see the dark moving lines of waggons with an occasional flash of steel from the escort. There could, apart from my promise, be no indiscretion in admitting that which was already obvious.

'He will retreat,' said I.

'By Coimbra?'

'I believe so.'

'But the army of Clausel?'

I shrugged my shoulders.

'Every path to the south is blocked. No message can reach them. If Massena falls back the army of Clausel is doomed.'

'It must take its chance,' said I.

'How many men has he?'

'I should say about fourteen thousand.'

'How much cavalry?'

'One brigade of Montbrun's Division.'

'What regiments?'

'The 4th Chasseurs, the 9th Hussars, and a regiment of Cuirassiers.'

'Quite right,' said he, looking at his notebook. 'I can tell you speak the truth, and Heaven help you if you don't.' Then, division by division, he went over the whole army, asking the composition of each brigade. Need I tell you that I would have had my tongue torn out before I would have told him such things had I not a greater end in view? I would let him know all if I could but save the army of Clausel.

At last he closed his notebook and replaced it in his pocket. 'I am obliged to you for this information, which shall reach Lord Wellington tomorrow,' said he. 'You have done your share of the bargain; it is for me now to perform mine. How would you wish to die? As a soldier you would, no doubt, prefer to be shot, but some think that a jump over the Merodal precipice is really an easier death. A good few have taken it, but we were, unfortunately, never able to get an opinion from them afterwards. There is the saw, too, which does not appear to be popular. We could hang you, no doubt, but it would involve the inconvenience of going down to the wood. However, a promise is a promise, and you seem to be an excellent fellow, so we will spare no pains to meet your wishes.'

'You said,' I answered, 'that I must die before midnight. I will choose, therefore, just one minute before that hour.'

'Very good,' said he. 'Such clinging to life is rather childish, but your wishes shall be met.'

'As to the method,' I added, 'I love a death which all the world can see. Put me on yonder pile of faggots and burn me alive, as saints and martyrs have been burned before me. That is no common end, but one which an Emperor might envy.'

The idea seemed to amuse him very much.

'Why not?' said he. 'If Massena has sent you to spy upon us, he may guess what the fire upon the mountains means.'

'Exactly,' said I. 'You have hit upon my very reason. He will guess, and all will know, that I have died a soldier's death.'

'I see no objection whatever,' said the brigand, with his abominable smile. 'I will send some goat's flesh and wine into your hut. The sun is sinking, and it is nearly eight o'clock. In four hours be ready for your end.'

It was a beautiful world to be leaving. I looked at the golden haze below, where the last rays of the sinking sun shone upon the blue waters of the winding Tagus and gleamed upon the white sails of the English transports. Very beautiful it was, and very sad to leave; but there are things more beautiful than that. The death that is died for the sake of others, honour, and duty, and loyalty, and love—these are the beauties far brighter than any which the eye can see. My breast was filled with admiration for my own most noble conduct, and with wonder whether any soul would ever come to know how I had placed myself in the heart of the beacon which saved the army of Clausel. I hoped so and I prayed so, for what a consolation it would be to my mother, what an example to the army, what a pride to my Hussars! When De Pombal came at last into my hut with the food and the wine, the first request I made him was that he would write an account of my death and send it to the French camp. He answered not a word, but I ate my supper with a better appetite from the thought that my glorious fate would not be altogether unknown.

I had been there about two hours when the door opened again, and the chief stood looking in. I was in darkness, but a brigand with a torch stood beside him, and I saw his eyes and his teeth gleaming as he peered at me.

'Ready?' he asked.

'It is not yet time.'

'You stand out for the last minute?'

'A promise is a promise.'

'Very good. Be it so. We have a little justice to do among ourselves, for one of my fellows has been misbehaving. We have a strict rule of our own which is no respecter of persons, as De Pombal here could tell you. Do you truss him and lay him on the faggots, De Pombal, and I will return to see him die.'

De Pombal and the man with the torch entered, while I heard the steps of the chief passing away. De Pombal closed the door.

'Colonel Gerard,' said he, 'you must trust this man, for he is one of my party. It is neck or nothing. We may save you yet. But I take a great risk, and I want a definite promise. If we save you, will you guarantee that we have a friendly reception in the French camp and that all the past will be forgotten?'

'I do guarantee it.'

'And I trust your honour. Now, quick, quick, there is not an instant to lose! If this monster returns we shall die horribly, all three.'

I stared in amazement at what he did. Catching up a long rope he wound it round the body of my dead comrade, and he tied a cloth round his mouth so as to almost cover his face.

'Do you lie there!' he cried, and he laid me in the place of the dead body. 'I have four of my men waiting, and they will place this upon the beacon.' He opened the door and gave an order. Several of the brigands entered and bore out Duplessis. For myself I remained upon the floor, with my mind in a turmoil of hope and wonder.

Five minutes later De Pombal and his men were back.

'You are laid upon the beacon,' said he; 'I defy any one in the world to say it is not you, and you are so gagged and bound that no one can expect you to speak or move. Now, it only remains to carry forth the body of Duplessis and to toss it over the Merodal precipice.'

Two of them seized me by the head and two by the heels and carried me, stiff and inert, from the hut. As I came into the open air I could have cried out in my amazement. The moon had risen, above the beacon, and there, clear outlined against its silver light, was the figure of the man stretched upon the top. The brigands were either in their camp or standing round the beacon, for none of them stopped or questioned our little party. De Pombal led them in the direction of the precipice. At the brow we were out of sight, and there I was allowed to use my feet once more. De Pombal pointed to a narrow, winding track.

'This is the way down,' said he, and then, suddenly, 'Dios mio, what is that?'

A terrible cry had risen out of the woods beneath us. I saw that De Pombal was shivering like a frightened horse.

'It is that devil,' he whispered. 'He is treating another as he treated me. But on, on, for Heaven help us if he lays his hands upon us!'

One by one we crawled down the narrow goat track. At the bottom of the cliff we were back in the woods once more. Suddenly a yellow glare shone above us, and the black shadows of the tree-trunks started out in front. They had fired the beacon behind us. Even from where we stood we could see that impassive body amid the flames, and the black figures of the guerillas as they danced, howling like cannibals, round the pile. Ha! how I shook my fist at them, the dogs, and how I vowed that one day my Hussars and I would make the reckoning level!

De Pombal knew how the outposts were placed and all the paths which led through the forest. But to avoid these villains we had to plunge among the hills and walk for many a weary mile. And yet how gladly would I have walked those extra leagues if only for one sight which they brought to my eyes! It may have been two o'clock in the morning when we halted upon the bare shoulder of a hill over which our path curled. Looking back we saw the red glow of the embers of the beacon as if volcanic fires were bursting from the tall peak of Merodal. And then, as I gazed, I saw something else—something which caused me to shriek with joy and to fall upon the ground, rolling in my delight. For, far away upon the southern horizon, there winked and twinkled one great yellow light, throbbing and flaming, the light of no house, the light of no star, but the answering beacon of Mount d'Ossa, which told that the army of Clausel knew what Etienne Gerard had been sent to tell them.

Rudyard Kipling

Red Dog

For our white and our excellent nights—for the nights of swift
  running,
  Fair ranging, far seeing, good hunting, sure cunning!
For the smells of the dawning, untainted, ere dew has departed!
For the rush through the mist, and the quarry blind-started!
For the cry of our mates when the sambhur has wheeled and is standing
  at bay,
  For the risk and the riot of night!
  For the sleep at the lair-mouth by day
  It is met, and we go to the fight.
  Bay! O Bay!

It was after the letting in of the Jungle that the pleasantest part
of Mowgli's [1] life began. He had the good conscience that comes
from paying debts; all the Jungle was his friend, and just a little
afraid of him. The things that he did and saw and heard when he
was wandering from one people to another, with or without his
four companions, would make many many stories, each as long
as this one. So you will never be told how he met the Mad Elephant of Mandla, who killed two-and-twenty bullocks drawing
eleven carts of coined silver to the Government Treasury, and
scattered the shiny rupees in the dust; how he fought Jacala, the
Crocodile, all one long night in the Marshes of the North, and
broke his skinning-knife on the brute's back-plates; how he found
a new and longer knife round the neck of a man who had been

[1] See notes on names at the end of this story.

killed by a wild boar, and how he tracked that boar and killed him as a fair price for the knife; how he was caught up once in the Great Famine, by the moving of the deer, and nearly crushed to death in the swaying hot herds; how he saved Hathi the Silent from being once more trapped in a pit with a stake at the bottom, and how, next day, he himself fell into a very cunning leopard-trap, and how Hathi broke the thick wooden bars to pieces above him; how he milked the wild buffaloes in the swamp, and how——

But we must tell one tale at a time. Father and Mother Wolf died, and Mowgli rolled a big boulder against the mouth of their cave, and cried the Death Song over them; Baloo grew very old and stiff, and even Bagheera, whose nerves were steel and whose muscles were iron, was a shade slower on the kill than he had been. Akela turned from gray to milky white with pure age; his ribs stuck out, and he walked as though he had been made of wood, and Mowgli killed for him. But the young wolves, the children of the disbanded Seeonee Pack, throve and increased, and when there were about forty of them, masterless, full-voiced, clean-footed five-year-olds, Akela told them that they ought to gather themselves together and follow the Law, and run under one head, as befitted the Free People.

This was not a question in which Mowgli concerned himself, for, as he said, he had eaten sour fruit, and he knew the tree it hung from; but when Phao, son of Phaona (his father was the Gray Tracker in the days of Akela's headship), fought his way to the leadership of the Pack, according to the Jungle Law, and the old calls and songs began to ring under the stars once more, Mowgli came to the Council Rock for memory's sake. When he chose to speak the Pack waited till he had finished, and he sat at Akela's side on the rock above Phao. Those were days of good hunting and good sleeping. No stranger cared to break into the jungles that belonged to Mowgli's people, as they called the Pack, and the young wolves grew fat and strong, and there were many cubs to bring to the Looking-over. Mowgli always attended a Looking-over, remembering the night when a black panther brought a naked brown baby into the pack, and the long call, 'Look, look well, O Wolves,' made his heart flutter. Otherwise, he would be far away in the Jungle with his four brothers, tasting, touching, seeing, and feeling new things.

One twilight when he was trotting leisurely across the ranges to give Akela the half of a buck that he had killed, while the Four jogged behind him, sparring a little, and tumbling one another over for joy of being alive, he heard a cry that had never been heard since the bad days of Shere Khan. It was what they call in the Jungle the *pheeal*, a hideous kind of shriek that the jackal gives when he is hunting behind a tiger, or when there is a big killing afoot. If you can imagine a mixture of hate, triumph, fear, and despair, with a kind of leer running through it, you will get some notion of the *pheeal* that rose and sank and wavered and quavered far away across the Waingunga. The Four stopped at once, bristling and growling. Mowgli's hand went to his knife, and he checked, the blood in his face, his eyebrows knotted.

'There is no Striped One dare kill here,' he said.

'That is not the cry of the Forerunner,' answered Gray Brother. 'It is some great killing. Listen!'

It broke out again, half sobbing and half chuckling, just as though the jackal had soft human lips. Then Mowgli drew deep breath, and ran to the Council Rock, overtaking on his way hurrying wolves of the Pack. Phao and Akela were on the Rock together, and below them, every nerve strained, sat the others. The mothers and the cubs were cantering off to their lairs; for when the *pheeal* cries it is no time for weak things to be abroad.

They could hear nothing except the Waingunga rushing and gurgling in the dark, and the light evening winds among the tree tops, till suddenly across the river a wolf called. It was no wolf of the Pack, for they were all at the Rock. The note changed to a long, despairing bay; and 'Dhole!' it said, 'Dhole! dhole! dhole!' They heard tired feet on the rocks, and a gaunt wolf, streaked with red on his flanks, his right fore-paw useless, and his jaws white with foam, flung himself into the circle and lay gasping at Mowgli's feet.

'Good hunting! Under whose Headship?' said Phao gravely.

'Good hunting! Won-tolla am I,' was the answer. He meant that he was a solitary wolf, fending for himself, his mate, and his cubs in some lonely lair, as do many wolves in the south. Won-tolla means an Outlier—one who lies out from any Pack. Then he panted, and they could see his heart-beats shake him backward and forward.

'What moves?' said Phao, for that is the question all the Jungle asks after the *pheeal* cries.

'The dhole, the dhole of the Dekkan—Red Dog, the Killer! They came north from the south saying the Dekkan was empty and killing out by the way. When this moon was new there were four to me—my mate and three cubs. She would teach them to kill on the grass plains, hiding to drive the buck, as we do who are of the open. At midnight I heard them together, full tongue on the trail. At the dawn-wind I found them stiff in the grass—four, Free People, four when this moon was new. Then sought I my Blood-Right and found the dhole.'

'How many?' said Mowgli quickly; the Pack growled deep in their throats.

'I do not know. Three of them will kill no more, but at the last they drove me like the buck; on my three legs they drove me. Look, Free People!'

He thrust out his mangled fore-foot, all dark with dried blood. There were cruel bites low down on his side, and his throat was torn and worried.

'Eat,' said Akela, rising up from the meat Mowgli had brought him, and the Outlier flung himself on it.

'This shall be no loss,' he said humbly, when he had taken off the first edge of his hunger. 'Give me a little strength, Free People, and I also will kill. My lair is empty that was full when this moon was new, and the Blood Debt is not all paid.'

Phao heard his teeth crack on a haunch-bone and grunted approvingly.

'We shall need those jaws,' said he. 'Were there cubs with the dhole?'

'Nay, nay. Red Hunters all: grown dogs of their Pack, heavy and strong for all that they eat lizards in the Dekkan.'

What Won-tolla had said meant that the dhole, the red hunting-dog of the Dekkan, was moving to kill, and the Pack knew well that even the tiger will surrender a new kill to the dhole. They drive straight through the Jungle, and what they meet they pull down and tear to pieces. Though they are not as big nor half as cunning as the wolf, they are very strong and very numerous. The dhole, for instance, do not begin to call themselves a pack till they are a hundred strong; whereas forty wolves make a very fair pack indeed. Mowgli's wanderings had taken him to the edge of the high grassy downs of the Dekkan, and he had seen the fearless dholes sleeping and playing and scratching themselves in the little hollows and tussocks that they use for lairs. He despised and hated them because they did not smell like the Free People, because they did not live in caves, and, above all, because they had hair between their toes while he and his friends were clean-footed. But he knew, for Hathi had told him, what a terrible thing a dhole hunting-pack was. Even Hathi moves aside from their line, and until they are killed, or till game is scarce, they will go forward.

Akela knew something of the dholes, too, for he said to Mowgli quietly, 'It is better to die in a Full Pack than leaderless and alone. This is good hunting, and—my last. But, as men live, thou hast very many more nights and days, Little Brother. Go north and lie down, and if any live after the dhole has gone by he shall bring thee word of the fight.'

'Ah,' said Mowgli, quite gravely, 'must I go to the marshes and catch little fish and sleep in a tree, or must I ask help of the *Bandar-log* and crack nuts, while the Pack fight below?'

'It is to the death,' said Akela. 'Thou hast never met the dhole —the Red Killer. Even the Striped One——'

'*Aowa! Aowa!*' said Mowgli pettingly. 'I have killed one striped ape, and sure am I in my stomach that Shere Khan would have left his own mate for meat to the dhole if he had winded a pack across three ranges. Listen now: There was a wolf, my father, and there was a wolf, my mother, and there was an old gray wolf (not too wise: he is white now) was my father and my mother. Therefore I—' he raised his voice, 'I say that when the dhole come, and if the dhole come, Mowgli and the Free People are of one skin for that hunting; and I say, by the Bull that bought me—by the Bull Bagheera paid for me in the old days which ye of the Pack do not remember—*I* say, that the Trees and the River may hear and hold fast if I forget; *I* say that this my knife shall be as a tooth to the Pack—and I do not think it is so blunt. This is my Word which has gone from me.'

'Thou dost not know the dhole, man with a wolf's tongue,' said Won-tolla. 'I look only to clear the Blood Debt against them ere they have me in many pieces. They move slowly, killing out as they go, but in two days a little strength will come back to me and I turn again for the Blood Debt. But for *ye*, Free People, my word is that ye go north and eat but little for a while till the dhole are gone. There is no meat in this hunting.'

'Hear the Outlier!' said Mowgli with a laugh. 'Free People, we must go north and dig lizards and rats from the bank, lest by any chance we meet the dhole. He must kill out our hunting-grounds, while we lie hid in the north till it please him to give us our own again. He is a dog—and the pup of a dog—red, yellow-bellied, lairless, and haired between every toe! He counts his cubs six and eight at the litter, as though he were Chikai, the little leaping rat. Surely we must run away, Free People, and beg leave of the peoples of the north for the offal of dead cattle! Ye know the saying: "North are the vermin; south are the lice. *We* are the Jungle." Choose ye, O choose. It is good hunting! For the Pack—for the Full Pack—for the lair and the litter; for the in-kill and the out-kill; for the mate that drives the doe and the little, little cub within the cave; it is met!—it is met!—it is met!'

The Pack answered with one deep, crashing bark that sounded in the night like a big tree falling. 'It is met!' they cried.

'Stay with these,' said Mowgli to the Four. 'We shall need every tooth. Phao and Akela must make ready the battle. I go to count the dogs.'

'It is death!' Won-tolla cried, half rising. 'What can such a hairless one do against the Red Dog? Even the Striped One, remember——'

'Thou art indeed an Outlier,' Mowgli called back; 'but we will speak when the dholes are dead. Good hunting all!'

He hurried off into the darkness, wild with excitement, hardly looking where he set foot, and the natural consequence was that he tripped full length over Kaa's great coils where the python lay watching a deer-path near the river.

'*Kssha!*' said Kaa angrily. 'Is this jungle-work, to stamp and tramp and undo a night's hunting—when the game are moving so well, too?'

'The fault was mine,' said Mowgli, picking himself up. 'Indeed I was seeking thee, Flathead, but each time we meet thou art longer and broader by the length of my arm. There is none like thee in the Jungle, wise, old, strong, and most beautiful Kaa.'

'Now whither does *this* trail lead?' Kaa's voice was gentler. 'Not a moon since there was a Manling with a knife threw stones at my head and called me bad little tree-cat names, because I lay asleep in the open.'

'Ay, and turned every driven deer to all the winds, and Mowgli was hunting, and this same Flathead was too deaf to hear his whistle, and leave the deer-roads free,' Mowgli answered composedly, sitting down among the painted coils.

'Now this same Manling comes with soft, tickling words to this same Flathead, telling him that he is wise and strong and beautiful, and this same old Flathead believes and makes a place, thus, for this same stone-throwing Manling, and——Art thou at ease now? Could Bagheera give thee so good a resting-place?'

Kaa had, as usual, made a sort of soft half-hammock of himself under Mowgli's weight. The boy reached out in the darkness, and gathered in the supple cable-like neck till Kaa's head rested on his shoulder, and then he told him all that had happened in the Jungle that night.

'Wise I may be,' said Kaa at the end; 'but deaf I surely am. Else I should have heard the *pheeal*. Small wonder the Eaters of Grass are uneasy. How many be the dhole?'

'I have not yet seen. I came hot-foot to thee. Thou art older than Hathi. But oh, Kaa,'—here Mowgli wriggled with sheer joy—'it will be good hunting. Few of us will see another moon.'

'Dost *thou* strike in this? Remember thou art a Man; and remember what Pack cast thee out. Let the Wolf look to the Dog. *Thou* art a Man.'

'Last year's nuts are this year's black earth,' said Mowgli. 'It is true that I am a Man, but it is in my stomach that this night I have said that I am a Wolf. I called the River and the Trees to remember. I am of the Free People, Kaa, till the dhole has gone by.'

'Free People,' Kaa grunted. 'Free thieves! And thou hast tied thyself into the death-knot for the sake of the memory of the dead wolves? This is no good hunting.'

'It is my Word which I have spoken. The Trees know, the River knows. Till the dhole have gone by my Word comes not back to me.'

'*Ngssh!* This changes all trails. I had thought to take thee away with me to the northern marshes, but the Word—even the Word of a little, naked, hairless Manling—is the Word. Now I, Kaa, say——'

'Think well, Flathead, lest thou tie thyself into the death-knot also. I need no Word from thee, for well I know——'

'Be it so, then,' said Kaa. 'I will give no Word; but what is in thy stomach to do when the dhole come?'

'They must swim the Waingunga. I thought to meet them with my knife in the shallows, the Pack behind me; and so stabbing and thrusting, we a little might turn them down-stream, or cool their throats.'

'The dhole do not turn and their throats are hot,' said Kaa. 'There will be neither Manling nor Wolf-cub when that hunting is done, but only dry bones.'

'*Alala!* If we die, we die. It will be most good hunting. But my stomach is young, and I have not seen many Rains. I am not wise nor strong. Hast thou a better plan, Kaa?'

'I have seen a hundred and a hundred Rains. Ere Hathi cast his milk-tushes my trail was big in the dust. By the First Egg, I am older than many trees, and I have seen all that Jungle has done.'

'But *this* is new hunting,' said Mowgli. 'Never before have the dhole crossed our trail.'

'What is has been. What will be is no more than a forgotten year striking backward. Be still while I count those my years.'

For a long hour Mowgli lay back among the coils, while Kaa, his head motionless on the ground, thought of all that he had seen and known since the day he came from the egg. The light seemed to go out of his eyes and leave them like stale opals, and now and again he made little stiff passes with his head, right and left, as though he were hunting in his sleep. Mowgli dozed quietly, for he knew that there is nothing like sleep before hunting, and he was trained to take it at any hour of the day or night.

Then he felt Kaa's back grow bigger and broader below him as the python puffed himself out, hissing with the noise of a sword drawn from a steel scabbard.

'I have seen all the dead seasons,' Kaa said at last, 'and the great trees and the old elephants, and the rocks that were bare and sharp-pointed ere the moss grew. Art *thou* still alive, Manling?'

'It is only a little after moonset,' said Mowgli. 'I do not understand——'

'*Hssh!* I am again Kaa. I knew it was but a little time. Now we will go to the river, and I will show thee what is to be done against the dhole.'

He turned, straight as an arrow, for the main stream of the Waingunga, plunging in a little above the pool that hid the Peace Rock, Mowgli at his side.

'Nay, do not swim. I go swiftly. My back, Little Brother.'

Mowgli tucked his left arm round Kaa's neck, dropped his right close to his body, and straightened his feet. Then Kaa breasted the current as he alone could, and the ripple of the checked water stood up in a frill round Mowgli's neck, and his feet were waved to and fro in the eddy under the python's lashing sides. A mile or two above the Peace Rock the Waingunga narrows between a gorge of marble rocks from eighty to a hundred feet high, and the current runs like a mill-race between and over all manner of ugly stones. But Mowgli did not trouble his head about the water; little water in the world could have given him a moment's fear. He was looking at the gorge on either side and sniffing uneasily, for there was a sweetish-sourish smell in the air, very like the smell of a big ant-hill on a hot day. Instinctively he lowered himself in the water, only raising his head to breathe from time to time, and Kaa came to anchor with a double twist of his tail round a sunken rock, holding Mowgli in the hollow of a coil, while the water raced on.

'This is the Place of Death,' said the boy. 'Why do we come here?'

'They sleep,' said Kaa. 'Hathi will not turn aside for the Striped One. Yet Hathi and the Striped One together turn aside for the dhole, and the dhole they say turn aside for nothing. And yet for whom do the Little People of the Rocks turn aside? Tell me, Master of the Jungle, who is the Master of the Jungle?'

'These,' Mowgli whispered. 'It is the Place of Death. Let us go.'

'Nay, look well, for they are asleep. It is as it was when I was not the length of thy arm.'

The split and weatherworn rocks of the gorge of the Waingunga had been used since the beginning of the Jungle by the
Little People of the Rocks—the busy, furious, black wild bees of
India; and, as Mowgli knew well, all trails turned off half a mile
before they reached the gorge. For centuries the Little People
had hived and swarmed from cleft to cleft, and swarmed again,
staining the white marble with stale honey, and made their combs
tall and deep in the dark of the inner caves, where neither man
nor beast nor fire nor water had ever touched them. The length
of the gorge on both sides was hung as it were with black shim-
mery velvet curtains, and Mowgli sank as he looked, for those
were the clotted millions of the sleeping bees. There were other
lumps and festoons and things like decayed tree-trunks studded
on the face of the rock, the old combs of past years, or new cities
built in the shadow of the windless gorge, and huge masses of
spongy, rotten trash had rolled down and stuck among the trees
and creepers that clung to the rock-face. As he listened he heard
more than once the rustle and slide of a honey-loaded comb turning over or falling away somewhere in the dark galleries; then a
booming of angry wings, and the sullen drip, drip, drip, of the
wasted honey, guttering along till it lipped over some ledge in
the open air and sluggishly trickled down on the twigs. There was
a tiny little beach, not five feet broad, on one side of the river,
and that was piled high with the rubbish of uncounted years.
There were dead bees, drones, sweepings, and stale combs, and
wings of marauding moths that had strayed in after honey, all
tumbled in smooth piles of the finest black dust. The mere sharp
smell of it was enough to frighten anything that had no wings, and
knew what the Little People were.

Kaa moved upstream again till he came to a sandy bar at the
head of the gorge.

'Here is this season's kill,' said he. 'Look!'

On the bank lay the skeletons of a couple of young deer and
a buffalo. Mowgli could see that neither wolf nor jackal had
touched the bones, which were laid out naturally.

'They came beyond the line; they did not know the Law,'
murmured Mowgli, 'and the Little People killed them. Let us
go ere they wake.'

'They do not wake till the dawn,' said Kaa. 'Now I will tell thee. A hunted buck from the south, many, many Rains ago, came hither from the south, not knowing the Jungle, a Pack on his trail. Being made blind by fear, he leaped from above, the Pack running by sight, for they were hot and blind on the trail. The sun was high, and the Little People were many and very angry. Many, too, were those of the Pack who leaped into the Waingunga, but they were dead ere they took water. Those who did not leap died also in the rocks above. But the buck lived.'

'How?'

'Because he came first, running for his life, leaping ere the Little People were aware, and was in the river when they gathered to kill. The Pack, following, was altogether lost under the weight of the Little People.'

'The buck lived?' Mowgli repeated slowly.

'At least he did not die *then*, though none waited his coming down with a strong body to hold him safe against the water, as a certain old fat, deaf, yellow Flathead would wait for a Manling—yea, though there were all the dholes of the Dekkan on his trail. What is in thy stomach?' Kaa's head was close to Mowgli's ear; and it was a little time before the boy answered.

'It is to pull the very whiskers of Death, but—Kaa, thou art, indeed, the wisest of all the Jungle.'

'So many have said. Look now, if the dhole follow thee——'

'As surely they will follow. Ho! ho! I have many little thorns under my tongue to prick into their hides.'

'If they follow thee hot and blind, looking only at thy shoulders, those who do not die up above will take water either here or lower down, for the Little People will rise up and cover them. Now the Waingunga is hungry water, and they will have no Kaa to hold them, but will go down, such as live, to the shallows by the Seeonee Lairs, and there thy Pack may meet them by the throat.'

'*Ahai! Eowawa!* Better could not be till the Rains fall in the dry season. There is now only the little matter of the run and the leap. I will make me known to the dholes, so that they shall follow me very closely.'

'Hast thou seen the rocks above thee? From the landward side?'

'Indeed, no. That I had forgotten.'

'Go look. It is all rotten ground, cut and full of holes. One of thy clumsy feet set down without seeing would end the hunt. See, I leave thee here, and for thy sake only I will carry word to the Pack that they may know where to look for the dhole. For myself, I am not of one skin with *any* wolf.'

When Kaa disliked an acquaintance he could be more unpleasant than any of the Jungle People, except perhaps Bagheera. He swam down-stream, and opposite the Rock he came on Phao and Akela listening to the night noises.

'*Hssh!* Dogs,' he said cheerfully. 'The dholes will come downstream. If ye be not afraid ye can kill them in the shallows.'

'When come they?' said Phao. 'And where is my Man-cub?' said Akela.

'They come when they come,' said Kaa. 'Wait and see. As for *thy* Man-cub, from whom thou hast taken a Word and so laid him open to Death, *thy* Man-cub is with *me*, and if he be not already dead the fault is none of thine, bleached dog! Wait here for the dhole, and be glad that the Man-cub and I strike on thy side.'

Kaa flashed upstream again, and moored himself in the middle of the gorge, looking upward at the line of the cliff. Presently he saw Mowgli's head move against the stars, and then there was a whizz in the air, the keen, clean *schloop* of a body falling feet first, and next minute the boy was at rest again in the loop of Kaa's body.

'It is no leap by night,' said Mowgli quietly. 'I have jumped twice as far for sport; but that is an evil place above—low bushes and gullies that go down very deep, all full of the Little People. I have put big stones one above the other by the side of three gullies. These I shall throw down with my feet in running, and the Little People will rise up behind me, very angry.'

'That is Man's talk and Man's cunning,' said Kaa. 'Thou art wise, but the Little People are always angry.'

'Nay, at twilight all wings near and far rest for a while. I will play with the dhole at twilight, for the dhole hunts best by day. He follows now Won-tolla's blood-trail.'

'Chil does not leave a dead ox, nor the dhole the blood-trail,' said Kaa.

'Then I will make him a new blood-trail, of his own blood, if I can, and give him dirt to eat. Thou wilt stay here, Kaa, till I come again with my dholes?'

'Ay, but what if they kill thee in the Jungle, or the Little People kill thee before thou canst leap down to the river?'

'When tomorrow comes we will kill for tomorrow,' said Mowgli, quoting a Jungle saying; and again, 'When I am dead it is time to sing the Death Song. Good hunting, Kaa!'

He loosed his arm from the python's neck and went down the gorge like a log in a freshet, paddling toward the far bank, where he found slack-water, and laughing aloud from sheer happiness. There was nothing Mowgli liked better than, as he himself said, 'to pull the whiskers of Death,' and make the Jungle know that he was their overlord. He had often, with Baloo's help, robbed bees' nests in single trees, and he knew that the Little People hated the smell of wild garlic. So he gathered a small bundle of it, tied it up with a bark string, and then followed Won-tolla's blood-trail, as it ran southerly from the Lairs, for some five miles, looking at the trees with his head on one side, and chuckling as as he looked.

'Mowgli the Frog have I been,' said he to himself; 'Mowgli the Wolf have I said that I am. Now Mowgli the Ape must I be before I am Mowgli the Buck. At the end I shall be Mowgli the Man. Ho!' and he slid his thumb along the eighteen-inch blade of his knife.

Won-tolla's trail, all rank with dark blood-spots, ran under a forest of thick trees that grew close together and stretched away north-eastward, gradually growing thinner and thinner to within two miles of the Bee Rocks. From the last tree to the low scrub of the Bee Rocks was open country, where there was hardly cover enough to hide a wolf. Mowgli trotted along under the trees, judging distances between branch and branch, occasionally climbing up a trunk and taking a trial leap from one tree to another till he came to the open ground, which he studied very carefully for an hour. Then he turned, picked up Won-tolla's trail where he had left it, settled himself in a tree with an outrunning branch some eight feet from the ground, and sat still, sharpening his knife on the sole of his foot and singing to himself.

A little before midday, when the sun was very warm, he heard the patter of feet and smelt the abominable smell of the dhole-pack as they trotted pitilessly along Won-tolla's trail. Seen from above, the red dhole does not look half the size of a wolf, but

Mowgli knew how strong his feet and jaws were. He watched the sharp bay head of the leader snuffing along the trail, and gave him 'Good hunting!'

The brute looked up, and his companions halted behind him, scores and scores of red dogs with low-hung tails, heavy shoulders, weak quarters, and bloody mouths. The dholes are a very silent people as a rule, and they have no manners even in their own Jungle. Fully two hundred must have gathered below him, but he could see that the leaders sniffed hungrily on Won-tolla's trail, and tried to drag the Pack forward. That would never do, or they would be at the Lairs in broad daylight, and Mowgli meant to hold them under his tree till dusk.

'By whose leave do ye come here?' said Mowgli.

'All Jungles are our Jungle,' was the reply, and the dhole that gave it bared his white teeth. Mowgli looked down with a smile, and imitated perfectly the sharp chitter-chatter of Chikai, the leaping rat of the Dekkan, meaning the dholes to understand that he considered them no better than Chikai. The Pack closed up round the tree-trunk and the leader bayed savagely, calling Mowgli a tree-ape. For an answer Mowgli stretched down one naked leg and wriggled his bare toes just above the leader's head. That was enough, and more than enough, to wake the Pack to stupid rage. Those who have hair between their toes do not care to be reminded of it. Mowgli caught his foot away as the leader leaped up, and said sweetly: 'Dog, red dog! Go back to the Dekkan and eat lizards. Go to Chikai thy brother—dog, dog—red, red dog! There is hair between every toe!' He twiddled his toes a a second time.

'Come down ere we starve thee out, hairless ape!' yelled the Pack, and this was exactly what Mowgli wanted. He laid himself down along the branch, his cheek to the bark, his right arm free, and there he told the Pack what he thought and knew about them, their manner, their customs, their mates, and their puppies. There is no speech in the world so rancorous and so stinging as the language the Jungle People use to show scorn and contempt. When you come to think of it you will see how this must be so. As Mowgli told Kaa, he had many little thorns under his tongue, and slowly and deliberately he drove the dholes from silence to growls, from growls to yells, and from yells to hoarse slavery ravings. They tried to answer his taunts, but a cub might as well have tried to answer Kaa in a rage; and all the while Mowgli's right hand lay crooked at his side, ready for action, his feet locked round the branch. The big bay leader had leaped many time in the air, but Mowgli dared not risk a false blow. At last, made furious beyond his natural strength, he bounded up seven or eight feet clear of the ground. Then Mowgli's hand shot out like the head of a tree-snake, and gripped him by the scruff of his neck, and the branch shook with the jar as his weight fell back, almost wrenching Mowgli to the ground. But he never loosed his grip, and inch by inch he hauled the beast, hanging like a drowned jackal, up on the branch. With his left hand he reached for his knife and cut off the red, bushy tail, flinging the dhole back to earth again. That was all he needed. The Pack would not go forward on Wontolla's trail now till they had killed Mowgli or Mowgli had killed them. He saw them settle down in circles with a quiver of the haunches that meant they were going to stay, and so he climbed to a higher crotch, settled his back comfortably, and went to sleep.

After three or four hours he waked and counted the Pack. They were all there, silent, husky, and dry, with eyes of steel. The sun was beginning to sink. In half an hour the Little People of the Rocks would be ending their labours, and, as you know, the dhole does not fight best in the twilight.

'I did not need such faithful watchers,' he said politely, standing up on a branch, 'but I will remember this. Ye be true dholes, but to my thinking over much of one kind. For that reason I do not give the big lizard-eater his tail again. Art thou not pleased, Red Dog?'

'I myself will tear out thy stomach!' yelled the leader, scratching at the foot of the tree.

'Nay, but consider, wise rat of the Dekkan. There will now be many litters of little tailless red dogs, yea, with raw red stumps that sting when the sand is hot. Go home, Red Dog, and cry that an ape has done this. Ye will not go? Come, then, with me, and I will make you very wise!'

He moved, *Bandar-log* fashion, into the next tree, and so on into the next and the next, the Pack following with lifted hungry heads. Now and then he would pretend to fall, and the Pack would

Then Mowgli's hand shot out . . . and gripped him by the scruff of his neck

tumble one over the other in their haste to be at the death. It was a curious sight—the boy with the knife that shone in the low sunlight as it sifted through the upper branches, and the silent Pack with their red coats all aflame, huddling and following below. When he came to the last tree he took the garlic and rubbed himself all over carefully, and the dholes yelled with scorn. 'Ape with a wolf's tongue, dost thou think to cover thy scent?' they said. 'We follow to the death.'

'Take thy tail,' said Mowgli, flinging it back along the course he had taken. The Pack instinctively rushed after it. 'And follow now—to the death.'

He had slipped down the tree-trunk, and headed like the wind in bare feet for the Bee Rocks, before the dholes saw what he would do.

They gave one deep howl, and settled down to the long, lobbing canter that can at the last run down anything that runs. Mowgli knew their pack-pace to be much slower than that of the wolves, or he would never have risked a two-mile run in full sight. They were sure that the boy was theirs at last, and he was sure that he held them to play with as he pleased. All his trouble was to keep them sufficiently hot behind him to prevent their turning off too soon. He ran cleanly, evenly, and springily; the tailless leader not five yards behind him; and the Pack tailing out over perhaps a quarter of a mile of ground, crazy and blind with the rage of slaughter. So he kept his distance by ear, reserving his last effort for the rush across the Bee Rocks.

The Little People had gone to sleep in the early twilight, for it was not the season of late blossoming flowers; but as Mowgli's first footfalls rang hollow on the hollow ground he heard a sound as though all the earth were humming. Then he ran as he had never run in his life before, spurned aside one—two—three of the piles of stones into the dark, sweet-smelling gullies; heard a roar like the roar of the sea in a cave; saw with the tail of his eye the air grow dark behind him; saw the current of the Waingunga far below, and a flat, diamond-shaped head in the water; leaped outward with all his strength, the tailless dhole snapping at his shoulder in mid-air, and dropped feet first to the safety of the river, breathless and triumphant. There was not a sting upon him, for the smell of the garlic had checked the Little People for just the few seconds that he was among them. When he rose Kaa's coils were steadying him and things were bounding over the edge of the cliff—great lumps, it seemed, of clustered bees falling like plummets; but before any lump touched water the bees flew upward and the body of a dhole whirled downstream. Overhead they could hear furious short yells that were drowned in a roar like breakers—the roar of the wings of the Little People of the Rocks. Some of the dholes, too, had fallen into the gullies that communicated with the underground caves, and there choked and fought and snapped among the tumbled honeycombs, and at last, borne up, even when they were dead, on the heaving waves of bees beneath them, shot out of some hole in the river-face, to roll over on the black-rubbish-heaps. There were dholes who had leaped short into the trees on the cliffs, and the bees blotted out their shapes; but the greater number of them, maddened by the stings, had flung themselves into the river; and, as Kaa said, the Waingunga was hungry water.

Kaa held Mowgli fast till the boy had recovered his breath.

'We may not stay here,' he said. 'The Little People are roused indeed. Come!'

Swimming low and diving as often as he could, Mowgli went down the river, knife in hand.

'Slowly, slowly,' said Kaa. 'One tooth does not kill a hundred unless it be a cobra's, and many of the dholes took water swiftly when they saw the Little People rise.'

'The more work for my knife, then. *Phai!* How the Little People follow!' Mowgli sank again. The face of the water was blanketed with wild bees, buzzing sullenly and stinging all they found.

'Nothing was ever yet lost by silence,' said Kaa—no sting could penetrate his scales—'and thou hast all the long night for the hunting. Hear them howl!'

Nearly half the pack had seen the trap their fellows rushed into, and turning sharp aside had flung themselves into the water where the gorge broke down in steep banks. Their cries of rage and their threats against the 'tree-ape' who had brought them to their shame mixed with the yells and growls of those who had been punished by the Little People. To remain ashore was death, and every dhole knew it. Their pack was swept along the current, down to the deep eddies of the Peace Pool, but even there the angry Little People followed and forced them to the water again. Mowgli could hear the voice of the tailless leader bidding his people hold on and kill out every wolf in Seeonee. But he did not waste his time in listening.

'One kills in the dark behind us!' snapped a dhole. 'Here is tainted water!'

Mowgli had dived forward like an otter, twitched a struggling dhole under water before he could open his mouth, and dark rings rose as the body plopped up, turning on its side. The dholes tried to turn, but the current prevented them, and the Little People darted at the heads and ears, and they could hear the challenge of the Seeonee Pack growing louder and deeper in the gathering darkness. Again Mowgli dived, and again a dhole went under, and rose dead, and again the clamour broke out at the rear of the pack; some howling that it was best to go ashore, others calling on their leader to lead them back to the Dekkan, and others bidding Mowgli show himself and be killed.

'They come to the fight with two stomachs and several voices,' said Kaa. 'The rest is with thy brethren below yonder. The Little People go back to sleep. They have chased us far. Now I, too, turn back, for I am not of one skin with any wolf. Good hunting, Little Brother, and remember the dhole bites low.'

A wolf came running along the bank on three legs, leaping up and down, laying his head sideways close to the ground, hunching his back, and breaking high into the air, as though he were playing with his cubs. It was Won-tolla, the Outlier, and he said never a word, but continued his horrible sport beside the dholes. They had been long in the water now, and were swimming wearily, their coats drenched and heavy, their bushy tails dragging like sponges, so tired and shaken that they, too, were silent, watching the pair of blazing eyes that moved abreast.

'This is no good hunting,' said one, panting.

'Good hunting!' said Mowgli, as he rose boldly at the brute's side, and sent the long knife home behind the shoulder, pushing hard to avoid his dying snap.

'Art thou there, Man-cub?' said Won-tolla across the water.

'Ask of the dead, Outlier,' Mowgli replied. 'Have none come downstream? I have filled these dogs' mouths with dirt; I have

88

tricked them in the broad daylight, and their leader lacks his
tail, but here be some few for thee still. Whither shall I drive
them?'

'I will wait,' said Won-tolla. 'The night is before me.'

Nearer and nearer came the bay of the Seeonee wolves. 'For the
Pack, for the Full Pack it is met!' and a bend in the river drove
the dholes forward among the sands and shoals opposite the Lairs.

Then they saw their mistake. They should have landed half a
mile higher up, and rushed the wolves on dry ground. Now it
was too late. The bank was lined with burning eyes, and except
for the horrible *pheeal* that had never stopped since sundown, there
was no sound in the Jungle. It seemed as though Won-tolla were
fawning on them to come ashore; and 'Turn and take hold!' said
the leader of the dholes. The entire Pack flung themselves at the
shore, threshing and squattering through the shoal water, till the
face of the Waingunga was all white and torn, and the great
ripples went from side to side, like bow-waves from a boat.
Mowgli followed the rush, stabbing and slicing as dholes, huddled
together, rushed up the river-beach in one wave.

Then the long fight began, heaving and straining and splitting
and scattering and narrowing and broadening along the red, wet
sands, and over and between the tangled tree-roots, and through
and among the bushes, and in and out of the grass clumps; for
even now the dholes were two to one. But they met wolves
fighting for all that made the Pack, and not only the short, high,
deep-chested, white-tusked hunters of the Pack, but the anxious-
eyed lahinis—the she-wolves of the lair, as the saying is—fighting
for their litters, with here and there a yearling wolf, his first coat
still half woolly, tugging and grappling by their sides. A wolf, you
must know, flies at the throat or snaps at the flank, while a dhole,
by preference, bites at the belly; so when the dholes were struggling out of the water and had to raise their heads, the odds were
with the wolves. On dry land the wolves suffered; but in the
water or ashore, Mowgli's knife came and went without ceasing.
The Four had worried their way to his side. Gray Brother,
crouched between the boy's knees, was protecting his stomach,
while the others guarded his back and either side, or stood over
him when the shock of a leaping, yelling dhole who had thrown
himself full on the steady blade bore him down. For the rest, it

was one tangled confusion—a locked and swaying mob that moved from right to left and from left to right along the bank; and also ground round and round slowly on its own centre. Here would be a heaving mound, like a water-blister in a whirlpool, which would break like a water-blister, and throw up four or five mangled dogs, each striving to get back to the centre; here would be a single wolf borne down by two or three dholes, laboriously dragging them forward, and sinking the while; here a yearling cub would be held up by the pressure round him, though he had been killed early, while his mother, crazed with dumb rage, rolled over and over, snapping, and passing on: and in the middle of the thickest press, perhaps, one wolf and one dhole, forgetting everything else, would be manœuvring for first hold till they were whirled away by a rush of furious fighters. Once Mowgli passed Akela, a dhole on either flank, and his all but toothless jaws closed over the loins of a third; and once he saw Phao, his teeth set in the throat of a dhole, tugging the unwilling beast forward till the yearling could finish him. But the bulk of the fight was blind flurry and smother in the dark; hit, trip, and tumble, yelp, groan, and worry-worry-worry, round him and behind him and above him. As the night wore on, the quick, giddy-go-round motion increased. The dholes were cowed and afraid to attack the stronger wolves, but did not yet dare to run away. Mowgli felt that the end was coming soon, and contented himself with striking merely to cripple. The yearlings were growing bolder; there was time now and again to breathe, and pass a word to a friend, and the mere flicker of the knife would sometimes turn a dog aside.

'The meat is very near the bone,' Gray Brother yelled. He was bleeding from a score of flesh-wounds.

'But the bone is yet to be cracked,' said Mowgli. '*Eowawa!* Thus do we do in the Jungle!' The red blade ran like a flame along the side of a dhole whose hind-quarters were hidden by the weight of a clinging wolf.

'My kill!' snorted the wolf through his wrinkled nostrils. 'Leave him to me.'

'Is thy stomach still empty, Outlier?' said Mowgli. Won-tolla was fearfully punished, but his grip had paralysed the dhole, who could not turn round and reach him.

'By the Bull that bought me,' said Mowgli, with a bitter laugh, 'it is the tailless one!' And indeed it was the big bay-coloured leader.

'It is not wise to kill cubs and lahinis,' Mowgli went on philosophically, wiping the blood out of his eyes, 'unless one has also killed the Outlier; and it is in my stomach that this Won-tolla kills thee.'

A dhole leaped to his leader's aid; but before his teeth had found Won-tolla's flank, Mowgli's knife was in his throat, and Gray Brother took what was left.

'And thus do we do in the Jungle,' said Mowgli.

Won-tolla said not a word, only his jaws were closing and closing on the backbone as his life ebbed. The dhole shuddered, his head dropped, and he lay still, and Won-tolla dropped above him.

'*Huh!* The Blood Debt is paid,' said Mowgli. 'Sing the song, Won-tolla.'

'He hunts no more,' said Gray Brother; 'and Akela, too, is silent this long time.'

'The bone is cracked!' thundered Phao, son of Phaona. 'They go! Kill, kill out, O hunters of the Free People!'

Dhole after dhole was slinking away from those dark and bloody sands to the river, to the thick Jungle, upstream or downstream as he saw the road clear.

'The debt! The debt!' shouted Mowgli. 'Pay the debt! They have slain the Lone Wolf! Let not a dog go!'

He was flying to the river, knife in hand, to check any dhole who dared to take water, when, from under a mound of nine dead, rose Akela's head and forequarters, and Mowgli dropped on his knees beside the Lone Wolf.

'Said I not it would be my last fight?' Akela gasped. 'It is good hunting. And thou, Little Brother?'

'I live, having killed many.'

'Even so. I die, and I would—I would die by thee, Little Brother.'

Mowgli took the terrible scarred head on his knees, and put his arms round the torn neck.

'It is long since the old days of Shere Khan, and a Man-cub that rolled naked in the dust.'

'Nay, nay, I am a wolf. I am of one skin with the Free People,' Mowgli cried. 'It is no will of mine that I am a man.'

'Thou art a man, Little Brother, wolfling of my watching. Thou art a man, or else the Pack had fled before the dhole. My life I owe to thee, and today thou hast saved the Pack even as once I saved thee. Hast thou forgotten? All debts are paid now. Go to thine own people. I tell thee again, eye of my eye, this hunting is ended. Go to thine own people.'

'I will never go. I will hunt alone in the Jungle. I have said it.'

'After the summer come the Rains, and after the Rains comes the spring. Go back before thou art driven.'

'Who will drive me?'

'Mowgli will drive Mowgli. Go back to thy people. Go to Man.'

'When Mowgli drives Mowgli I will go,' Mowgli answered.

'There is no more to say,' said Akela. 'Little Brother, canst thou raise me to my feet? I also was a leader of the Free People.'

Very carefully and gently Mowgli lifted the bodies aside, and raised Akela to his feet, both arms round him, and the Lone Wolf drew a long breath, and began the Death Song that a leader of the Pack should sing when he dies. It gathered strength as he went on, lifting and lifting, and ringing far across the river, till it came to the last 'Good hunting!' and Akela shook himself clear of Mowgli for an instant, and, leaping into the air, fell backward dead upon his last and most terrible kill.

Mowgli sat with his head on his knees, careless of anything else, while the remnant of the flying dholes were being overtaken and run down by the merciless lahinis. Little by little the cries died away, and the wolves returned limping, as their wounds stiffened, to take stock of the losses. Fifteen of the Pack, as well as half a dozen lahinis, lay dead by the river, and of the others not one was unmarked. And Mowgli sat through it all till the cold daybreak, when Phao's wet, red muzzle was dropped in his hand, and Mowgli drew back to show the gaunt body of Akela.

'Good hunting!' said Phao, as though Akela were still alive, and then over his bitten shoulder to the others: 'Howl, dogs! A Wolf has died tonight!'

But of all the Pack of two hundred fighting dholes, whose boast was that all Jungles were their Jungle, and that no living thing could stand before them, not one returned to the Dekkan to carry that word.

Notes on the names in 'Red Dog'

Many years after the stories were written, Rudyard Kipling supplied some 'Author's Notes on the Names in *The Jungle Books*', from which the following have been taken to explain all those mentioned in 'Red Dog':

'Mowgli' is a name I made up. It does not mean 'frog' in any language that I know of. It is pronounced *Mow-glee* (accent on the *Mow*). ['Mow rhymes with *cow*', wrote Kipling on another occasion.]

Shere Khan is pronounced *Sheer Karn*. 'Shere' means 'Tiger' in some of the Indian dialects, and 'Khan' is a title, more or less of distinction, to show that he was a chief among tigers.

The Waingunga is a real river in Central India. It is pronounced Wine-gunger (accent on *gung*, I think).

Akela, which means 'Alone', is pronounced *Uk-kay-la* (accent on *kay*).

Baloo is Hindustani for 'Bear'. Pronounced *Bar-loo* (accent on *Bar*).

Bagheera is Hindustani for a panther or leopard. It is a sort of diminutive of BAGH, which is Hindustani for 'Tiger'. Pronounced *Bug-eer-a* (accent on the *eer*).

Kaa is pronounced *Kar*. A made-up name, from the queer open-mouthed hiss of a big snake.

Hathi is pronounced *Huttee*, or say nearly so. One of the Indian names for 'Elephant'.

Chil, the Indian Kite, pronounced *Cheel*.

Phaou is pronounced *Fayou*: he was son of *Fay-owner*. A made-up name.

The Pheeal, pronounced *Fe-arl*, is a noise that a jackal sometimes makes when he is following or going before a hunting tiger. It is, men have told me, quite different from his regular cry and not nice to listen to.

Dhole is *Dole*, and is one of the native names for the Wild Hunting Dog of India.

Won-Tolla is pronounced *Woon-toller* (accent on *tol*).

The Dekkan is part of the big Central Plain of India. Look it up on the map.

Bee Rocks. There are some rocks above a river near Jubbulpore in India where wild bees have lived for many years. Nobody goes near them if he can avoid it, for sometimes they attack and kill men and horses.

Lahini, pronounced *Lar-hee-ney*, is a made-up name for she-wolves (accent on *hee*).

Anthony Hope

The Sin of the Bishop of Modenstein

In the days of Rudolf III there stood on the hill opposite the Castle of Zenda, and on the other side of the valley in which the town lies, on the site where the château of Tarlenheim now is situated, a fine and strong castle belonging to Count Nikolas of Festenburg. He was a noble of very old and high family, and had great estates; his house being, indeed, second only to the Royal House in rank and reputation. He himself was a young man of great accomplishments, of a domineering temper, and of much ambition; and he had gained distinction in the wars that marked the closing years of the reign of King Henry the Lion. With King Rudolf he was not on terms of cordial friendship, for he despised the King's easy manners and carelessness of dignity, while the King had no love for a gentleman whose one object seemed to be to surpass and outshine him in the eyes of his people, and who never rested from extending and fortifying his castle until it threatened to surpass Zenda itself both in strength and magnificence. Moreover Nikolas, although maintaining a state ample and suitable to his rank, was yet careful and prudent, while Rudolf spent all that he received and more besides, so that the Count grew richer and the King poorer. But in spite of these causes of difference, the Count was received at Court with apparent graciousness, and no open outburst of enmity had yet occurred, the pair being, on the contrary, often together, and sharing their sports and pastimes with one another.

Now most of these diversions were harmless, or, indeed, becoming and proper, but there was one among them full of danger to a man of hot head and ungoverned impulse such as King Rudolf was. And this one was diceing, in which the King took great delight, and in which Count Nikolas was very ready to encourage him. The King, who was generous and hated to win from poor men or those who might be playing beyond their means in order to give him pleasure, was delighted to find an opponent whose purse was as long or longer than his own, and thus gradually came to pass many evenings with the boxes in Nikolas's company. And the more evenings he passed the deeper he fell into the Count's debt; for the King drank wine, while the Count was content with small beer, and when the King was losing he doubled his stakes, whereas the Count took in sail if the wind seemed adverse. Thus always and steadily the debt grew, till at last Rudolf dared not reckon how large it had become, nor did he dare to disclose it to his advisers. For there were great public burdens already imposed by reason of King Henry's wars, and the citizens of Strelsau were not in a mood to bear fresh exaction, nor to give their hard earnings for the payment of the King's gambling debts; in fine, although they loved the Elphbergs well enough, they loved their money more. Thus the King had no resource except in his private possessions, and these were of no great value, saving the Castle and estate of Zenda.

At length, when they had sat late one night and the throws had gone all the evening against the King and for Nikolas, the King flung himself back in his chair, drained his glass, and said impatiently:

'I am weary of the game! Come, my lord, let us end it.'

'I would not urge you, sire, a moment beyond what you desire. I play but for your pleasure.'

'Then my pleasure has been your profit,' said the King with a vexed laugh, 'for I believe I am stripped of my last crown. What is my debt?'

The Count, who had the whole sum reckoned on his tablets, took them out, and showed the King, the amount of the debt.

'I cannot pay it,' said Rudolf. 'I would play you again, to double the debt or wipe it out, but I have nothing of value enough to stake.'

The desire which had been nursed for long in the Count's heart now saw the moment of its possible realization.

He leant over the table, and, smoothing his beard with his hand, said gently:

'The amount is no more than half the value of your Majesty's Castle and demesne of Zenda.'

The King started and forced a laugh.

'Aye, Zenda spoils the prospect from Festenburg, does it?' said he. 'But I will not risk Zenda. An Elphberg without Zenda would seem like a man robbed of his wife. We have had it since we have had anything or been anything. I should not seem King without it.'

'As you will, sire. Then the debt stands?' He looked full and keenly into the King's eyes, asking without words, 'How will you pay it?' and adding without words, 'Paid it must be.' And the King read the unspoken words in the eyes of Count Nikolas.

The King took up his glass, but finding it empty flung it angrily on the floor, where it shivered into fragments at Count Nikolas's feet; and he shifted in his chair and cursed softly under his breath. Nikolas sat with the dice-box in his hand and a smile on his lips; for he knew that the King could not pay, and therefore must play, and he was in the vein, and did not doubt of winning from the King Zenda and its demesne. Then he would be the greatest lord in the kingdom, and hold for his own a kingdom within the kingdom, and the two strongest places in all the land. And a greater prize might then dangle in reach of his grasp.

'The devil spurs and I gallop,' said the King at last. And he took up the dice-box and rattled it.

'Fortune will smile on you this time, sire, and I shall not grieve at it,' said Count Nikolas with a courteous smile.

'Curses on her!' cried the King. 'Come, my lord, a quick ending to it! One throw, and I am a free man, or you are master of my castle!'

'One throw let it be, sire, for it grows late,' assented Nikolas with a careless air; and they both raised the boxes and rattled the dice inside them. The King threw; his throw was a six and a five, and a sudden gleam of hope lit up his eyes; he leant forward in his chair, gripping the elbows of it with his hands; his cheeks flushed and his breath came quickly. With a bow Count Nikolas raised his hand and threw. The dice fell and rolled on the table.

The King sank back; and the Count said with a smile of apology and a shrug of his shoulders:

'Indeed I am ashamed. For I cannot be denied tonight.'

For Count Nikolas of Festenburg had thrown sixes, and thereby won from the King the Castle and demesne of Zenda.

He rose from his chair, and, having buckled on his sword that had lain on the table by him, and taken his hat in his hand, stood looking down on the King with a malicious smile on his face. And he said with a look that had more mockery than respect in it:

'Have I your Majesty's leave to withdraw? For ere day dawn, I have matters to transact in Strelsau, and I would be at my Castle of Zenda tonight.'

The King Rudolf took a sheet of paper and wrote an order that the Castle, and all that was in it, and all the demesne should be surrendered to Count Nikolas of Festenburg on his demand, and he gave the paper to Nikolas. Then he rose up and held out his hand, which Nikolas kissed, smiling covertly, and the King said with grace and dignity:

'Cousin, my castle has found a more worthy master. God give you joy of it.'

And he motioned with his hand to be left alone. Then, when the Count had gone, he sat down in his chair again, and remained there till it was full day, neither moving nor yet sleeping. There he was found by his gentlemen when they came to dress him, but none asked him what had passed.

Count Nikolas, now Lord of Zenda, did not so waste time, and the matters that he had spoken of did not keep him long in Strelsau; but in the early morning he rode out, the paper which the King had written in his belt.

First he rode with all speed to his own house of Festenburg, and there he gathered together all his followers, servants, foresters, and armed retainers, and he told them that they were to ride with him to Zenda, for that Zenda was now his and not the King's. At this they were greatly astonished, but they ate the fine dinner and drank the wine which he provided, and in the evening they rode down the hill very merry, and trotted, nearly a hundred strong, through the town, making a great noise, so that they disturbed the Bishop of Modenstein, who was lying that night at the inn in the course of a journey from his See to the Capital; but nobody could tell the Bishop why they rode to Zenda, and presently the Bishop, being wearied with travelling, went to his bed.

Now King Rudolf, in his chagrin and dismay, had himself forgotten, or had at least neglected to warn the Count of Festenburg, that his sister Princess Osra was residing at the Castle of Zenda; for it was her favourite resort, and she often retired from the Court and spent many days there alone. There she was now with two of her ladies, a small retinue of servants, and no more than a half a dozen guards; and when Count Nikolas came to the gate, it being then after nine, she had gone to her own chamber, and sat before the mirror, dressed in a loose white gown, with her ruddy hair unbound and floating over her shoulders. She was reading an old story book, containing tales of Helen of Troy, of Cleopatra, of Berenice, and other lovely ladies, very elegantly related and embellished with fine pictures. And the Princess, being very much absorbed in the stories, did not hear nor notice the arrival of the Count's company, but continued to read, while Nikolas roused the watchmen, and the bridge was let down, and the steward summoned. Then Nikolas took the steward aside, and showed him the King's order, bearing the King's seal, and the steward, although both greatly astonished and greatly grieved, could not deny the letter or the seal, but declared himself ready to obey and to surrender the Castle; and the sergeant in command of the guard said the same; but, they added, since the Princess was in the Castle, they must inform her of the matter, and take her commands.

'Aye, do,' said Nikolas, sitting down in the great hall. 'Tell her not to be disturbed, but to give me the honour of being her host for as long as she will, and say that I will wait on her, if it be her pleasure.'

But he smiled to think of the anger and scorn with which Osra would receive the tidings when the steward delivered them to her.

In this respect the event did not fall short of his expectations, for she was so indignant and aghast that, thinking of nothing but the tidings, she flung away the book and cried: 'Send the Count here to me,' and stood waiting for him there in her chamber, in her white gown and with her hair unbound and flowing down over her shoulders. And when he came she cried: 'What is this, my lord?' and listened to his story with parted lips and flashing

99

eyes, and thus read the King's letter and saw the King's seal. And her eyes filled with tears, but she dashed them away with her hand. Then the Count said, bowing to her as mockingly as he had bowed to her brother:

'It is the fortune of the dice, madame.'

'Yes, my lord, as you play the game,' said she.

His eyes were fixed on her, and it seemed to him that she was more beautiful in her white gown and with her hair unbound over her shoulders, than he had ever felt her to be before, and he eyed her closely. Suddenly she looked at him, and for a moment she averted his eyes; but he looked again and her eyes met his. For several moments she stood rigid and motionless. Then she said:

'My lord, the King has lost the Castle of Zenda, which is the home and cradle of our House. It was scarcely the King's alone to lose. Have I no title in it?'

'It was the King's, madame, and now it is mine,' smiled Nikolas.

'Well, then, it is yours,' said she, and taking a step towards him, she said: 'Have you a mind to venture it again, my lord?'

'I would venture it only against a great stake,' said he, smiling still, while his eyes were fixed on her face and marked every change in the colour of her cheeks.

'I can play dice as well as the King,' she cried. 'Are we not all gamblers, we Elphbergs?' And she laughed bitterly.

'But what would your stake be?' he asked sneeringly.

Princess Osra's face was now very pale, but her voice did not tremble and she did not flinch; for the honour of her House and of the throne was as sacred to her as her salvation, and more than her happiness.

'A stake, my lord,' said she, 'that many gentlemen have thought above any castle in preciousness.'

'Of what do you speak?' he asked and his voice quivered a little, as a man's does in excitement. 'For, pardon me, madame, but what have you of such value?'

'I have what the poorest girl has, and it is of the value that it pleased God to make it and pleases men to think it,' said Osra. 'And all of it I will stake against the King's Castle of Zenda and its demesne.'

Count Nikolas's eyes flashed and he drew nearer to her; he

took his dice-box from his pocket, and he held it up before her, and he whispered in an eager hoarse voice:

'Name this great stake, madame; what is it?'

'It is myself, my lord,' said Princess Osra.

'Yourself?' he cried wondering, though he had half guessed.

'Aye. To be the Lord of Zenda is much. Is it not more to be husband to the King's sister?'

'It is more,' said he, 'when the King's sister is the Princess Osra.' And he looked at her now with open admiration. But she did not heed his glance, but with face pale as death she seized a small table and drew it between them and cried: 'Throw then, my lord! We know the stakes.'

'If you win, Zenda is yours. If I win, you are mine.'

'Yes, I and Zenda also,' said she. 'Throw, my lord!'

'Shall we throw thrice, madame, or once, or how often?'

'Thrice, my lord,' she answered, tossing back her hair behind her neck, and holding one hand to her side. 'Throw first,' she added.

The Count rattled the box; and the throw was seven. Osra took the box from him, looked keenly and defiantly in his eyes, and threw.

'Fortune is with you, madame,' said he, biting his lips. 'For a five and a four make nine, or I err greatly.'

He took the box from her; his hand shook, but hers was firm and steady; and again he threw.

'Ah, it is but five,' said he impatiently, and a frown settled on his brow.

'It is enough, my lord,' said Osra, and pointed to the dice that she had thrown, a three and a one.

The Count's eyes gleamed again; he sprang towards her, and was about to seize the box. But he checked himself suddenly, and bowed, saying:

'Throw first this time, I pray you, madame, if it be not disagreeable to you.'

'I do not care which way it is,' said Osra, and she shook and made her third cast. When she lifted the box, the face of the dice showed seven. A smile broadened on the Count's lips, for he thought surely he could beat seven, he that had beaten eleven and thereby won the Castle of Zenda, which now he staked against the Princess Osra. But his eyes were very keenly and attentively on her, and he held the box poised, shoulder-high, in his right hand.

Then a sudden faintness and sickness seized on the Princess, and the composure that had hitherto upheld her failed; she could not meet his glance, nor could she bear to see the fall of the dice; but she turned away her head before he threw, and stood thus with averted face. But he kept attentive eyes on her, and drew very near to the table so that he stood right over it. And the Princess Osra caught sight of her own face in the mirror, and started to see herself pallid and ghastly, and her features drawn as though she were suffering some great pain. Yet she uttered no sound.

The dice rattled in the box; they rattled on the table; there was a pause while a man might quickly count a dozen; and then Count Nikolas of Festenburg cried out in a voice that trembled and tripped over the words:

'Eight, eight, eight!'

But before the last of the words had left his shaking lips, the Princess Osra faced round on him like lightning. She raised her hand so that the loose white sleeve fell back from her rounded arm, and her eyes flashed, and her lips curled as she outstretched her arm at him, and cried:

'Foul play!'

For, as she watched her own pale face in the mirror—the mirror which Count Nikolas had not heeded—she had seen him throw, she had seen him stand for an instant over the dice he had thrown with gloomy and maddened face; and then she had seen a slight swift movement of his left hand, as his fingers deftly darted down and touched one of the dice and turned it. And all this she had seen before he had cried eight. Therefore now she turned on him, and cried. 'Foul play!' and before he could speak, she darted by him towards the door. But he sprang forward, and caught her by the arm above the wrist and gripped her, and his fingers bit into the flesh of her arm, as he gasped, 'You lie! Where are you going?' But her voice rang out clear and loud in answer:

'I am going to tell all the world that Zenda is ours again, and I am going to publish in every city in the kingdom that Count Nikolas of Festenburg is a common cheat and rogue, and should be whipped at the cart's tail through the streets of Strelsau. For I

saw you in the mirror, my lord, I saw you in the mirror!' And
she ended with a wild laugh that echoed through the room.

Still he gripped her arm, and she did not flinch; for an instant
he looked full in her eyes; covetousness, and desire, and shame,
came all together upon him, and overmastered him, and he hissed
between set teeth:

'You shan't! By God, you shan't!'

'Aye, but I will, my lord,' said Osra. 'It is a fine tale for the
King and for your friends in Strelsau.'

An instant longer he held her where she was; and he gasped
and licked his lips. Then he suddenly dragged her with him
towards a couch; seizing up a coverlet that lay on the couch he
flung it round her, and he folded it tight about her, and he drew
it close over her face. She could not cry out nor move. He lifted
her up and swung her over his shoulder, and, opening the door
of the room, dashed down the stairs towards the great hall.

In the great hall were six of the King's Guard, and some of the
servants of the castle, and many of the people who had come with
Count Nikolas; they all sprang to their feet when they saw him.
He took no heed of them, but rushed at a run through the hall,
and out under the portcullis and across the bridge, which had not
been raised since he entered. There at the end of the bridge a
lackey held his horse; and he leapt on his horse, setting one hand
on the saddle, and still holding Osra; and then he cried aloud:

'My men follow me! To Festenburg!'

And all his men ran out, the King's Guard doing nothing to
hinder them, and jumping on their horses and setting them at a
gallop, hurried after the Count. He, riding furiously, turned towards the town of Zenda, and the whole company swept down
the hill, and, reaching the town, clattered and dashed through it at
full gallop, neither drawing rein nor turning to right or left; and
again they roused the Bishop of Modenstein, and he turned in his
bed, wondering what the rush of mounted men meant. But they,
galloping still, climbed the opposite hill and came to the Castle
of Festenburg with their horses spent and foundered. In they all
crowded, close on one another's heels; the bridge was drawn up;
and there in the entrance they stood looking at one another, asking
mutely what their master had done, and who was the lady whom
he carried wrapped in the coverlet. But he ran on till he reached

the stairs, and he climbed them, and entering a room in the gate-tower, looking over the moat, he laid the Princess Osra on a couch, and standing over her he smote one hand upon the other, and he swore loudly:

'Now, as God lives, Zenda I will have, and her I will have, and it shall be her husband whom she must, if she will, proclaim a cheat in Strelsau!'

Then he bent down and lifted the coverlet from her face. But she did not stir nor speak, nor open her eyes. For she had fallen into a swoon as they rode, and did not know what had befallen her, nor where she had been brought, nor that she was now in the Castle of Festenburg, and in the power of a desperate man. Thus she lay still and white, while Count Nikolas stood over her and bit his nails in rage. And it was then just on midnight.

On being disturbed for the third time, the Bishop of Moden-stein, whose temper was hot and cost him continual prayers and penances from the mastery it strove to win over him, was very impatient; and since he was at once angry and half asleep, it was long before he could or would understand the monstrous news with which his terrified host came trembling and quaking to his bedside in the dead of the night. A servant-girl, stammered the frightened fellow, had run down half dressed and panting from the Castle of Zenda, and declared that whether they chose to believe her or not—and, indeed, she could hardly believe such a thing herself, although she had seen it with her own eyes from her own window—yet Count Nikolas of Festenburg had come to the castle that evening, had spoken with Princess Osra, and now (they might call her a liar if they chose) had carried off the Princess with him on his horse to Festenburg, alive or dead none knew; and the men-servants were amazed and terrified, and the soldiers were at their wits' end, talking big and threatening to bring ten thousand men from Strelsau and to leave not one stone upon another at Festenburg, and what not. But all the while and for all their big talk nothing was done; and the Princess was at Festenburg, alive or dead or in what strait none knew. And, finally, nobody but one poor servant-girl had had the wit to run down and rouse the town.

The Bishop of Modenstein sat up in his bed and he fairly roared at the innkeeper:

'Are there no men, then, who can fight in the town, fool?'

'None, none, my lord—not against the Count. Count Nikolas is a terrible man. Please God, he has not killed the Princess by now.'

'Saddle my horse,' said the Bishop, 'and be quick with it.'

And he leapt out of bed with sparkling eyes. For the Bishop was a young man, but a little turned of thirty, and he was a noble of the old house of Hentzau. Now some of the Hentzaus (of whom history tells us of many) have been good, and some have been bad; and the good fear God, while the bad do not; but neither the good nor the bad fear anything in the world besides. Hence, for good or ill, they do great deeds and risk their lives as another man risks a penny. So the Bishop, leaving his bed, dressed himself in breeches and boots, and set a black hat with a violet feather on his head, and, staying to put on nothing else but his shirt and his cloak over it, in ten minutes was on his horse at the door of the inn. For a moment he looked at a straggling crowd that had gathered there; then with a toss of his head and a curl of his lip he told them what he thought of them, saying openly that he thanked heaven they were not of his diocese, and in an instant he was galloping through the streets of the town towards the Castle of Festenburg, with his sword by his side, and a brace of pistols in the holsters of the saddle. Thus he left the gossipers and vapourers behind, and rode alone as he was up the hill, his blood leaping and his heart beating quick; for, as he went, he said to himself:

'It is not often a Churchman has a chance like this.'

On the stroke of half-past twelve he came to the bridge of the castle moat, and the bridge was up. But the Bishop shouted, and the watchman came out and stood in the gateway across the moat, and, the night being fine and clear, he presented an excellent aim.

'My pistol is straight at your head,' cried the Bishop. 'Let down the bridge. I am Frederick of Hentzau; that is, I am the Bishop of Modenstein, and I charge you, if you are a dutiful son of the Church, to obey me. The pistol is full at your head.'

The watchman knew the Bishop, but he also knew the Count his master.

'I dare not let down the bridge without an order from my lord,' he faltered.

'Then before you can turn round, you're a dead man,' said the Bishop.

'Will you hold me harmless with my lord, if I let it down?'

'Aye, he shall not hurt you. But if you do not immediately let it down, I'll shoot you first and refuse you Christian burial afterwards. Come, down with it.'

So the watchman, fearing that, if he refused, the Bishop would spare neither body nor soul, but would destroy the one and damn the other, let down the bridge, and the Bishop, leaping from his horse, ran across with his drawn sword in one hand and a pistol in the other. Walking into the hall, he found a great company of Count Nikolas's men, drinking with one another, but talking uneasily and seeming alarmed. And the Bishop raised the hand that held the sword above his head in the attitude of benediction, saying, 'Peace be with you!'

Most of them knew him by his face, and all knew him as soon as a comrade whispered his name, and they sprang to their feet, uncovering their heads and bowing. And he said:

'Where is your master the Count?'

'The Count is upstairs, my lord,' they answered. 'You cannot see him now.'

'Nay, but I will see him,' said the Bishop.

'We are ordered to let none pass,' said they, and although their manner was full of respect, they spread themselves across the hall, and thus barred the way to the staircase that rose in the corner of the hall. But the Bishop faced them in great anger, crying:

'Do you think I do not know what has been done? Are you all, then, parties in this treachery? Do you all want to swing from the turrets of the Castle when the King comes with a thousand men from Strelsau?'

At this they looked at him and at one another with great uneasiness; for they knew that the King had no mercy when he was roused, and that he loved his sister above everybody in the world. And the Bishop stept up close to their rank. Then one of them drew his sword half-way from its scabbard. But the Bishop, perceiving this, cried:

'Do you all do violence to a lady, and dare to lay hands on the King's sister? Aye, and here is a fellow that would strike a Bishop of God's Church!' And he caught the fellow a buffet with the flat of his sword, that knocked him down. 'Let me pass, you rogues,' said the Bishop. 'Do you think you can stop a Hentzau?'

'Let us go and tell the Count that my lord the Bishop is here,' cried the house-steward, thinking that he had found a way out of the difficulty; for they dared neither to touch the Bishop nor yet to let him through; and the steward turned to run towards the staircase. But the Bishop sprang after him, quick as an arrow, and, dropping the pistol from his left hand, caught him by the shoulder and hurled him back. 'I want no announcing,' he said. 'The Church is free to enter everywhere.' And he burst through them at the point of the sword, reckless now what might befall him so that he made his way through. But they did not venture to cut him down; for they knew that nothing but death would stop him, and for their very souls' sake they dared not kill him. So he, kicking one and pushing another and laying about him with the flat of his sword and with his free hand, and reminding them all the while of their duty to the Church and of his sacred character, at last made his way through and stood alone, unhurt, at the foot of the staircase, while they cowered by the walls or looked at him in stupid helplessness and bewilderment. And the Bishop swiftly mounted the stairs.

At this instant in the room in the gate-tower of the Castle overlooking the moat there had fallen a moment of dead silence. Here Count Nikolas had raised the Princess, set her on a couch, and waited till her faintness and fright were gone. Then he had come near to her, and in brief harsh tones told her his mind. For him, indeed, the dice were now cast; in his fury and fear he had dared all. He was calm now, with the calmness of a man at a great turn of fate. That room, he told her, she should never leave alive, save as his promised wife, sworn and held to secrecy and silence by the force of that bond and of her oath. If he killed her he must die, whether by his own hand or the King's mattered little. But he would die for a great cause and in a great venture. 'I shall not be called a cheating gamester, madame,' said he, a smile on his pale face. 'I choose death sooner than disgrace. Such is my choice. What is yours? It stands between death and silence; and no man but your husband will dare to trust your silence.'

'You do not dare to kill me,' said she defiantly.

'Madame, I dare do nothing else. They may write "murderer" on my tomb; they shall not throw "cheat" in my living face.'

'I will not be silent,' cried Osra, springing to her feet. 'And rather than be your wife I would die a thousand times. For a cheat you are—a cheat—a cheat!' Her voice rose, till he feared that she would be heard, if any one chanced to listen, even from so far off as the hall. Yet he made one more effort, seeking to move her by an appeal to which women are not wont to be insensible.

'A cheat, yes!' said he. 'I, Nikolas of Festenburg, am a cheat. I say it, though no other man shall while I live to hear him. But to gain what stake?'

'Why, my brother's Castle of Zenda.'

'I swear to you it was not,' he cried, coming nearer to her. 'I did not fear losing on the cast, but I could not endure not to win. Not my stake, madame, but yours lured me to my foul play. Have you your face, and yet do not know to what it drives men?'

'If I have a fair face, it should inspire fair deeds,' said she. 'Do not touch me, sir, do not touch me. I loathe breathing the same air with you, or so much as seeing your face. Aye, and I can die. Even the women of our House know how to die.'

At her scorn and contempt a great rage came upon him, and he gripped the hilt of his sword, and drew it from the scabbard. But she stood still, facing him with calm eyes. Her lips moved for a moment in prayer, but she did not shrink.

'I pray you,' said he in trembling speech, mastering himself for an instant. 'I pray you!' But he could say no more.

'I will cry your cheating in all Strelsau,' said she.

'Then commend your soul to God. For in one minute you shall die.'

Still she stood motionless; and he began to come near to her, his sword now drawn in his hand. Having come within the distance from which he could strike her, he paused and gazed into her eyes. She answered him with a smile. Then there was for an instant the utter stillness in the room; and in that instant the Bishop of Modenstein set his foot on the staircase and came running up. On a sudden Osra heard the step, and a gleam flashed in her eye. The Count heard it also, and his sword was arrested in its stroke. A smile came on his face. He was glad at the coming of someone whom he might kill in fight; for it turned him sick to butcher her unresisting. Yet he dared not let her go, to cry his cheating in the streets of Strelsau. The steps came nearer.

He dropped his sword on the floor and sprang upon her. A shriek rang out, but he pressed his hand on her mouth and seized her in his arms. She had no strength to resist, and he carried her swiftly across the room to a door in the wall. He pulled the door open—it was very heavy and massive—and he flung her down roughly on the stone floor of a little chamber, square and lofty, having but one small window high up, through which the moonlight scarcely pierced. She fell with a moan of pain. Unheeding, he turned on his heel and shut the door. And, as he turned, he heard a man throw himself against the door of the room. It also was strong and twice the man hurled himself with all his force against it. At last it strained and gave way; and the Bishop of Modenstein burst into the room breathless. And he saw no trace of the Princess's presence, but only Count Nikolas standing sword in hand in front of the door in the wall with a sneering smile on his face.

The Bishop of Modenstein never loved to speak afterwards of what followed, saying always that he rather deplored than gloried in it, and that when a man of sacred profession was forced to use the weapons of this world it was a matter of grief to him, not of vaunting. But the King compelled him by urgent requests to describe the whole affair, while the Princess was never weary of telling all that she knew, or of blessing all bishops for the sake of the Bishop of Modenstein. Yet the Bishop blamed himself; perhaps, if the truth were known, not for the necessity that drove him to do what he did, as much as for a secret and ashamed joy which he detected in himself. For certainly, as he burst into the room now, there was no sign of reluctance or unwillingness in his face; he took off his feathered hat, bowed politely to the Count, and resting the point of his sword on the floor asked:

'My lord, where is the Princess?'

'What do you want here, and who are you?' cried the Count with a blasphemous oath.

'When we were boys together, you knew Frederick of Hentzau. Do you not now know the Bishop of Modenstein?'

'Bishop! This is no place for bishops. Get back to your prayers, my lord.'

'It wants some time yet before matins,' answered the Bishop. 'My lord, where is the Princess?'

'What do you want with her?'

'I am here to escort her wherever it may be her pleasure to go.'

He spoke confidently, but he was in his heart alarmed and uneasy because he had not found the Princess.

'I do not know where she is,' said Nikolas of Festenburg.

'My lord, you lie,' said the Bishop of Modenstein.

The Count had wanted nothing but an excuse for attacking the intruder. He had it now, and an angry flush mounted in his cheeks as he walked across to where the Bishop stood.

Shifting his sword, which he had picked up again, to his left hand, he stuck the Bishop on the face with his gloved hand. The Bishop smiled and turned the other cheek to Count Nikolas, who struck him again with all his force, so that he reeled back, catching hold of the open door to avoid falling, and the blood started dull red under the skin of his face. But he still smiled, and bowed, saying:

'I find nothing about the third blow in Holy Scripture.'

At this instant the Princess Osra, who had been half stunned by the violence with which Nikolas had thrown her on the floor, came to her full senses, and, hearing the Bishop's voice, she cried out loudly for help. He, hearing her, darted in an instant across the room, and was at the door of the little chamber before the Count could stop him. He pulled the door open and Osra sprang out to him, saying:

'Save me! Save me!'

'You are safe, madame, have no fear,' answered the Bishop. And turning to the Count, he continued: 'Let us go outside, my lord, and discuss this matter. Our dispute will disturb and perhaps alarm the Princess.'

And a man might have read the purpose in his eyes, though his manner and words were gentle; for he had sworn in his heart that the Count should not escape.

But the Count cared as little for the presence of the Princess as he had for her dignity, her honour, or her life: and now that she was no longer wholly at his mercy, but there was a new chance that she might escape, his rage and the fear of exposure lashed him to fury, and, without more talking, he made at the Bishop, crying:

'You first, and then her! I'll be rid of the pair of you!'

The Bishop faced him, standing between Princess Osra and his assault, while she shrank back a little, sheltering herself behind the heavy door. For although she had been ready to die without fear, yet the sight of men fighting frightened her, and she veiled her face with her hands, and waited in dread to hear the sound of their swords clashing. But the Bishop looked very happy, and, setting his hat on his head with a jaunty air, he stood on guard. For ten years or more he had not used his sword, but the secret of its mastery seemed to revive, fresh and clear in his mind, and let his soul say what it would, his body rejoiced to be at the exercise again, so that his blood kindled and his eyes gleamed in the glee of strife. Thus he stepped forward, guarding himself, and thus he met the Count's impetuous onset; he neither flinched nor gave back, but finding himself holding his own, he pressed on and on, not violently attacking and yet never resting, and turning every thrust with a wrist of iron. And while Osra now gazed with wide eyes and close-held breath and Count Nikolas muttered oaths and grew more furious, the Bishop seemed as gay as when he talked to the King more gaily, may be, than Bishops should. Again his eye danced as in the days when he had been called the wildest of the Hentzaus. And still he drove Count Nikolas back and back.

Now behind the Count was a window, which he himself had caused to be enlarged and made low and wide, in order that he might look from it over the surrounding country; in time of war it was covered with a close and strong iron grating. But now the grating was off and the window open, and beneath the window was a fall of fifty feet or hard upon it into the moat below. The Count, looking into the Bishop's face and seeing him smile, suddenly recollected the window, and fancied it was the Bishop's design to drive him on it so that he could give back no more; and since he knew by now that the Bishop was his master with the sword, a despairing rage settled upon him; determining to die swiftly, since die he must, he rushed forward, making a desperate lunge at his enemy. But the Bishop parried the lunge, and, always seeming to be about to run the Count through the body, again forced him to retreat till his back was close to the opening of the window. Here Nikolas stood, his eyes glaring like a madman's; then a sudden devilish smile spread over his face.

. . . finding himself holding his own, he pressed on

'Will you yield yourself, my lord?' cried the Bishop, putting a restraint on the wicked impulse to kill the man, and lowering his point for an instant.

In that short moment the Count made his last throw; for all at once, as it seemed, and almost in one motion, he thrust and wounded the Bishop in the left side of his body, high in the chest near the shoulder, and, though the wound was slight, the blood flowed freely; then drawing back his sword, he seized it by the blade half-way up and flung it like a javelin at the Princess, who stood still by the door, breathlessly watching the fight. By an ace it missed her head, and it pinned a tress of her hair to the door and quivered deep-set in the wood of the door. When the Bishop of Modenstein saw this, hesitation and mercy passed out of his heart, and though the man had now no weapon, he thought of sparing him no more than he would have spared any cruel and savage beast, but he drove his sword into his body, and the Count, not being able to endure the thrust without flinching, against his own will gave back before it. Then came from his lips a loud cry of dismay and despair; for at the same moment that the sword was in him he, staggering back, fell wounded to death through the open window. The Bishop looked out after him, and Princess Osra heard the sound of a great splash in the water of the moat below; for very horror she sank against the door, seeming to be held up more by the sword that had pinned her hair than by her own strength. Then came up through the window, from which the Bishop still looked with a strange smile, the clatter of a hundred feet, running to the gate of the Castle. The bridge was let down; the confused sound of many men talking, of whispers, of shouts, and of cries of horror, mounted up through the air. For the Count's men in the hall also had heard the splash, and run out to see what it was, and there they beheld the body of their master, dead in the moat; their eyes were wide open, and they could hardly lay their tongues to the words as they pointed to the body and whispered to one another, very low: 'The Bishop has killed him—the Bishop has killed him.' But the Bishop saw them from the window, and leant out, crying:

'Yes, I have killed him. So perish all such villains!'

When they looked up, and saw in the moonlight the Bishop's face, they were amazed. But he hastily drew his head in, so that

 Anthony Hope

they might not see him any more. For he knew that his face had been fierce, and exultant, and joyful. Then, dropping his sword, he ran across to the Princess; he drew the Count's sword, which was wet with his own blood, out of the door, releasing the Princess's hair; and, seeing that she was very faint, he put his arm about her, and led her to the couch; she sank upon it, trembling and white as her white gown, and murmuring: 'Fearful, fearful!' and she clutched his arm, and for a long while she would not let him go; and her eyes were fixed on the Count's sword that lay on the floor by the entrance of the little room.

'Courage, madame,' said the Bishop softly. 'All danger is past. The villain is dead, and you are with the most devoted of your servants.'

'Yes, yes,' she said, and pressed his arm and shivered. 'Is he really dead?'

'He is dead. God have mercy on him,' said the Bishop.

'And you killed him?'

'I killed him. If it were a sin, pray God forgive me!'

Up through the window still came the noise of voices and the stir of men moving; for they were recovering the body of the Count from the moat; yet neither Osra nor the Bishop noticed any longer what was passing; he was intent on her, and she seemed hardly yet herself; but suddenly, before he could interpose, she threw herself off the couch and on to her knees in front of him, and, seizing hold of his hand, she kissed first the episcopal ring that he wore and then his hand. For he was both Bishop and a gallant gentleman, and a kiss she gave him for each; and after she had kissed his hand, she held it in both of hers as though for safety's sake she clung to it. But he raised her hastily, crying to her not to kneel before him, and, throwing away his hat, he knelt before her, kissing her hands many times. She seemed now recovered from her bewilderment and terror; for as she looked down on him kneeling, she was half-way between tears and smiles, and with curving lips but wet shining eyes she said very softly:

'Ah, my lord, who made a bishop of you?' And her cheeks grew in an instant from dead white into suddenly red, and her hand moved over his head as if she would fain have touched him with it. And she bent down ever so little towards him. Yet, per-

114

haps, it was nothing; any lady, who had seen how he bore himself, and knew that it was in her cause, for her honour and life, might well have done the same.

The Bishop of Modenstein made no immediate answer; his head was still bowed over her hand, and after a while he kissed her hand again; and he felt her hand press his. Then suddenly, as though in alarm, she drew her hand away, and he let it go easily. Then he raised his eyes and met the glance of hers, and he smiled; and Osra also smiled. For an instant they were thus. Then the Bishop rose to his feet, and he stood before her with bent head and eyes that sought the ground in becoming humility.

'It is by God's infinite goodness and divine permission that I hold my sacred office,' said he. 'I would that I were more worthy of it! But today I have taken pleasure in the killing of a man.'

'And in the saving of a lady, sir,' she added softly, 'who will ever count you among her dearest friends and the most gallant of her defenders. Is God angry at such a deed as that?'

'May He forgive us all our sins,' said the Bishop gravely; but what other sins he had in his mind he did not say, nor did the Princess ask him.

Then he gave her his arm, and they two walked together down the stairs into the hall; the Bishop, having forgotten both his hat and his sword, was bareheaded and had no weapon in his hand. The Count's men were all collected in the hall, being crowded round a table that stood by the wall; for on the table lay the body of Count Nikolas of Festenburg, and it was covered with a horsecloth that one of the servants had thrown over it. But when the men saw the Princess and the Bishop, they made way for them and stood aside, bowing low as they passed.

'You bow now,' said Osra, 'but, before, none of you would lift a finger for me. To my lord the Bishop alone do I owe my life; and he is a Churchman, while you were free to fight for me. For my part, I do not envy your wives such husbands'; and with a most scornful air she passed between their ranks, taking great and ostentatious care not to touch one of them even with the hem of her gown. At this they grew red and shuffled on their feet; and one or two swore under their breath; and thanked God their wives were not such shrews, being indeed very much ashamed of themselves, and very uneasy at thinking what these same wives of theirs would say to them when the thing came to be known. But Osra and the Bishop passed over the bridge, and he set her on his horse. The summer morning had just dawned, clear and fair, so that the sun caught her ruddy hair as she mounted in her white gown. But the Bishop took the bridle of the horse and led it at a foot's pace down the hill and into the town.

Now by this time the news of what had chanced had run all through the town and the people were out in the streets, gossiping and guessing. And when they saw the Princess Osra safe and sound and smiling, and the Bishop in his shirt—for he had given his cloak to her—leading the horse, they broke into great cheering. The men cheered the Princess, while the women thrust themselves to the front rank of the crowd, and blessed the Bishop of Modenstein. But he walked with his head down and his eyes on the ground, and would not look up, even when the women cried out in great fear and admiration on seeing that his shirt was stained with his blood and with the blood of Nikolas of Festenburg that had spurted out upon it. But one thing the Princess heard, which sent her cheeks red again: for a buxom girl glanced merrily at her, and made bold to say in a tone that the Princess could not but hear:

'By the Saints, here's waste! If he were not a Churchman, now!' And her laughing eye travelled from the Princess to him, and back to the Princess again.

'Shall we go a little faster?' whispered Osra, bending down to the Bishop. But the girl only thought that she whispered something else, and laughed the more.

At last they passed the town, and with a great crowd still following them came to the Castle. At the gate of it the Bishop stopped, and aided the Princess to alight. Again he knelt and kissed her hand, saying only:

'Madame, farewell!'

'Farewell, my lord,' said Osra softly; and she went hastily into the Castle, while the Bishop returned to his inn in the town, and though the people stood round the inn the best part of the day, calling and watching for him, he would not show himself.

In the evening of that day the King, having heard the tidings of the crime of Count Nikolas, came in furious haste with a troop of horse from Strelsau. And when he heard how Osra had played at dice with the Count, and staking herself against the Castle of Zenda had won it back, he was ashamed, and swore an oath that he would play dice no more, which oath he faithfully observed. But in the morning of the next day he went to Festenburg, where he flogged soundly every man who had not run away before his coming; and all the possessions of Count Nikolas he confiscated, and he pulled down the Castle of Festenburg, and filled up the moat that had run round its walls.

Then he sent for the Bishop of Modenstein, and thanked him, offering to him all the demesne of Count Nikolas; but the Bishop would not accept it, nor any mark of the King's favour, not even the Order of the Red Rose. Therefore the King granted the ground on which the Castle stood, and all the lands belonging to it, to Francis of Tarlenheim, brother-in-law to the wife of Prince Henry, who built the château which now stands there and belongs to the same family to this day.

But the Bishop of Modenstein, having been entertained by the King with great splendour for two days, would not stay longer, but set out to pursue his journey, clad now in his ecclesiastical garments. And Princess Osra sat by her window, leaning her head on her hand, and watching him till the trees of the forest hid him; and once, when he was on the edge of the forest, he turned his face for an instant, and looked back at her where she sat watching in the window. Thus he went to Strelsau; and when he was come there, he sent immediately for his confessor, and the confessor, having heard him, laid upon him a severe penance, which he performed with great zeal, exactness, and contrition. But whether the penance were for killing Count Nikolas of Festenburg (which in a layman, at least, would have seemed but a venial sin) or for what else, who shall say?

Andrew Lang

Captain Pink

I

The leaden light of a noon in early December hardly sufficed for Molly Vaughan's needlework, and for Kate Wogan's reading it seemed not to suffice at all. The two cousins were sitting by themselves in the library of the Castle, a long narrow room on the first floor; outside ran a railed gallery, above the old hall.

Molly was perched on a stool in the deep window niche; the stool she had set on a narrow platform, to which you climbed by five steps from the level of the library floor. The window, that overlooked the avenue, had been cut when James I was king, out of the thickness of the wall of the gate-tower; and the gate-tower, under the Red William, had been built for the keep of a Norman settler on the wild Marches of Wales. The black Jacobean panelling of the library and the brown backs of the books on the shelves sucked up the pallid light. Molly, in the window, could see to stitch her scraps of a white silk petticoat into cockades; but Kate, it seemed, could not see to read the *Adventures of Pamela* that lay in her lap, and was new to her, Mr Richardson having published his famous book in 1741, when Miss Wogan happened to be in France. The young lady, her hands clasped across her knees, was gazing into the fire of logs in the deep chimney-place. Now and again she shivered slightly; the day was bitterly cold.

Nevertheless the door of the library had been left half open, and, whenever the outer door of the hall below was opened to admit a visitor, the frosty wind brought up with it a gale of the strong tobacco which the assembled squires were moodily smoking. Always came the muffled sounds of men's voices—now low, now loud, and the grating of heavy oaken chairs as they were shifted on the stone floor of the hall, beneath their anxious occupants. Any one could feel that something was going to happen, and that something not so pleasant to everybody as the drinking of toasts to the King over the water.

Molly, in the window recess, would pause from her work and listen, now and then, to the voices from the hall beneath, or would rise and look through the window behind her down the avenue. This she did whenever horses' hoofs clattered on the frozen road. Then she would watch the stranger who was welcomed at the door, and hearken while the voices in the hall rose louder and more eager, to die again in a kind of anxious disappointed hush.

'Nobody but a neighbour, of the Cycle Club [1]—Mr Williams of the Barrow,' said Molly, after one of these arrivals; and the snip of her scissors sounded again, as she trimmed and twisted odds and ends of white silk into a cockade.

Kate did not answer.

'The adventures of chaste Pamela do not seem to hold your attention, Kate,' the sewing girl said again; adding, 'I am not surprised: greater adventures than a waiting-maid's are at the doors. I wonder how you can keep so mum and still.'

Her own voice was trembling with eagerness: her fingers were quivering as she snipped, or sewed in the gold thread which made the heart of her white roses. There are some of them still to be seen among the relics in old Welsh houses; the silk is darkened, and the tarnished gold has long lost its glitter. It is many a year since 'Aunt Molly's roses' withered in a day.

'If you won't read, and despise fidgeting, Kate,' said the sewing girl, who could neither be still nor silent, 'at least you might work as I do. Oh, why can't I do more? How can the men sit smoking and prosing when they should rise and ride?'

'Whither should they be riding?' said Kate, picking up a dry twig from the hearth and tossing it on the flames.

'They might ride northward till they heard the guns,' said Molly, flushing: 'perhaps today they are fighting at Preston.'

'They say the third time is lucky,' said Kate; 'I am sure I do not know. Preston has twice brought ill fortune to the Stuarts.'

[1] A Welsh Jacobite society.

119

'And, Kate, you do not seem to care—you that have been in France, and had a kiss of the Prince's hand: you, a Wogan!'

'There are Wogans and Wogans,' said the other girl listlessly. 'We have had a regicide in our family, you know, as well as a Cavalier. We had Uncle Tom, as well as Uncle Ned.'

She leaned forward and watched the flames again; she was lithe and tall, of the dark, brilliant type of the Irish.

The sewing girl rose and threw down a lapful of scraps of silk and golden thread. She came to her moody friend, knelt beside her, and coaxing laid her brown head on the red silk that draped the dark girl's knees. 'Dear Cousin Kate, what ails you? Why are you so still and sad when the Prince may be within a short day's ride? Five years ago, when we were young, you were all on fire for the Cause.'

'It is very cold today,' muttered Kate, shivering.

'Then you were with us, summer or winter, hot or cold.'

The dark girl lowered her grey eyes to the other's kind face. 'Molly, I am so silent because . . . because I have too much to say. Heart and soul! I have no heart in my body, except for you.'

'I was afraid of that, Kate, ever since you came back from France,' murmured Molly, her brown head buried on her cousin's breast. She was sorry, and she was curious. 'Do you want to tell me, dear?' she whispered.

'Something in me seems to keep forcing me to tell you. Heart and soul! Molly, I learned many things in France besides French.'

'You learned to draw, I know, and to play the spinet, and sing to charm "fish out of the water, and water out of a stone," and to ride better than any of us girls—oh, and to fence as well as Dick! Oh, Kate, and the same man taught you all of these things! I understand, dear Kate!'

'Yes,' said Kate dreamily: 'it was the old story. I learned my lesson from one who knew much though he was young. He taught me a world of things for little fee. Silver and gold had I none, but what I had I gave. So now, Molly, I have no heart; and Molly, they made me believe, in France, that we have no souls. Nothing is true that the priests have told us.'

Molly jumped up and crossed herself. A Catholic of Wales, she knew little of the happy discoveries then recent and fashionable in France.

'Oh, hush, Kate!' cried Molly. 'You are in a fever, you are hot and cold, you don't know what you speak! Some wicked man in France has said these words in your hearing. Let me bring Father Walsh to you: he is in the Oratory, praying for the Cause. He is a doctor, as well as a priest. Let me go'; for Kate had clasped her round the waist. Kate was the stronger by far, and held her firmly.

'No,' she whispered—'let me confess to you, not to a priest.'

What she confessed was bitter enough to hear—the new creed philosophical.

'Can men believe these things and live?' cried Molly.

'We call them *philosophes*,' said Kate. 'They live very merrily. How Monsieur Arouet used to make us laugh at the old Bible stories! Yes, all the ladies used to laugh! I was too happy, for one, to care for heaven or hell, death or judgment, true stories or fairy tales. And then there came another woman and took away my teacher, and did me a worse wrong, even, that I cannot tell you, Molly. Where my heart was, there is only the gnawing of pain and shame.'

'Shame, Kate!'

'It was an unbearable wrong and wickedness. A man would have known what to do, but we are women. Am I to forgive? A saint would not have forgiven.'

Kate hid her face in her hands and sobbed.

Molly also was puzzled and miserable. She did not want to know more. The silence grew: they could hear the great clock tick in the hall, for below the men were strangely quiet.

Kate lifted her hand without looking up, and the other girl caught it and laid it against her own cheek, which was wet.

'After all I had something left of my own,' said Kate—'I had my secret. Now I have given it to you—the last thing that I had to give, except my love, that you had long ago. But you will keep my secret, won't you?'

'I shall keep it while I keep my love for you, and that is till I die, and after. And my love, and Dick's love, Kate, shall give you back your heart, and you will forget these wicked French lies, and Dick will right your wrong . . .'

'My wrong no man can right,' muttered Kate, 'and no woman may. Oh, it is not fair!'

Molly suddenly leaped to her window-seat, and looked down the road; as swiftly Kate was deep in *Pamela*.

They had heard on the stairs the footfalls of a booted man. He entered, a young fellow—manifestly, by the resemblance of features and complexion, the brother of the girl in the window-seat.

'Molly is in her watch-tower,' he said, 'but I doubt she will see no more than Sister Anne did, in *Bluebeard*.'

'Have you no news?' said Kate, looking up from her *Pamela*.

'Nothing but reports: the Prince is within two days' march of Derby, with all Cheshire and Lancashire behind him, say some; or he has turned off to the Midlands to meet the Duke; or he is away northward again, as fast as the red shanks of his Highlanders can carry them. Every one has a different tale. Nothing certain: never a word for Sir Watkin and Wales! Was ever enterprise so ill guided? And here we sit . . .' he said, moodily flicking his boot with his riding-whip.

'We are more active,' said Kate. 'Here'—she stooped and took a white cockade from the heap—'is a badge for you, Cousin Dick. Wear it where it will be seen by the rebels—the Hanoverian's men—or keep it till you may wear it at Court.'

'I shall keep it while I live, Cousin Kate, as you wrought it; though I hope it may be black with powder before the week is out.'

Kate did not disclaim having been the artificer of the silken knot; and Molly, who had turned round to speak, caught her glance and was silent.

There was no madness in Kate's manner now, but there was what Molly liked no better, and dreaded even more.

'I can be still nowhere, not even with you, Kate,' said Dick, rising to go; 'and I do so reek of tobacco from the pipes of a dozen wavering squires that I am no fit company for ladies. Here comes another neighbour—with cross-news, or cross-questions. By the sound of the horse's hoofs he comes alone. But I must see him.'

Dick leaped to the window-seat, where Molly was still gazing down the road. A single horseman on a weary grey turned the corner and came in view. 'It is young Morgan of the Weld,' said Dick, 'as far as I can smoke him under his heavy riding-cloak. But I never saw his horse before. And, egad, if it is Morgan, he has more courage than all the rest. He is the only man of them that has ridden in wearing the white coackade. I wonder if he wore it all the way?'

He ran from the room, leaving the door open. Molly watched the horseman. Kate sat still; she had dropped her book again, and seemed listless as ever.

'It is not Tom Morgan,' said Molly. 'It is no one whom we know—indeed, we know no man half so handsome; though, by the patch on his chin, he has cut himself in shaving. He is young, and looks very daring. Can it be a rider from the Prince, at last? Can it be—the Prince himself?'

She spoke to herself, not to Kate. She ran out onto the gallery and stooped behind the railings that were draped with tapestry, whence she could see into the hall. There was a noise of welcoming the newcomer; out of many voices his came singularly clear and sweet, with an accent strange to the watching girl; it seemed to be French with a touch, for those who could recognize it, of the soft West Highland brogue. The words were of a broken English. The Prince, she knew, spoke English with the English accent; and, little as she had hoped, she felt a sinking of the heart. Molly crept back into the panelled room. Kate was crouched by the half-open door, her face averted. Molly looked strangely at her; the fancy entered her mind, would this voice be that of the man whom Kate called her teacher? Kate rose, went up to the window-seat, and gazed down the empty avenue, drumming with her fingers on the pane.

'From the voice,' Kate said listlessly, 'a stranger has come at last. He does not speak English or Welsh, whatever he speaks. Run back to your eavesdropping, Molly; I am ashamed of mine.'

Molly, without replying, flitted to her shelter behind the gallery railing, and Kate, noiselessly descending from the window-seat, crouched again in the shelter of the open door, listening. Men were putting questions to the stranger, now in English, now in Welsh, to little purpose. A squire had just ended a Welsh sentence. The stranger spoke: *Est-ce-que c'est le Gallois que j'écoute*—would it be de Gaelic she would be? *Excusez, je n'entends pas.* Have you *personne qui parle Français*—no French speaking?'

'Begad, he's right,' cried the old Squire: 'we shall never make him out at this rate. What English he has is Scotch, and what

Welsh he has is Gaelic, as hard as Hebrew; but he rattles out French quick enough, if any of us knew it. There is Father Walsh, or—no, what a fool I am!—there is Kate: she patters parleyvoo like any monsieur of the lot, damn them all. Dick, run upstairs and ask Kate to come down and interpret.'

In a moment Molly was on her window-seat, Kate had retreated and ensconced herself in the armchair by the fire, and then Dick ran up and entered the room.

'The Prince has sent a messenger,' he explained, 'an officer in French service, who speaks no human language but French. I suppose he is of Scotch blood, born in France, and so he is safe as a prisoner of war if he is taken. They would hang any prisoner they could make out to be a British subject. But we can only understand one word out of five that he says, so the Squire asks you, Kate, to come down and translate him.'

He took her hand. 'Why, how cold you are! Your blood must have gone back to your heart,' said Dick.

'It is at the Prince's service, wherever it may be,' said Kate, blushing; while Molly liked her way less than ever.

'Well, the colour shows in your face now, that never I saw so pretty. This Captain Pink-o'-the-fashion in his French clothes looks coxcomb enough to believe you show your colour for *him*.'

Dick turned and ran downstairs. Kate followed more slowly; she swiftly picked up a white cockade from the floor, and pinned it above her heart.

The stranger, his booted legs stretched out wearily, sat uncloaked in the hall—a shining presence among the plain squires, in his gay French clothes, unsoiled by war. But there were three little stains of blood on the lace band round his throat. Nothing else marred his elegance, and he fingered the patch where he had cut his chin. He seemed about Dick's age; but his eyes were as hard as they were handsome. Seeing Kate as she descended the last steps into the hall, he raised a silver cup and drank a long draught of claret. '*A la santé du Prince et de Mademoiselle!*' he said, and next moment was performing a deep French bow to Kate. She curtisied to the ground, stately, remote, and pale as snow.

The stranger, bowing, handed to Kate a letter which the company had already seen. It briefly bade Sir Arthur Vaughan trust the bearer, Captain Macdonald de Juvigny, and was signed

'Charles P. R.' The girl kissed the signature, and the stranger, smiling oddly, murmured words in French which sent the colour angrily back to her face, while her black brows contracted fiercely.

The words, which no man present understood, were: '*Vous portez encore la rose blanche! Miracle de fidélité! On retrouve la belle brebis égaree!*'

Kate's hand flew with a clutch to the white cockade above her heart.

To Dick, who was watching her, it seemed as if the girl only checked herself by an effort from wrenching the cockade from her bosom. A moment, Dick divined, and she would have torn off the emblem and tossed it in the Frenchman's face.

'What the devil has he said to Kate?' muttered Dick audibly; but his cousin was listening now with quiet attention, and a face blank of expression, while Captain Pink, as Dick called him, spoke rapidly and aloud, in French.

She began to interpret. 'Monsieur Macdonald de Juvigny tells me that he has seen me in Paris, though I do not remember his face. He has just left my uncle, Colonel Nicholas Wogan, who is, I know, with his Royal Highness, and now rides to raise Wales for the Cause.'

'Hurrah for old one-armed Nick!' cried Dick Vaughan.

De Juvigny spoke again.

'The gentleman says,' Kate interpreted, while the Frenchman fingered the cut on his chin, 'that his orders are to report to my uncle, Sir Arthur, alone. Sir Arthur will communicate what he is charged with to the rest of the gentlemen. He has news of importance.'

'Orders must be obeyed, friends,' remarked Sir Arthur. 'You must excuse me for a quarter of an hour. Kate, lead Monsieur Macdonald—I can speak the first half of his name easiest—to the summer parlour. I'll follow as fast as my gout will let me. Faith, I scarce feel as if the saddle was the place for me this winter morning.'

M. de Juvigny, one hand on his heart, swept a bow with his hat to the company. Kate led him out of the hall; he was whispering to her rapidly; she, with head erect, gave no sign that she heard him. Dick glared after them angrily.

The Squire hobbled after, very slow and lame, leaning a gouty red hand on tables as he passed. When the door at last closed behind him, Dick turned fiercely to a young man in the throng. 'Was I so unfortunate,' he asked, 'as to hear Mr Williams say that Sir Arthur's gout was mighty convenient?'

'Was mighty inconvenient, Mr Vaughan, was what I took the freedom to observe. Does any gentleman here dissent from my expression of sympathy?'

'Sir, I beg your pardon for my mistake,' said Dick, in the coldest of tones; and the company began to talk all at once and very loud to cover the incident. Dick sat down, silent, toying with his sword-hilt. Whatever the rest might feel, Dick was on fire to fight somebody—anybody, white cockade or black. That French coxcomb, he was sure, had been insulting his cousin.

When the side door was opening again, Dick sped from the hall by another way. He ran along a passage till he saw Kate's skirt turning the corner of a staircase, and followed her eagerly. He heard her sob.

'Kate, what is it? Tell me!'

'Bad news from Spain: our uncle Charles very ill,' answered Kate, entering her room. Dick heard the bolt ring in the staple.

'That is a girl's lie,' thought honest Dick to himself. 'She never saw my uncle—none of us ever did. But my father had a letter from him, at La Mancha, later than any news that could have reached the Prince from Spain. How can I get even with that coward Captain Pink-o'-the-fashion? He is in my father's house. I cannot tread on his toe, or pick a quarrel over the cards. By George, I have a plan! Nobody will know that we have quarrelled, if this Captain Pink has the heart of a mouse.'

Dick found his way to the library without crossing the hall. Molly was sitting by the fire; she had been crying.

'What possesses the women this day?' thought Dick; but what he said was, 'Molly, where is the French dictionary?'

Molly went to a shelf and found it. 'What do you want?' she asked.

'Something I have to ask of that French officer. He has said a word she does not like to Kate. Go and see her—she is in her room.'

'Dick, you won't quarrel?'

'In my father's house?' asked Dick. 'Is it likely? But I want to understand. That is the way, my uncle Nick says, to avoid a misunderstanding. I am sure Kate needs you.'

Molly went off reluctantly. She knew that her brother could be obstinate.

Dick seized on the French dictionary, and, not without labour, discovered some words that he wanted. Then he opened a drawer in a card-table, and took out a card—the ace of hearts. On this he wrote very distinctly the words which he had found, and threw the rest of the incomplete pack behind a bookcase. The card on which he had written he placed in a pocket in the breast of his coat. Then he sauntered down into the hall.

Horses were being brought to the door; guests with rather pale faces were taking the stirrup cup; others, five or six, were to stay for the night.

Sir Arthur beckoned Dick into a corner, where he sat beside a tankard. 'Dick, you whelp, where have you been? I've sent the Mounseer to your room to unboot himself, and put his neat feet in a pair of your sprawling pumps, and to change his linen— though, faith, you have none fine enough for his wear.'

'He is very welcome, sir. I am sorry I was away, but you came back to the hall before I expected you. May I ask his news?'

'We must rise and ride, those of us who can mount a horse,' said the Squire, looking tenderly at his gouty foot. 'I would rather be ordering my carriage to carry me to the Bath, but needs must when somebody drives. The Prince has spoken very candid and fair, I must say. If we can join him the day after tomorrow, or promise to join him the day after, he will make for London. If not, he cannot keep the faces of the Highland chiefs to the South for another day. The Cheshire gentry have flinched. Of Lancashire only a mob from Manchester has come in. He has hopes from his brother Henry, and the French, but no certain news. Barry has gone to my Lord Barrymore and Sir Watkin; French officers, like our Mounseer, are riding to warn all the Cycle Club.'

The Squire had seldom told a tale so long and so plain: he told it mournfully, and comforted himself with flagons.

'We are all ready here, sir: do we ride tonight?' asked Dick.

'The others are not ready, except for a few near neighbours, who will dine and sleep here; the rest go home, and muster here tomorrow. Bring Molly to me in the blue study: let us eat and drink, for tomorrow——' The Squire sighed, and did not finish the text.

'Should I mount at once?' thought Dick, as he went on his errand. 'No, I must settle first with Captain Pink.'

A troop of servants and gentlemen cantered down the avenue and away.

2

Molly sat at the head of the table at dinner: beside her the French officer, very courtly and gallant. Molly had a little French, and she did her best to amuse him; her mind all the while was with Kate, who had refused to see her, and had sent to say that she was ill and must keep her room. Dick, watching closely, saw no touch of insolence in the Frenchman's words and looks—nothing more than the accustomed and honourable gallantry of the time. The squires drank deep enough to forget care; and Molly, when the dishes were removed, curtsied and left them to their wine. Dick moved up beside Monsieur de Juvigny; the usual loyal toasts were honoured: Dick doing his best, as he had scarce any French, to keep the visitor's glass full. But this was an easy task, for the officer never really emptied it, merely putting his lips to the wine.

'Father,' said Dick, stepping to the Squire in his great chair, 'we cannot well talk to our guest, but the cards speak a language that all gentlemen understand.'

'Cards!' cried the Squire; and the servants, drawing up another table of green baize, brought clean glasses and a box holding several packs.

De Juvigny rose with alacrity, lugging out a heavy purse and pouring a heap of louis d'or before him on the table. The others did likewise, and a huge bowl of punch was set down.

The night sped, amid shouts of laughter and oaths from the wild squires. More than one fell sound asleep amidst the din; others played eagerly—they had brought money for their expedition. Fortune went and came in varying tides: the gold crossed with the tides from place to place on the table. The hours ran by, unnoted; but the night had begun early, and by eleven o'clock :

Dick and the Frenchman were the only sober men in the room, the only men who, strictly speaking, could keep their feet if they rose. Two were under the table vaguely quarrelling. De Juvigny smiled over a considerable heap of gold at the young man opposite, beside whom lay two or three pieces. The rest were cleared out.

Dick called the servants: they helped their defeated and half-unconscious masters away to bed. The gouty Squire, babbling hospitalities, was wheeled off in an armchair specially constructed for that purpose. One of the servants of the house handed a sealed note to Dick.

Bowing to De Juvigny for permission, he opened it, read it, thrust it in his pocket, and murmured a word to the man, who left the room. Then, with the sweetest of smiles, Dick took up two of the candlesticks, and, again bowing to De Juvigny, waved his hand, and moved towards the door.

'*Dormez, dormez, chers amours,*' hummed Dick, laughing. He had no French, but the words came in a song that Kate used to sing.

The Frenchman laughed back: he rather liked this intelligent young barbarian. He crammed the captive gold into his wide pockets. A dozen pieces slipped from his fingers and rolled on the carpet. De Juvigny looked at the servants, and pointed to the floor with a gesture of permission. The men, who had been gazing with greedy eyes at so great a treasure, glanced at Dick, and when he smiled, began to hunt for the fallen pieces, whispering eagerly in Welsh. But one was watching the movements of the Frenchman.

De Juvigny laid his hand affectionately on the lad's shoulder, as if to steady himself, and followed his candle-bearer. Dick led him to his room, bowed to him to enter first, and surveyed all with the attentive eye of the host. The bed lay white and inviting; the fire flickered a lullaby; a pile of letters, one unfinished, was heaped on the bureau: all was well.

Then Dick, setting down one candle on a table by the bed, lit from the flame of the other an illumination through the room, on walls, chimneypiece, and dressing-table. Last, he drew his card from his pocket and, bowing, handed it to the Frenchman, who read—

'*Vous insultez une femme. Vous êtes un lâche.*'

The Frenchman read, and smiled. '*L'Amour n'est pas si aveugle!*'

he murmured to himself. Then, taking from his fob a watch that burned with diamonds, he placed his white ringed finger at a figure on the dial.

Dick looked at the figure indicated, smiled, bowed again, profoundly, and lit his way, with his one candle, through the long black corridors, to his own room.

'Clever of him to give me the hour of meeting in that way,' said Dick aloud to himself. 'If one did not know better, one might think the brute a gentleman.'

A door was open: the dim light from a low fire within showed a woman's figure in the doorway. Kate stood there, and beckoned to Dick to enter.

He hesitated.

'Come: you must come!' she whispered imperiously.

Dick looked right and left: there was no light and no sound in the corridor—the house was wondrous still. He entered; Kate softly closed the door, and stood with her back against it.

'Dick, I was watching and listening: I heard what you said to yourself.'

Her face, in her fallen black hair, was white, her eyes shining in the light of the candle which was in Dick's hand.

His hand trembled. 'I am sorry that you heard,' said he.

'Dick, dear Dick, you must not do what you intend. You must not meet that man. It will harm the Cause.'

'Your honour, our honour, come before the Cause. He insulted you under our roof. We two quarrelled over the cards when the rest had gone: it is easily explained. Goodnight.' He tried to pass her.

She stood firm. 'Dick, you cannot fight! If you fall by his sword, your memory will be a mockery while men remember. If he falls by your sword, your honour is lost for ever.'

'I don't know what you mean, but I can take care of my honour,' said Dick. 'Kate,' he went on, 'you know what you are to me: to you I am Molly's brother. This is not a matter for women's meddling.'

Kate paused one moment; then her face altered. She looked as Dick had never thought to see her look. Her eyes fell; then, as she raised them to his face, they softened and glowed. 'What you are to me? Oh, Dick, don't you know? You are everything.'

She caught him in a wild embrace, she laid her cheek against his; then, with a little low laughter, she blew out the candle.

In that moment Dick's love for Kate Wogan fell dead. He was very young, very inexperienced, but he was certain that love for him was not in her heart. Was she playing this strange part for the first time? He shook in her embrace, but he undid her arms from his neck. 'I am very sorry,' he said, with a kind of sob. 'But your honour is mine.'

He moved her from her place, he went forth, shutting the door very carefully. He groped his way down the corridor for six paces; then he stood and listened, while he took off his shoes. All was deathly still. When perfectly assured that no one was stirring, he went stealthily to his room, feeling his way by the walls of the corridors. His door was open, the firelight shone out from it. He entered, locked his door, and threw himself, face down, on his bed.

Molly, awakened in the deep of the night, heard the clatter of horses' hoofs galloping down the way from the stables—the hoofs of two horses, she thought. She drew her repeater from below her pillow, and pressed the spring. There was no tinkle of the tiny silver bells. She had forgotten to wind her watch, and it had run down. She dared not go from her room to consult a clock; Kate's door, she knew, was bolted—no help there.

The girl tossed and turned, tormented by many thoughts, and unwittingly at last fell asleep. The early sounds of folk astir in the castle before the dawn did not arouse her. When she awoke it was in the yellow light and among the dancing shadows of a candle held in an old woman's trembling hand.

'Nurse, Winifred, what is it? why so early?' cried the girl. Then she went on: 'Oh, I remember—they ride today. The Saints give me courage, and to them safety, and to the Prince victory,' she murmured, sitting up and crossing herself.

The old woman fell into a chair by the bed, moaning, and rocking her body to and fro.

'Courage, dear old Winnie!' said the girl, in Welsh. 'We must be brave today, till they have ridden.'

'One will never ride out,' said the old woman, with the pleasure old women take in 'breaking the news.'

'Who? Is it Dick? is it my father?' cried the girl, leaping from bed.

'Master Dick is flown, his grey gelding and the big brown horse, Rupert, are gone from the stables, and the Squire is but now come out of his fit, and crying like a child over the honour of the house.'

'Oh, do speak: what honour? Is any one dead?' Molly shook the old woman. 'Speak! speak!' she said. She could not believe that Dick had fled from the enterprise of the day, and that this news had smitten his father. That could not be. But she had heard the horses' feet that bore her brother through the night.

'The French officer is dead,' the old woman answered.

'How?' screamed Molly, trying to dress with hands numb and trembling.

'Mat, the Squire's man, was up by six; most of the household were up. He had orders to call the French officer, and as he walked along the yellow gallery, he saw a great light that streamed from his open chamber door. And there, fallen across the bed, in shirt and drawers, was the Frenchman, a sword-thrust in his side, and another had grazed his ribs. His own sword, drawn, lay on the floor: and a table had fallen, and golden coins were glittering all over the carpet, and every candle in the room was lit, as if it had been for a ball. Mat ran for me; for I know about treating sword-wounds—many a one have I tended when the Squire was young and the gentlemen would quarrel over their cards. I was up and stirring when Mat came to me, and he took me to the room. I put my hand on the Frenchman's heart: he was hardly cold, but never a flutter of the heart. Miss Molly,' said the old nurse, dropping her voice to a low whisper in the girl's ear, '*the Frenchman was a woman!*'

Peal upon peal of the cruel agony of laughter that seems as if it would never cease rang from Molly's lips. She fell back on her bed, mastered by the mad mirth that possessed and tormented her—a laughing devil that for long would not go out, despite all the old wife's arts of rousing and soothing.

The skirts of frightened women came fluttering to the door, maids drawn by the frightful laughter. The old woman bade them leave her fosterling to her. Kate entered on tiptoe, pale and cool, and whispered with Winifred.

'Tell her, when you can, that her father is himself again,' Kate said, and passed to her own adjacent room.

And there fallen across the bed, in shirt and drawers, was the Frenchman

The dawn was grey in the chamber before Molly's shaking head was still and her wild lips were silent.

'Now I may bring you a cup of chocolate, dear,' said the nurse.

Life was come into the room again, and common things and memory returned. Molly lay and thought; escaped from the mad mockery of the strange event. Her brother had been angry with the Frenchman, she reflected. They had fought a duel, no doubt, by candlelight, without witnesses; it was nothing so very unusual in these days. After the fatal sword-thrust Dick had found that his enemy was a woman. Many ladies rode all the way with the Prince's troops: some, the English believed, rode in male attire, and armed, like Jenny Cameron. The horror of the discovery had driven Dick to fly—whither? Perhaps to give himself up to the justice of his rightful Prince.

So Molly reasoned with herself, languidly, when her eyes fell on a card, the ace of hearts, that lay on a table beside her pillow. There was writing along the length of the card. She looked at it more closely; the writing was in Dick's hand.

'*Vous insultez une femme. Vous êtes un lâche.*'

Then Molly knew: her guess was now a proved fact; there lay the challenge.

The old nurse opened the door.

'What is this card, Winnie? how came it here?' Molly asked, with a desperate calmness.

'I found it on the Frenchwoman's table, and brought it to show you, before you had your bad turn.'

Molly thrust the card into the bosom of her bedgown. She would destroy it when she had the chance. 'What do they say downstairs, Winnie?' she asked.

'The gentlemen all rode away when they heard the news. They said that Stewart of Glenbucky was pistoled in his bed in Arnprior's house—it is not known by whom—as he went to join the Prince, and that now this Frenchwoman has been killed here strangely; and so they say that there is a curse on the Cause.'

'Cowards!' said Molly. 'And what do our own people think?'

'The serving-men said at first, dearie, that the stranger and Master Dick were the only two gentlemen in the house who could stand on their feet last night, and that Master Dick was flown. So they thought that these two, playing alone at the cards, must have quarrelled and fought. It was when the Squire heard *that*, that he swooned away; but Father Walsh bled him, and he came to again. And then they wakened David Price, the stable-boy, that had slept through all the morning noise in his loft; and he showed a written line that Master Dick had left with him for the Squire, when he saddled the horses. It was no more than "I will be back again before nine," and that comforted the Squire. For Master Dick, if he had fought with a lady, not knowing, and unhappily had killed her and ridden off, would not be riding back in the morning, to be sure. And back he will come; Master Dick never lied in his life.'

'Thank the Saints,' said Molly. Dick would answer for himself. Dick was guiltless.

'And now,' said Winifred, 'the men do not know what to think, and each is suspecting the other, for they quarrelled last night over some gold that the Frenchwoman let fall on the floor and told them to scramble for. And her window was found open, and marks of blood on the carpet, as if some one had stepped on tiptoe out of the pool of blood to the window, and let himself down by a sheet that is fastened to a table and hanging out of the window.'

'Are there footmarks on the ground below?' asked Molly.

'There could not be—the ground is frozen as hard as steel. Father Walsh guesses that someone attacked the Mounseer in the night for the money, and that he—I mean she—defended herself, and that the thief was somebody in the house, a serving-man, who had knotted the sheet to the table to escape by. But something must have disturbed him, and he had not time to pick up the gold, but probably got back into the castle by a way that the young men use when they go courting.'

'But a thief would not light all the candles,' said Molly.

'No; but Father Walsh thinks that the Frenchwoman had lit them, and sat up writing letters. Many letters lay on her table— Father Walsh burned them all—and one was unfinished. The Father told me, that I might tell you; he has known me for forty years, the blessed man. It is all to show you that Master Dick did not do it. He was never the one for mean tricks like these.'

'Never Dick!' said Molly, pondering over the theory of the

Jesuit. It seemed to meet all the circumstances. A greedy servant, probably the servant of one of the neighbours in the house, had seen the pile of gold; had hoped to seize it in the night, and escape in the confusion of the times. He could easily find a sword—nay, probably was armed, to ride with his master to the war. He had unexpectedly found the Prince's messenger up and awake, writing. They had fought, and the man had killed the woman, whom he took for a man. He had then been disturbed, probably by the noise of Dick moving through the house before he rode away, and had preferred to escape by the window, and then re-enter the house, rather than risk being found in the passages. It appeared the only solution of the mystery.

But why had Dick ridden away? and why with two horses?

'What o'clock is it, Winnie?' Molly asked.

'It was near nine, dear, when I passed the great clock on the stairs.'

'Help me to dress,' said Molly; and being dressed, she drank her chocolate, and ran along the gallery to her old perch in the window-seat of the library. She had not long to wait. Again there came the longed-for sound of two horses galloping up the avenue. The girl fled down to the hall, passing one or two frightened men-servants, already somewhat bemused with beer. Along the avenue she flitted, bare-headed; she was past the corner, was alone beneath the trees. The trample of the hoofs came nearer; she stooped and hid among the low shrubs and hollies beside the road. Two horse-men came in sight, galloping: the foremost, who rode the grey, was Dick Vaughan; the huge one-armed man on brown Rupert could be none but Molly's uncle, whom she had never seen. Kate's uncle, too—the half-mythic hero of the family, the daring jolly Irish Chevalier Nicholas Wogan.

Through thirty years—all Europe knew it—Nick had fought for the Cause, by land and sea. A lad of fifteen, he had shown the steady courage of a veteran at Preston. A veteran of forty five, he had displayed the fighting fury of a lad, at Fontenoy, with the conquering Irish brigade.

The girl leaped up from her hiding-place; stood in the centre of the avenue, and stretched out her arms as a signal to the riders to stop.

The men checked their steaming horses.

'Oh, Dick, stop, stop!' the girl cried. 'Do not go to the house; I must speak to you first alone!'

'Not without your uncle, Miss Molly. You must be niece Molly!' quoth Nicholas Wogan, leaping down from the saddle. His one arm was round her in a moment.

'Turn, and walk beside me away from the house,' said Molly, as her uncle kissed her.

Dick looked at his watch. 'Five minutes to nine, Uncle Nicholas,' said he.

'Never mind, Dick: 'tis for once a fair occasion to be late at a tryst with a lady. Think of it, Molly,' cried the Chevalier, letting a great laugh out of him; 'your brother rode in the night to bring me a beast that could carry a man of my inches; my nag had broken down at an inn twelve miles away, and I sent a lad on a country pony, late last night, to bid Dick come with a remount.'

He patted Rupert's neck. 'So your brother's first word to his long-lost uncle was—what do you think?—was to ask me to second him in a duel this morning! It is myself that always was a a peacemaker, and glad I was to be of use so soon in my own family.'

'But who is your man?' says I to Dick; 'and what is the quarrel? Not that it matters much between gentlemen.'

'Says Dick to me, "He insulted my cousin Kate."'

'Says I, "I have fought more than once on that head, when I was with the Army in Flanders. Some enemy my niece has, and I was compelled to silence lying tales that came to us from Versailles—tales that we cannot tell niece Molly. But your man?" I asked again.

'Says Dick, "A Scotch French officer—the Prince's messenger, Monsieur Macdonald de Juvigny."

'Lord, niece, at that I lay back in my chair in the *auberge*, and laughed till the chair was killed under me. When I had dug myself out of the ruins, "Dick," says I, "your man's a woman! She came over in the same barque as myself, with d'Eguilles. I knew it, knew what she was, by a chance, and one other knows it; but in the camp there is never a whisper of it. The cunning wench acts the man well, and now and again cuts her chin with a razor, as if she had shaved badly in a hurry, *comme à la guerre*."'

Nicholas laughed again, till the bare woods rang, and rubbed his own black-bristled chin. He ran on. 'But, Dick, you took a risk when you challenged my lady. I have seen her use the foils; she might have been fencer to the Sophy, like the lady in Shakespeare's play,' and he laughed once more.

Dick did not laugh.

'Let's back and to breakfast,' said Nicholas. 'I daresay the wench no more insulted your cousin, you fire-eater, than she had a right to the breeches.'

Molly stopped, fronted her uncle, and held up her hand. 'Oh, uncle, for the sake of charity do not laugh. She, that woman in man's dress, is lying dead in the red room; a sword-thrust through her heart, her own sword bare beside her. Every candle in the room was left lighted: it shone brighter than the day. Gold won at cards was scattered all over the floor. She fell in a fight. My God! with whom?'

Dick staggered; his face was deadly white.

Nick Wogan's broad brown face could not pale, but his jaw drooped. 'The honour of the house—the honour of the old house! A woman slain in the house!' he gasped, and leaned against his horse's side, as if a bullet had struck him.

There was silence. Dick said no word; he was trembling.

'Molly, it cannot be,' said Nick at last. 'I see it all. He, the woman I would say, had won all the gold in the house, all our friends' gold, at cards. A servant has killed her for the money—killed her in her sleep, and left the candles all alight, and her own sword drawn beside her, to give the appearance of a duel. Oh, damn the infernal villain!'

Dick Vaughan groaned.

'That is just what Father Walsh guessed,' said Molly, 'or something very like that. He thinks that the Frenchwoman was writing, late in the night; that she attacked the thief, who had a sword; that the thief killed her, but was disturbed, perhaps by the noise Dick made when he went out to the stables. Then the thief let himself out of the window by a sheet, and came back into the house by a way which, Winnie says, the servants sometimes use.'

'That's it!' cried Nicholas. 'Dick, we must find the fellow. Well guessed, the Jesuit! Cheer up, Dick: it is better, black as it is, now we know the secret of it. Why, man, you look as if you had seen a ghost. I don't wonder: you might have fought a woman, though she was a man's match with the foils.'

Dick turned a white face on his uncle. 'It must be so—you are right,' he said; and between his teeth he muttered, 'unless——'

'Unless what, you *omadhaun*?' thundered Nicholas.

There was a rustling of dry beech-leaves and a snapping of twigs in the shrubbery.

'My uncle Nicholas is welcome,' came in Kate's voice. She had stolen on them through the underwood. She was in riding-habit as if for a journey, her right hand was thrust into the breast of her coat. She went on: 'This is, perhaps, no safe place for confidences. The servants are talking about the sound of horses' hoofs that came so near and strangely died away. Some speak of the omen of the phantom coach; but bolder spirits are heartening themselves to walk down the avenue and investigate. Let us hurry on. It were a pity if the horses caught cold.'

'Niece Kate,' said Nicholas, 'I have heard of you often, but never seen you. You are the best man of us. Let us jog.' He walked in advance, his arm round Molly's trembling waist; she led Rupert.

Dick followed, Kate beside him, speaking low. 'Dick,' she said, 'I have listened for some minutes. I seem to have got a habit of listening, in these late times. You said "unless!" But Molly guesses nothing, does she?'

Dick looked at her. His tongue was dry; he could hardly utter the words, 'It was so, then?'

'It was so—in fair fight,' said Kate. She bared her right fore-arm. There was blood on a bandage above the wrist. 'My *maître d'armes* taught me to use the left hand,' she said, 'or I had not been here. We fought *à outrance*. We had the same master, in France. I knew that we were of equal force. You guessed, I think, when our sonorous uncle said, "She is a man's match with the foils." You knew that I was.'

'I guessed sooner,' said Dick. 'Why was this done?'

'Could I leave it to you? You now know why I could not. I do not love you, Dick,' said Kate, her white face angrily flushed. She hid her face with her hands. 'I could not leave this to you, this shame to the house. I would have taken shame on myself; it was a choice of shames, and I was mad, and I was shamed by you. By that woman I would not again be shamed. I hated her to the death, and she me. She knew I was here, and came to ruin me. In France she did me the greatest wrong that one woman can do another. I endured it. Then she gave out, Dick, lies against me; said that I was a spy on the Prince. The lies were believed. She was the granddaughter of that Macdonald called "The Tailor," who dealt with Stair when the King was young. Poison was in her blood. She was believed. I had to leave France. In this house she insulted me.'

'I knew it,' said Dick.

Kate went on: 'She threatened to tell her old lies, and new lies, to my uncle and all the gentlemen, today. Your Cause has been betrayed; she learned it on her way hither. The Scots are running home. And she told me that she would denounce me as the traitress, the informer. She had a great protector, who would have believed her story. Could I let her speak? If my hand might help me, could I let her live? You could not stop her in *your* way; no man could meet her, in a man's way, and no man knew that. I sat and thought, when you left me. How could I make good my story? How could I live, if she lived to tell hers? You might have stopped her, if I had left you free, but shame would have fallen on you—to have slain a woman—dishonour among men. To save you from that, if I could, I did a great wrong, a bitter wrong, to you and to myself, Dick. We can never meet again. Do you forgive me? I may say goodbye to Molly? I shall never see her more.'

Dick could not speak. He held out his hand, and she kissed it.

'Now let us join the rest,' said Kate. 'I am quite safe in life, and'—she said with a strange smile—'in honour. The Jesuit's guess will be believed. I arranged the sheet at the window, when all was done, to that very end. But no man will suffer for me; if any man is in danger I shall tell all. I go today to my people in Essex.'

'They are bitter Protestants,' said Dick.

'The better for me. Protestants do not confess, and you have heard my last confession. Let us go in.'

Little moan was made, and no inquest was held on the body of a Jacobite officer, dying where it was no man's interest to proclaim that he had been. In the old castle they still speak of the mysterious 'Captain Pink,' as they call him. They tell you how gallantly attired he came to the house, how he won the gold of his hosts at cards, how, next morning, he was found strangely slain, and how, mystery of mysteries, Captain Pink was a woman. They show you the room in which she lay—no one has lain there since—and the stained mattress on which she died. But even the date of these events has been forgotten by tradition, which still guesses vaguely at the problem of the slaying of Captain Pink.

A E W Mason

The Cruise of the *Willing Mind*

The cruise happened before the steam trawler ousted the smack from the North Sea. A few newspapers recorded it in half a dozen lines of small print which nobody read. But it became and—though nowadays the *Willing Mind* rots from month to month by the quay—remains staple talk at Gorleston alehouses on winter nights.

The crew consisted of Weeks, three fairly competent hands, and a baker's assistant, when the *Willing Mind* slipped out of Yarmouth. Alexander Duncan, the photographer from Derby, joined the smack afterwards under peculiar circumstances. Duncan was a timid person, but aware of his timidity. He was quite clear that his paramount business was to be a man; and he was equally clear that he was not successful in his paramount business. Meanwhile he pretended to be, hoping that on some miraculous day a sudden test would prove the straw man he was to have become real flesh and blood. A visit to a surgeon and the flick of a knife quite shattered that illusion. He went down to Yarmouth afterwards fairly disheartened. The test had been applied and he had failed.

Now Weeks was a particular friend of Duncan's. They had chummed together on Gorleston Quay some years before, perhaps because they were so dissimilar. Weeks had taught Duncan to sail a boat, and had once or twice taken him for a short trip on his smack; so that the first thing that Duncan did on his arrival at Yarmouth was to take the tram to Gorleston and to make inquiries.

A fisherman lounging against a winch replied to them——

'If Weeks is a friend o' yours I should get used to missin' 'im, as I tell his wife.'

There was at that time an ingenious system by which the skipper might buy his smack from the owner on the instalment plan—as people buy their furniture—only with a difference: for people sometimes get their furniture. The instalments had to be completed within a certain period. The skipper could do it—he could just do it; but he couldn't do it without running up one little bill here for stores, and another little bill there for sail mending. The owner worked in with the sailmaker, and just as the skipper was putting out to earn his last instalment he would find the bailiffs on board, his cruise would be delayed, he would be consequently behindhand with his instalment, and back would go the smack to the owner with a present of four-fifths of its price. Weeks had still to pay two hundred pounds, and had eight weeks to earn it in. The time was sufficient, although no more than sufficient. But he got the straight tip that his sailmaker would stop him; and getting together any sort of crew he could he slipped out at night with half his stores.

'Now the No'th Sea,' concluded the fisherman, 'in November and December ain't a bobby's job.'

Duncan walked forward to the pierhead. He looked out at a grey tumbled sky shutting down on a grey tumbled sea. There were flecks of white cloud in the sky, flecks of white breakers on the sea, and it was all most dreary. He stood at the end of the jetty, and his great possibility came out of the grey to him. Weeks was shorthanded. Cribbed within a few feet of the smack's deck, there would be no chance for any man to shirk. Duncan acted on the impulse. He bought a fisherman's outfit at Gorleston, travelled up to London, got a passage the next morning on a Billingsgate fish-carrier, and that night went throbbing down the great water street of the Swin, past the green globes of the Mouse. The four flashes of the Outer Gabbard winked him goodbye away on the starboard, and at eleven o'clock the next night far out in the North Sea he saw the little city of lights swinging on the Dogger.

The *Willing Mind*'s boat came aboard the next morning, and Captain Weeks with it, who smiled grimly while Duncan explained how he had learnt that the smack was shorthanded.

'I can't put you ashore in Denmark,' said Weeks knowingly.

'There'll be seven weeks, it's true, for things to blow over; but I'll have to take you back to Yarmouth. And I can't afford a passenger. If you come, you come as a hand. I mean to own my smack at the end of this voyage.'

Duncan climbed after him into the boat. The *Willing Mind* had now six for her crew: Weeks; his son Willie, a lad of sixteen; Upton, the first hand; Deakin, the decky; Rall, the baker's assistant, and Alexander Duncan. And of these six four were almost competent. Deakin, it is true, was making only his second voyage; but Willie Weeks, though young, had begun early; and Upton, a man of forty, knew the banks and currents of the North Sea as well as Weeks.

'It's all right,' said the skipper, 'if the weather holds.' And for a month the weather did hold, and the catches were good, and Duncan learned a great deal. He learnt how to keep a night watch from midnight till eight in the morning, and then stay on deck till noon: how to put his tiller up and down when his tiller was a wheel, and how to vary the order according as his skipper stood to windward or to lee; he learnt to box a compass and to steer by it; to gauge the leeway he was making by the angle of his wake and the black line in the compass; above all, he learnt to love the boat like a live thing, as a man loves his horse, and to want every scanty inch of brass on her to shine.

But it was not for this that Duncan had come down to the sea. He gazed out at night across the rippling starlit water and the smacks nestling upon it, and asked of his God: 'Is this all?' And his God answered him.

The beginning of it was the sudden looming of ships upon the horizon, very clear, till they looked like carved toys. The skipper got out his accounts and totted up his catches, and the prices they had fetched in Billingsgate Market. Then he went on deck and watched the sun set. There were no cloud-banks in the west, and he shook his head.

'It'll blow a bit from the east before morning,' said he, and he tapped on the barometer. Then he returned to his accounts and added them up again. After a little he looked up, and saw the first hand watching him with comprehension.

'Two or three really good hauls would do the trick,' suggested Weeks.

Upton nodded. 'If it was my boat I should chance it tomorrow before the weather blows up.'

Weeks drummed his fists on the table and agreed.

On the morrow the Admiral headed north for the Great Fisker Bank, and the fleet followed, with the exception of the *Willing Mind*. The *Willing Mind* lagged along in the rear without her top-sails till about halfpast two in the afternoon, when Captain Weeks became suddenly alert. He bore away till he was right before the wind, hoisted every scrap of sail he could carry; rigged out a spinnaker with his balloon foresail, and made a clean run for the coast of Denmark. Deakin explained the manœuvre to Duncan. 'The old man's goin' poachin'. He's after soles.'

'Keep a lookout, lads!' cried Weeks. 'It's not the Danish gunboat I'm afraid of: it's the fatherly English cruiser a-turning of us back.'

Darkness, however, found them unmolested. They crossed the three-mile limit at eight o'clock, and crept close in under the Danish headlands without a glimmer of light showing.

'I want all hands all night,' said Weeks; 'and there's a couple of pounds for him as first sees the bogey-man.'

'Meaning the Danish gunboat,' explained Deakin.

The trawl was down before nine. The skipper stood by his lead, Upton took the wheel, and all night they trawled in the shallows, creeping silently beneath the dark headlands, bumping on the grounds, with a sharp eye forward and aft for the Danish gun-boat. The wind veered round from the west. They hauled in at twelve and again at three and again at six, and they had just got their last catch on deck when Duncan saw by the first grey of the morning a dun-coloured trail of smoke hanging over a pro-jecting knoll.

'There she is!' he cried.

'Yes, that's the gunboat,' answered Weeks. 'She has waited too long. We can laugh at her with this wind.'

He put his smack about, and before the gunboat puffed round the headland, three miles away, was reaching northwards with his sails free. He rejoined the fleet that afternoon. 'Fifty-two boxes of soles!' said Weeks. And every one of them worth two pound ten in Billingsgate Market. This smack's mine!' and he stamped on the deck in all the pride of ownership. 'We'll take a reef in,' he added. 'There's a no'th-easterly gale blowin' up and I don't know anything worse in the No'th Sea. The sea piles in upon you from Noofoundland, piles in till it strikes the banks. Then it breaks. You were right, Upton; we'll be lying hove-to in the morning.'

They were lying hove-to before the morning. Duncan, tossing about in his canvas cot, heard the skipper stamping overhead, and in an interval of the wind caught a snatch of song bawled out in a high voice. The song was not reassuring, for the two lines which Duncan caught ran as follows——

> You never can tell when your death-bells are ringing,
> You never can know when you're going to die.

Duncan tumbled on to the floor, fell about the cabin as he pulled on his sea-boots and climbed up the companion. He clung to the mizzen runners in a night of extraordinary blackness. To port and to starboard the lights of the smacks rose on the crests and sank in the troughs with such violence they had the air of being tossed up into the sky and then extinguished in the water; while all round him there flashed little points of white which suddenly lengthened out into a horizontal line. There was one quite close to the quarter of the *Willing Mind*. It stretched about the height of the main-gaff in a line of white. The line suddenly descended towards him and became a sheet; and then a voice bawled, 'Water! Jump! Down the companion! Jump!' The line of white was a breaking wave.

There was a scamper of heavy boots, and a roar of water plunging over the bulwarks, as though so many loads of wood had been dropped on the deck. Duncan jumped for the cabin, Weeks and the mate jumped the next second and the water sluiced down after them, put out the fire, and washed them, choking and wrestling, about on the cabin floor. Weeks was the first to disentangle himself, and he turned fiercely on Duncan.

'What were you doing on deck? Upton and I keep the watch tonight. You stay below, and by God, I'll see you do it! I have fifty-two boxes of soles to put aboard the fish cutter in the morning, and I'm not going to lose lives before I do that! This smack's mine!'

Captain Weeks was transformed into a savage animal fighting for his own. All night he and the mate stood on the deck and plunged down the open companion with a torrent of water to hurry them. All night Duncan lay in his bunk listening to the bellowing of the wind, the great thuds of solid green wave on the deck, the horrid rush and roaring of the seas as they broke loose to leeward from under the smack's keel. And he listened to something more—the whimpering of the baker's assistant in the next bunk. 'Three inches of deck! What's the use of it! Lord ha' mercy on me, what's the use of it? No more than an eggshell! We'll be broken in afore morning, broken in like a man's skull under a bludgeon. . . . I'm no sailor, I'm not; I'm a baker. It isn't right I should die at sea!'

Duncan stopped his ears, and thought of the journey some one would have to make to the fish cutter in the morning. There were fifty-two boxes of soles to be put aboard.

He remembered the waves and the swirl of foam upon their crests and the wind. Two men would be needed to row the boat, and the boat must make three trips. The skipper and the first hand had been on deck all night. Accordingly he left them out of his reckoning. There remained four, or rather three, for the baker's assistant had ceased to count—Willie Weeks, Deakin, and himself, not a great number to choose from. He felt that he was within an ace of a panic, and not so far, after all, from that whimperer his neighbour. Two men to row the boat—two men! His hands clutched at the iron bar of his hammock; he closed his eyes tight; but the words were thundered out at him overhead in the whistle of the wind, and slashed at him by the water against the planks at his side. He found that his lips were framing excuses.

Nevertheless Duncan was on deck when the morning broke. It broke extraordinarily slowly, a niggardly filtering of grey sad light from the under edge of the sea. The bare topmasts of the smacks showed one after the other. Duncan watched each boat as it came into view with a keen suspense. This was a ketch, and that, and that other, for there was the peak of its reefed mainsail just visible, like a bird's wing, and at last he saw it—the thing he looked for, the steam fish cutter—lurching and rolling in the very middle of the fleet, whither she had crept up in the night. He stared at her; his belly was pinched with fear as a starveling's with hunger; and yet he was conscious that in a way he would have been disappointed if she had not been there.

'No other smack is shipping her fish,' quavered a voice at his elbow. It was the voice of the baker's assistant

'But this smack is,' replied Weeks, and he set his mouth hard. 'And, what's more, my Willie is taking it aboard. Now, who'll go with Willie?'

'I will.'

Weeks swung round on Duncan and stared at him. Then he stared out to sea. Then he stared again at Duncan.

'You?'

'When I shipped as a hand on the *Willing Mind,* I took all a hand's risks.'

'And brought the willing mind,' said Weeks with a smile. 'Go, then! Some one must go. Get the boat tackle ready forward. Here, Willie, put your lifebelt on. You, too, Duncan, though God knows lifebelts won't be of no manner of use; but they'll save your insurance. Steady with the punt there! If it slips inboard off the rail there will be a broken back! And, Willie, don't get under the cutter's counter. She'll come atop of you and smash you like an egg. I'll drop you as close as I can to windward, and pick you up as close as I can to leeward.'

The boat was slung over into the water and loaded up with fishboxes. Duncan and Willie Weeks took their places, and the boat slid away into a furrow. Duncan sat in the bow and rowed. Willie Weeks stood in the stern, facing him, and rowed and steered.

'Water!' said Willie every now and then and a wave curled over the bows and hit Duncan a stunning blow on the back.

'Row!' said Willie, and Duncan rowed and rowed. His hands were ice, he sat in water ice-cold, and his body perspired beneath his oilskins, but he rowed. Once, on the crest of a wave, he looked out and saw below them the deck of a smack, and the crew looking upwards at them as though they were a balloon. 'Row!' said Willie Weeks. Once, too, at the bottom of a slope down which they had bumped dizzily, Duncan again looked out, and saw the spar of a mainmast tossing high above his head just over the edge of a grey roller. 'Row!' said Weeks, and a moment later, 'Ship your oar!' and a rope caught him across the chest.

They were alongside the cutter.

Duncan made fast the rope.

'Push her off!' suddenly cried Willie, and grasped an oar. But he was too late. The cutter's bulwarks swung down towards him, disappeared under water, caught the punt fairly beneath the keel, and scooped it clean on to the deck, cargo and crew.

For a moment both men sat dazed upon their thwarts, stupidly staring. Then Willie exclaimed, 'And this is only the first trip!'

The two following trips however were made without accident, and Duncan found the work too arduous to allow him much thought of its danger.

'Fifty-two boxes at two pound ten,' Weeks chuckled as the boat was swung inboard. 'That's a hundred and four, and ten twos are twenty, and carry two, and ten fives are fifty, and two carried, and twenties into that makes twenty-six. One hundred and thirty pounds—this smack's mine, every rope on her. I tell you what, Duncan: you've done me a good turn today, and I'll do you another. I'll land you at Helsund in Denmark, and you shall get clear away. All we can do now is to lie out this gale.'

Before the afternoon the air was dark with a swither of foam and spray blown off the waves in the thickness of a fog. The heavy bows of the smack beat into the seas with a thud and a hiss—the thud of a steam hammer, the hiss of molten iron plunged into water; the waves raced exultingly up to the bows from windward, and roared angrily away in a spume of foam from the ship's keel to lee; and the thrumming and screaming of the storm in the rigging exceeded all that Duncan had ever imagined. He clung to the stays appalled. This storm was surely the perfect expression of anger too persistent for mere fury. There seemed to be a definite aim of destruction, a deliberate attempt to wear the boat down, in the steady follow of wave upon wave, and in the steady volume of the wind.

Captain Weeks, too, had lost of a sudden all his exhilaration. He stood moodily by Duncan's side, his mind evidently labouring like his ship. He told Duncan stories to which Duncan would rather not have listened—the story of the man who slipped as he stepped from the deck into the punt, and, weighted by his boots, had sunk visibly down and down and down through the clearest calmest water without a struggle; the story of the punt which got

This storm was surely the perfect expression of anger too persistent for mere fury

its painter under its keel and drowned three men; the story of the full rigged ship which was driven across the seven-fathom part of the Dogger—the part that looks like a man's leg in the chart—and which was turned upside down through the back breaking.

'The skipper and the mate,' said Weeks, 'got outside and clung to her bottom, and a steam cutter tried to get them off, but smashed them both with her iron counter instead. Look!' and he gloomily pointed his finger, 'I don't know why that breaker didn't hit us. I don't know what we should have done if it had. I can't think why it didn't hit us! Are you saved?'

Duncan was taken aback by the unexpected question, and answered vaguely——

'I hope so.'

'But you must know,' said Weeks, perplexed. The wind made a theological discussion difficult. Weeks curved his hand into a trumpet, and bawled into Duncan's ear: 'You are either saved or not saved! It's a thing one knows. You must know if you are saved, if you've felt the glow and illumination of it.' He suddenly broke off into a shout of triumph: 'But I got my fish on board the cutter. The *Willing Mind*'s the only boat that did.' Then he relapsed again into melancholy: 'But I'm troubled about the poachin'. The temptation was great but it wasn't right; and I'm not sure but what this storm ain't a judgment.'

He was silent for a little, and then cheered up. 'I tell you what. Since we're hove-to, we'll have a prayer meeting in the cabin tonight and smooth things over.'

The meeting was held after tea by the light of a smoking paraffin lamp with a broken chimney. The crew sat and smoked but with no thought of irreverence, the companion was open, so that the swish of the water and the man on deck alike joined in the hymns. Rall, the baker's assistant, who had once been a steady attendant at Revivalist meetings, led off with a Moody and Sankey hymn, and the crew followed, bawling at the top pitch of their lungs, with now and then some suggestion of a tune. The little stuffy smoke-laden cabin rang with the noise. It burst upwards through the companion way, loud and earnest and plaintive, and the winds caught it and carried it over the water, a thin and appealing cry. After the hymn Weeks prayed aloud, and extempore and most seriously. He prayed for each member of the crew by name, one by one, taking the opportunity to mention in detail each fault of which he had had to complain, and begging that the offender's chastisement might be light. Of Duncan he spoke in ambiguous terms.

'O Lord!' he prayed, and without any abatement of his sincerity, 'a strange gentleman, Mr Duncan, has come amongst us. O Lord! we do not know as much about Mr Duncan as You do, but still bless him, O Lord!' And so he came to himself: 'O Lord! this smack's mine, this little smack labouring in the No'th Sea is mine. Through my poachin' and Your lovin' kindness it's mine; and, O Lord, see that it don't cost me dear!' And the crew solemnly and fervently said 'Amen!'

But the smack was to cost him dear. For in the morning Duncan woke to find himself alone in the cabin. He thrust his head up the companion, and saw Weeks alone with a very grey face standing by the lashed wheel.

'Halloa!' said Duncan. 'Where's the binnacle?'

'Overboard,' said Weeks.

Duncan looked round the deck.

'Where's Willie and the crew?'

'Overboard,' said Weeks. 'All except Rall! He's below deck forward, and clean daft. Listen and you'll hear 'im. He's singing hymns for those in peril on the sea.'

Duncan stared in disbelief. The skipper's face drove the disbelief out of him.

'Why didn't you wake me?' he asked.

'What's the use? You want all the sleep you can get, because you an' me have got to sail my smack into Yarmouth. But I was minded to call you, lad,' he said, with a sort of cry leaping from his throat. 'The wave struck us at about twelve, and it's been mighty lonesome on deck since then with Willie callin' out of the sea. All night he's been callin' out of the welter of the sea. Funny that I haven't heard Upton or Deakin, but on'y Willie! All night until daybreak he called, first on one side of the smack and then on t'other. I don't think I'll tell his mother that. An' I don't see how I'm to put you on shore in Denmark, after all.'

What had happened Duncan put together from the curt utterances of Captain Weeks and the crazy lamentations of Rall. Weeks had roused all hands except Duncan to take the last reef in. They were forward by the mainmast at the time the wave struck them. Weeks himself was on the boom, threading the reefing rope through the eye of the sail. He shouted 'Water!' and the water roared on the deck, carrying the three men aft. Upton was washed over the taffrail. Weeks threw one end of the rope down, and Rall and Willie caught it and were swept overboard, dragging Weeks from the boom on to the deck and jamming him against the bulwarks.

The captain held on to the rope, setting his feet against the side. The smack lifted and dropped and tossed, and each movement wrenched his arms. He could not reach a cleat. Had he moved he would have been jerked overboard.

'I can't hold you both!' he cried, and then, setting his teeth and hardening his heart, he addressed his words to his son: 'Willie! I can't hold you both!' and immediately the weight upon the rope was less. With each drop of the stern the rope slackened, and Weeks gathered the slack in. He could now afford to move. He made the rope fast and hauled the one survivor on deck. He looked at him for a moment. 'Thank God, it's not my son!' he had the courage to say.

'And my heart's broke!' had gasped Rall. 'Fair broke.' And he had gone forward and sung hymns.

They saw little more of Rall. He came aft and fetched his meals away; but he was crazed and made a sort of kennel for himself forward, and the two men left on the smack had enough upon their hands to hinder them from waiting on him. The gale showed no sign of abatement; the fleet was scattered; no glimpse of the sun was visible at any time; and the binnacle was somewhere at the bottom of the sea.

'We may be making a bit of headway no'th, or a bit of leeway west,' said Weeks, 'or we may be doing a sternboard. All that I'm sure of is that you and me are one day going to open Gorleston Harbour. This smack's cost me too dear for me to lose her now. Lucky there's the tell-tale compass in the cabin to show us the wind hasn't shifted.'

All the energy of the man was concentrated upon this wrestle with the gale for the ownership of the *Willing Mind*; and he imparted his energy to his companion. They lived upon deck, wet and starved and perishing with the cold—the cold of December in the North Sea, when the spray cuts the face like a whipcord. They ate by snatches when they could, which was seldom; and they slept by snatches when they could, which was even less often. And at the end of the fourth day there came a blinding fall of snow and sleet, which drifted down the companion, sheeted the ropes with ice, and hung the yards with icicles, and which made every inch of brass a searing iron and every yard of the deck a danger to the foot.

It was when this storm began to fall that Weeks grasped Duncan fiercely by the shoulder.

'What is it you did on land?' he cried. 'Confess it, man! There may be some chance for us if you go down on your knees and confess it.'

Duncan turned as fiercely upon Weeks. Both men were over-strained with want of food and sleep.

'I'm not your Jonah—don't fancy it! I did nothing on land!'

'Then what did you come out for?'

'What did you? To fight and wrestle for your ship, eh? Well I came out to fight and wrestle for my immortal soul, and let it go at that!'

Weeks turned away, and as he turned, slipped on the frozen deck. A lurch of the smack sent him sliding into the rudder-chains, where to Duncan's despair he lay. Once he tried to rise, and fell back. Duncan hauled himself along the bulwarks to him.

'Hurt?'

'Leg broke. Get me down into the cabin. Lucky there's the tell-tale. We'll get the *Willing Mind* berthed by the quay, see if we don't.' That was still his one thought, his one belief.

Duncan hitched a rope round Weeks, underneath his arms, and lowered him as gently as he could down the companion.

'Lift me on to the table so that my head's just beneath the compass! Right! Now take a turn with the rope underneath the table, or I'll roll off. Push an oily under my head, and then go for'ard and see if you can find a fish-box. Take a look that the wheel's fast.'

It seemed to Duncan that the last chance was gone. There was just one inexperienced amateur to shift the sails and steer a seventy-ton ketch across the North Sea into Yarmouth Roads. He said nothing however of his despair to the indomitable man upon the table, and went forward in search of a fish-box. He split up the sides into rough splints and came aft with them.

'Thank 'ee, lad,' said Weeks. 'Just cut my boot away, and fix it up best you can.'

The tossing of the smack made the operation difficult and long. Weeks however never uttered a groan. Only Duncan once looked up and said——

'Halloa! You've hurt your face too. There's blood on your chin!'

'That's all right,' said Weeks with an effort. 'I reckon I've just bit through my lip.'

Duncan stopped his work.

'You've got a medicine chest, skipper, with some laudanum in it——?'

'Daren't!' replied Weeks. 'There's on'y you and me to work the ship. Fix up the job quick as you can, and I'll have a drink of Friar's Balsam afterwards. Seems to me the gale's blowing itself out, and if on'y the wind holds in the same quarter——' And thereupon he fainted.

Duncan bandaged up the leg, got Weeks round, gave him a drink of Friar's Balsam, set the teapot within his reach, and went on deck. The wind was certainly going down; the air was clearer of foam. He tallowed the lead and heaved it, and brought it down to Weeks. Weeks looked at the sand stuck on the tallow and tasted it, and seemed pleased.

'This gives me my longitude,' said he, 'but not my latitude, worse luck. Still, we'll manage it. You'd better get our dinner now; any odd thing in the way of biscuits or a bit of cold fish will do, and then I think we'll be able to run.'

After dinner Duncan said: 'I'll put her about now.'

'No; wear her and let her jibe,' said Weeks, 'then you'll on'y have to ease your sheets.'

Duncan stood at the wheel, while Weeks, with the compass swinging above his head, shouted directions through the companion. They sailed the boat all that night with the wind on her quarter, and at daybreak Duncan brought her to and heaved his lead again. There was rough sand with blackish specks upon the allow, and Weeks, when he saw it, forgot his broken leg.

'My word,' he cried, 'we've hit the Fisker Bank! You'd best lash the wheel, get our breakfast, and take a spell of sleep on deck. Tie a string to your finger and pass it down to me, so that I can wake you up.'

Weeks waked him up at ten o'clock, and they ran south-west with a steady wind till six, when Weeks shouted—

'Take another cast with your lead.'

The sand upon the tallow was white like salt.

'Yes,' said Weeks; 'I thought we was hereabouts. We're on the edge of the Dogger, and we'll be in Yarmouth by the morning.' And all through the night the orders came thick and fast from the cabin. Weeks was on his own ground; he had no longer any need of the lead; he seemed no longer to need his eyes; he felt his way across the currents from the Dogger to the English coast; and at daybreak he shouted—

'Can you see land?'

'There's a mist.'

'Lie to, then, till the sun's up.'

Duncan lay the boat to for a couple of hours, till the mist was tinged with gold and the ball of the sun showed red on his starboard quarter. The mist sank, the brown sails of a smack thrust upwards through it; coastwards it shifted and thinned and thickened, as though cunningly to excite expectation as to what it hid. Again Weeks called out—

'See anything?'

'Yes,' said Duncan in a perplexed voice. 'I see something. Looks like a sort of mediaeval castle on a rock.'

A shout of laughter answered him.

'That's the Gorleston Hotel. The harbour mouth's just beneath. We've hit it fine,' and while he spoke the mist swept clear, and the long treeless esplanade of Yarmouth lay there a couple of miles from Duncan's eyes, glistening and gilded in the sun like a row of doll's houses.

'Haul in your sheets a bit,' said Weeks. 'Keep no'th of the hotel, for the tide'll set you up and we'll sail her in without dawdlin' behind a tug. Get your mainsail down as best you can before you make the entrance.'

Half an hour afterwards the smack sailed between the pierheads.

'Who are you?' cried the harbour master.

'The *Willing Mind*.'

'The *Willing Mind*'s reported lost with all hands.'

'Well, here's the *Willing Mind*,' said Duncan, 'and here's one of the hands.'

The irrepressible voice bawled up the companion to complete the sentence——

'And the owner's reposin' in his cabin.' But in a lower key he added words for his own ears: 'There's the old woman to meet. Lord! but the *Willing Mind* has cost me dear.'

Baroness Orczy

A Question of Passports

Bibot was very sure of himself. There never was, never had been, there never would be again another such patriotic citizen of the Republic as was citizen Bibot of the Town Guard.

And because his patriotism was so well known among the members of the Committee of Public Safety, and his uncompromising hatred of the aristocrats so highly appreciated, citizen Bibot had been given the most important military post within the city of Paris.

He was in command of the Porte Montmartre, which goes to prove how highly he was esteemed, for, believe me, more treachery had been going on inside and out of the Porte Montmartre than in any other quarter of Paris. The last commandant there, citizen Ferney, was guillotined for having allowed a whole batch of aristocrats—traitors to the Republic, all of them—to slip through the Porte Montmartre and to find safety outside the walls of Paris. Ferney pleaded in his defence that these traitors had been spirited away from under his very nose by the devil's agency, for surely that meddlesome Englishman who spent his time in rescuing aristocrats—traitors, all of them—from the clutches of Madame la Guillotine must be either the devil himself or at any rate one of his most powerful agents.

'*Nom de Dieu!* Just think of his name! The Scarlet Pimpernel they call him! No one knows him by any other name! and he is preternaturally tall and strong and superhumanly cunning! And the power which he has of being transmuted into various personalities—rendering himself quite unrecognizable to the eyes of the most sharp-seeing patriot of France, must of a surety be a gift of Satan!'

But the Committee of Public Safety refused to listen to Ferney's explanations. The Scarlet Pimpernel was only an ordinary mortal —an exceedingly cunning and meddlesome personage it is true, and endowed with a superfluity of wealth which enabled him to break the thin crust of patriotism that overlay the natural cupidity of many Captains of the Town Guard—but still an ordinary man for all that, and no true lover of the Republic should allow either superstitious terror or greed to interfere with the discharge of his duties which at the Porte Montmartre consisted in detaining any and every person—aristocrat, foreigner, or otherwise traitor to the Republic—who could not give a satisfactory reason for desiring to leave Paris. Having detained such persons, the patriot's next duty was to hand them over to the Committee of Public Safety, who would then decide whether Madame la Guillotine would have the last word over them or not.

And the guillotine did nearly always have the last word to say, unless the Scarlet Pimpernel interfered.

The trouble was, that that same accursed Englishman interfered at times in a manner which was positively terrifying. His impudence, certes, passed all belief. Stories of his daring and of his impudence were abroad which literally made the lank and greasy hair of every patriot curl with wonder. 'Twas even whispered—not too loudly, forsooth—that certain members of the Committee of Public Safety had measured their skill and valour against that of the Englishman and emerged from the conflict beaten and humiliated, vowing vengeance which, of a truth, was still slow in coming.

Citizen Chauvelin, one of the most implacable and unyielding members of the Committee, was known to have suffered overwhelming shame at the hands of that daring gang, of whom the so-called Scarlet Pimpernel was the accredited chief. Some there were who said that citizen Chauvelin had for ever forfeited his prestige, and even endangered his head by measuring his well-known astuteness against that mysterious League of Spies.

But then Bibot was different!

He feared neither the devil nor any Englishman. Had the latter the strength of giants and the protection of every power of evil,

Bibot was ready for him. Nay! he was aching for a tussle, and
haunted the purlieus of the Committees to obtain some post
which would enable him to come to grips with the Scarlet
Pimpernel and his League.

Bibot's zeal and perseverance were duly rewarded, and anon
he was appointed to the command of the guard at the Porte
Montmartre.

A post of vast importance as aforesaid; so much so, in fact,
that no less a person than citizen Jean Paul Marat himself came to
speak with Bibot on that third day of Nivôse in the year I of the
Republic, with a view to impressing upon him the necessity of
keeping his eyes open, and of suspecting every man, woman and
child indiscriminately until they had proved themselves to be
true patriots.

'Let no one slip through your fingers, citizen Bibot,' Marat
admonished with grim earnestness. 'That accursed Englishman
is cunning and resourceful, and his impudence surpasses that of
the devil himself.'

'He'd better try some of his impudence on me!' commented
Bibot with a sneer, 'he'll soon find out that he no longer has a
Ferney to deal with. Take it from me, citizen Marat, that if a
batch of aristocrats escape out of Paris within the next few days,
under the guidance of the d——d Englishman, they will have to
find some other way than the Porte Montmartre.'

'Well said, citizen!' commented Marat. 'But be watchful
tonight . . . tonight especially. The Scarlet Pimpernel is rampant
in Paris just now.'

'How so?'

'The *ci-devant* Duc and Duchesse de Montreux and the whole
of their brood—sisters, brothers, two or three children, a priest
and several servants—a round dozen in all, have been condemned
to death. The guillotine for them tomorrow at daybreak! Would
it could have been tonight,' added Marat, whilst a demoniacal
leer contorted his face which already exuded lust for blood from
every pore. 'Would it could have been tonight. But the guillotine
has been busy; over four hundred executions today . . . and the
tumbrils are full—the seats bespoken in advance—and still they
come. . . . But tomorrow morning at daybreak Madame la Guillotine will have a word to say to the whole of the Montreux crowd!'

'But they are in the Conciergerie prison surely, citizen! out of the reach of that accursed Englishman?'

'They are on their way, an I mistake not, to the prison at this moment. I came straight on here after the condemnation, to which I listened with true joy. Ah, citizen Bibot! the blood of these hated aristocrats is good to behold when it drips from the blade of the guillotine. Have a care, citizen Bibot, do not let the Montreux crowd escape!'

'Have no fear, citizen Marat! But surely there is no danger! They have been tried and condemned! They are, as you say, even now on their way—well guarded, I presume—to the Conciergerie prison!—tomorrow at daybreak, the guillotine! What is there to fear?'

'Well! well!' said Marat, with a slight tone of hesitation, 'it is best, citizen Bibot, to be over-careful these times.'

Even whilst Marat spoke his face, usually so cunning and vengeful, had suddenly lost its look of devilish cruelty which was almost superhuman in the excess of its infamy, and a greyish hue —suggestive of terror—had spread over the sunken cheeks. He clutched Bibot's arm, and leaning over the table he whispered in his ear:

'The Public Prosecutor had scarce finished his speech today, judgment was being pronounced, the spectators were expectant and still, only the Montreux woman and some of the females and children were blubbering and moaning, when suddenly, it seemed from nowhere, a small piece of paper fluttered from out the assembly and alighted on the desk in front of the Public Prosecutor. He took the paper up and glanced at its contents. I saw that his cheeks had paled, and that his hand trembled as he handed the paper over to me.'

'And what did that paper contain, citizen Marat?' asked Bibot, also speaking in a whisper, for an access of superstitious terror was gripping him by the throat.

'Just the well-known accursed device, citizen, the small scarlet flower, drawn in red ink, and the few words: "Tonight the innocent men and women now condemned by this infamous tribunal will be beyond your reach!"'

'And no sign of a messenger?'

'None.'

'And when did——'

'Hush!' said Marat peremptorily, 'no more of that now. To your post, citizen, and remember—all are suspect! let none escape!'

The two men had been sitting outside a small tavern, opposite the Porte Montmartre, with a bottle of wine between them, their elbows resting on the grimy top of a rough wooden table. They had talked in whispers, for even the walls of the tumble-down cabaret might have had ears.

Opposite them the city wall—broken here by the great gate of Montmartre—loomed threateningly in the fast-gathering dusk of this winter's afternoon. Men in ragged red shirts, their unkempt heads crowned with Phrygian caps adorned with a tricolour cockade, lounged against the wall, or sat in groups on the top of piles of refuse that littered the street, with a rough deal plank between them and a greasy pack of cards in their grimy fingers. Guns and bayonets were propped against the wall. The gate itself had three means of egress; each of these was guarded by two men with fixed bayonets at their shoulders, but otherwise dressed like the others, in rags—with bare legs that looked blue and numb in the cold—the *sans-culottes* of revolutionary Paris.

Bibot rose from his seat, nodding to Marat, and joined his men.

From afar, but gradually drawing nearer, came the sound of a ribald song, with chorus accompaniment sung by throats obviously surfeited with liquor.

For a moment—as the sound approached—Bibot turned back once more to the Friend of the People.

'Am I to understand, citizen,' he said, 'that my orders are not to let anyone pass through these gates tonight?'

'No, no, citizen,' replied Marat, 'we dare not do that. There are a number of good patriots in the city still. We cannot interfere with their liberty or——'

And the look of fear of the demagogue—himself afraid of the human whirlpool which he had let loose—stole into Marat's cruel, piercing eyes.

'No, no,' he reiterated more emphatically, 'we cannot disregard the passports issued by the Committee of Public Safety. But examine each passport carefully, citizen Bibot! If you have any reasonable ground for suspicion, detain the holder, and if you have not——'

A Question of Passports

The sound of singing was quite near now. With another wink and a final leer, Marat drew back under the shadow of the *cabaret* and Bibot swaggered up to the main entrance of the gate.

'*Qui va là?*' he thundered in stentorian tones as a group of some half-dozen people lurched towards him out of the gloom, still shouting hoarsely their ribald drinking song.

The foremost man in the group paused opposite citizen Bibot, and with arms akimbo, and legs planted well apart, tried to assume a rigidity of attitude which apparently was somewhat foreign to him at this moment.

'Good patriots, citizen,' he said in a thick voice which he vainly tried to render steady.

'What do you want?' queried Bibot.

'To be allowed to go on our way unmolested.'

'What is your way?'

'Through the Porte Montmartre to the village of Barency.'

'What is your business there?'

This query, delivered in Bibot's most pompous manner, seemed vastly to amuse the rowdy crowd. He who was the spokesman turned to his friends and shouted hilariously:

'Hark at him, citizens! He asks me what is our business. Ohé, citizen Bibot, since when have you become blind? A dolt you've always been, else you had not asked the question.'

But Bibot, undeterred by the man's drunken insolence, retorted gruffly:

'Your business, I want to know.'

'Bibot! my little Bibot!' cooed the bibulous orator, now in dulcet tones, 'dost not know us, my good Bibot? Yet we all know thee, citizen—Captain Bibot of the Town Guard, eh, citizens! Three cheers for the citizen captain!'

When the noisy shouts and cheers from half a dozen hoarse throats had died down, Bibot, without more ado, turned to his own men at the gate.

'Drive these drunken louts away!' he commanded; 'no one is allowed to loiter here.'

Loud protest on the part of the hilarious crowd followed, then a slight scuffle with the bayonets of the Town Guard. Finally the spokesman, somewhat sobered, once more appealed to Bibot.

'Citizen Bibot! you must be blind not to know me and my mates! And let me tell you that you are doing yourself a deal of harm by interfering with the citizens of the Republic in the proper discharge of their duties, and by disregarding their rights of egress through this gate, a right confirmed by passports signed by two members of the Committee of Public Safety.'

He had spoken now fairly clearly and very pompously. Bibot, somewhat impressed and remembering Marat's admonitions, said very civilly:

'Tell me your business, then, citizen, and show me your passports. If everything is in order you may go your way.'

'But you know me, citizen Bibot?' queried the other.

'Yes, I know you—unofficially—citizen Durand.'

'You know that I and the citizens here are the carriers for citizen Legrand, the market gardener of Barency?'

'Yes, I know that,' said Bibot guardedly, 'unofficially.'

'Then, unofficially, let me tell you, citizen, that unless we get to Barency this evening, Paris will have to do without cabbages and potatoes tomorrow. So now you know that you are acting at your own risk and peril, citizen, by detaining us.'

'Your passports, all of you,' commanded Bibot.

He had just caught sight of Marat still sitting outside the tavern opposite, and was glad enough, in this instance, to shelve his responsibility on the shoulders of the popular 'Friend of the People.' There was general searching in ragged pockets for grimy papers with official seals thereon, and whilst Bibot ordered one of his men to take the six passports across the road to citizen Marat for his inspection, he himself, by the last rays of the setting winter sun, made close examination of the six men who desired to pass through the Porte Montmartre.

As the spokesman had averred, he—Bibot—knew every one of these men. They were the carriers to citizen Legrand, the Barency market gardener. Bibot knew every face. They passed with a load of fruit and vegetables in and out of Paris every day. There was really and absolutely no cause for suspicion, and when citizen Marat returned the six passports, pronouncing them to be genuine, and recognizing his own signature at the bottom of each, Bibot was at last satisfied, and the six bibulous carriers were allowed to pass through the gate, which they did, arm in arm,

'Your passports, all of you,' commanded Bibot

singing a wild *carmagnole*, and vociferously cheering as they emerged out into the open.

But Bibot passed an unsteady hand over his brow. It was cold, yet he was in a perspiration. That sort of thing tells on a man's nerves. He rejoined Marat, at the table outside the drinking booth, and ordered a fresh bottle of wine.

The sun had set now, and with the gathering dusk a damp mist descended on Montmartre. From the wall opposite, where the men sat playing cards, came occasional volleys of blasphemous oaths. Bibot was feeling much more like himself. He had half forgotten the incident of the six carriers, which had occurred nearly half an hour ago.

Two or three other people had, in the meanwhile, tried to pass through the gates, but Bibot had been suspicious and had detained them all.

Marat, having commended him for his zeal, took final leave of him. Just as the demagogue's slouchy, grimy figure was disappearing down a side street there was the loud clatter of hoofs from that same direction, and the next moment a detachment of the mounted Town Guard, headed by an officer in uniform, galloped down the ill-paved street.

Even before the troopers had drawn rein the officer had hailed Bibot.

'Citizen,' he shouted, and his voice was breathless, for he had evidently ridden hard and fast, 'this message to you from the citizen Chief Commissary of the Section. Six men are wanted by the Committee of Public Safety. They are disguised as carriers in the employ of a market gardener, and have passports for Barency ! . . . The passports are stolen: the men are traitors—escaped aristocrats—and their spokesman is that d——d Englishman, the Scarlet Pimpernel.'

Bibot tried to speak; he tugged at the collar of his ragged shirt; an awful curse escaped him.

'Ten thousand devils !' he roared.

'On no account allow these people to go through,' continued the officer. 'Keep their passports. Detain them ! . . . Understand?'

Bibot was still gasping for breath even whilst the officer, ordering a quick 'Turn !' reeled his horse round, ready to gallop away as far as he had come.

'I am for the St Denis Gate—Grosjean is on guard there!' he shouted. 'Same orders all round the city. No one to leave the gates! . . . Understand?'

His troopers fell in. The next moment he would be gone, and these cursed aristocrats well in safety's way.

'Citizen Captain!'

The hoarse shout at last contrived to escape Bibot's parched throat. As if involuntarily, the officer drew rein once more.

'What is it? Quick!—I've no time. That confounded Englishman may be at the St Denis Gate even now!'

'Citizen Captain,' gasped Bibot, his breath coming and going like that of a man fighting for his life. 'Here! . . . at this gate! . . . not half an hour ago . . . six men . . . carriers . . . market gardeners . . . I seemed to know their faces. . . .'

'Yes! yes! market gardener's carriers,' exclaimed the officer gleefully, 'aristocrats all of them . . . and that d——d Scarlet Pimpernel. You've got them? You've detained them? . . . Where are they? . . . Speak, man, in the name of hell! . . .'

'Gone!' gasped Bibot. His legs would no longer bear him. He fell backwards on to a heap of street *débris* and refuse, from which lowly vantage ground he contrived to give away the whole miserable tale.

'Gone! half an hour ago! Their passports were in order! . . . I seemed to know their faces! Citizen Marat was here. . . . He, too——'

In a moment the officer had once more swung his horse round, so that the animal reared, with wild forefeet pawing the air, with champing of bit, and white foam scattered around.

'A thousand million curses!' he exclaimed. 'Citizen Bibot, your head will pay for this treachery. Which way did they go?'

A dozen hands were ready to point in the direction where the merry party of carriers had disappeared half an hour ago; a dozen tongues gave rapid, confused explanations.

'Into it, my men!' shouted the officer; 'they were on foot! They can't have gone far. Remember the Republic has offered ten thousand francs for the capture of the Scarlet Pimpernel.'

Already the heavy gates had been swung open, and the officer's voice once more rang out clear through a perfect thunder-clap of fast galloping hoofs:

'*Ventre à terre!* Remember!—ten thousand francs to him who first sights the Scarlet Pimpernel!'

The thunder-clap died away in the distance, the dust of four score hoofs was merged in the fog and in the darkness; the voice of the captain was raised again through the mist-laden air. One shout . . . a shout of triumph . . . then silence once again.

Bibot had fainted on the heap of *débris*.

His comrades brought him wine to drink. He gradually revived. Hope came back to his heart; his nerves soon steadied themselves as the heavy beverage filtrated through into his blood.

'Bah!' he ejaculated as he pulled himself together, 'the troopers were well-mounted . . . the officer was enthusiastic; those carriers could not have walked very far. And, in any case, I am free from blame. Citoyen Marat himself was here and let them pass!'

A shudder of superstitious terror ran through him as he recollected the whole scene: for surely he knew all the faces of the six men who had gone through the gate. The devil indeed must have given the mysterious Englishman power to transmute himself and his gang wholly into the bodies of other people.

More than an hour went by. Bibot was quite himself again, bullying, commanding, detaining everybody now.

At that time there appeared to be a slight altercation going on on the farther side of the gate. Bibot thought it his duty to go and see what the noise was about. Someone wanting to get into Paris instead of out of it at this hour of the night was a strange occurrence.

Bibot heard his name spoken by a raucous voice. Accompanied by two of his men he crossed the wide gates in order to see what was happening. One of the men held a lanthorn, which he was swinging high above his head. Bibot saw standing there before him, arguing with the guard by the gate, the bibulous spokesman of the band of carriers.

He was explaining to the sentry that he had a message to deliver to the citizen commanding at the Porte Montmartre.

'It is a note,' he said, 'which an officer of the mounted guard gave me. He and twenty troopers were galloping down the great North Road not far from Barency. When they overtook the six of us they drew rein, and the officer gave me this note for citizen Bibot and fifty francs if I would deliver it tonight.'

'Give me the note!' said Bibot calmly.

But his hand shook as he took the paper; his face was livid with fear and rage.

The paper had no writing on it, only the outline of a small scarlet flower done in red—the device of the cursed Englishman, the Scarlet Pimpernel.

'Which way did the officer and the twenty troopers go?' he stammered, 'after they gave you this note?'

'On the way to Calais,' replied the other; 'but they had magnificent horses, and didn't spare them either. They are a league and more away by now!'

All the blood in Bibot's body seemed to rush up to his head, a wild buzzing was in his ears. . . .

And that was how the Duc and Duchesse de Montreux, with their servants and family, escaped from Paris on that third day of Nivôse in the year I of the Republic.

John Buchan

The Lemnian

He pushed the matted locks from his brow as he peered into the mist. His hair was thick with salt, and his eyes smarted from the green-wood fire on the poop. The four slaves who crouched beside the thwarts—Carians with thin birdlike faces—were in a pitiable case, their hands blue with oar-weals and the lash marks on their shoulders beginning to gape from sun and sea. The Lemnian himself bore marks of ill-usage. His cloak was still sopping, his eyes heavy with watching, and his lips black and cracked with thirst. Two days before the storm had caught him and swept his little craft into mid-Ægean. He was a sailor, come of sailor stock, and he had fought the gale manfully and well. But the sea had burst his water-jars, and the torments of drought had been added to his toil. He had been driven south almost to Scyros, but had found no harbour. Then a weary day with the oars had brought him close to the Eubœan shore, when a freshet of storm drove him seaward again. Now at last in this northerly creek of Sciathos he had found shelter and a spring. But it was a perilous place, for there were robbers in the bushy hills—mainland men who loved above all things to rob an islander; and out at sea, as he looked towards Pelion, there seemed something adoing which boded little good. There was deep water beneath a ledge of cliff, half covered by a tangle of wildwood. So Atta lay in the bows, looking through the trails of vine at the racing tides now reddening in the dawn.

The storm had hit others besides him, it seemed. The channel was full of ships, aimless ships that tossed between tide and wind. Looking closer, he saw that they were all wreckage. There had

been tremendous doings in the north, and a navy of some sort
had come to grief. Atta was a prudent man, and knew that a
broken fleet might be dangerous. There might be men lurking
in the maimed galleys who would make short work of the owner
of a battered but navigable craft. At first he thought that the
ships were those of the Hellenes. The troublesome fellows were
everywhere in the islands, stirring up strife and robbing the old
lords. But the tides running strongly from the east were bringing
some of the wreckage in an eddy into the bay. He lay closer and
watched the spars and splintered poops as they neared him. These
were no galleys of the Hellenes. Then came a drowned man,
swollen and horrible: then another—swarthy, hook-nosed fellows,
all yellow with the sea. Atta was puzzled. They must be the men
from the East about whom he had been hearing. Long ere he left
Lemnos there had been news about the Persians. They were
coming like locusts out of the dawn, swarming over Ionia and
Thrace, men and ships numerous beyond telling. They meant
no ill to honest islanders: a little earth and water were enough to
win their friendship. But they meant death to the ὕβρις [1] of the
Hellenes. Atta was on the side of the invaders; he wished them
well in their war with his ancient foes. They would eat them up,
Athenians, Lacedæmonians, Corinthians, Æginetans, men of
Argos and Elis, and none would be left to trouble him. But in the
meantime something had gone wrong. Clearly there had been
no battle. As the bodies butted against the side of the galley he
hooked up one or two and found no trace of a wound. Poseidon
had grown cranky, and had claimed victims. The god would be
appeased by this time, and all would go well.

Danger being past, he bade the men get ashore and fill the water-
skins. 'God's curse on all Hellenes,' he said, as he soaked up the
cold water from the spring in the thicket.

About noon he set sail again. The wind sat in the north-east,
but the wall of Pelion turned it into a light stern breeze which
carried him swiftly westward. The four slaves, still leg-weary and
arm-weary, lay like logs beside the thwarts. Two slept; one
munched some salty figs; the fourth, the headman, stared wearily
forward, with ever and again a glance back at his master. But the

[1] hubris = pride.

Lemnian never looked his way. His head was on his breast, as he steered, and he brooded on the sins of the Hellenes. He was of the old Pelasgian stock, the first lords of the land, who had come out of the soil at the call of God. The pillaging northmen had crushed his folk out of the mainlands and most of the islands, but in Lemnos they had met their match. It was a family story how every grown male had been slain, and how the women long after had slaughtered their conquerors in the night. 'Lemnian deeds,' said the Hellenes, when they wished to speak of some shameful thing: but to Atta the shame was a glory to be cherished for ever. He and his kind were the ancient people, and the gods loved old things, as those new folk would find. Very especially he hated the men of Athens. Had not one of their captains, Miltiades, beaten the Lemnians, and brought the island under Athenian sway? True, it was a rule only in name, for any Athenian who came alone to Lemnos would soon be cleaving the air from the highest cliff-top. But the thought irked his pride, and he gloated over the Persians' coming. The Great King from beyond the deserts would smite those outrageous upstarts. Atta would willingly give earth and water. It was the whim of a fantastic barbarian, and would be well repaid if the bastard Hellenes were destroyed. They spoke his own tongue, and worshipped his own gods, and yet did evil. Let the nemesis of Zeus devour them!

The wreckage pursued him everywhere. Dead men shouldered the sides of the galley, and the straits were stuck full of things like monstrous buoys, where tall ships had foundered. At Artemision he thought he saw signs of an anchored fleet with the low poops of the Hellenes, and sheered off to the northern shores. There, looking towards Œta and the Malian Gulf, he found an anchorage at sunset. The waters were ugly and the times ill, and he had come on an enterprise bigger than he had dreamed. The Lemnian was a stout fellow, but he had no love for needless danger. He laughed mirthlessly as he thought of his errand, for he was going to Hellas, to the shrine of the Hellenes.

It was a woman's doing, like most crazy enterprises. Three years ago his wife had laboured hard in childbirth, and had had the whims of labouring women. Up in the keep of Larisa, on the windy hillside, there had been heart-searching and talk about the gods. The little olive-wood Hermes, the very private and particu-

lar god of Atta's folk, was good enough in simple things like a
lambing or a harvest, but he was scarcely fit for heavy tasks.
Atta's wife declared that her lord lacked piety. There were mainland gods who repaid worship, but his scorn of all Hellenes made
him blind to the merits of those potent divinities. At first Atta
resisted. There was Attic blood in his wife, and he strove to argue
with her unorthodox craving. But the woman persisted, and a
Lemnian wife, as she is beyond other wives in virtue and comeli-
ness, excels them in stubbornness of temper. A second time she
was with child, and nothing would content her but that Atta
should make his prayers to the stronger gods. Dodona was far
away, and long ere he reached it his throat would be cut in the
hills. But Delphi was but two days' journey from the Malian
coast, and the god of Delphi, the Far-Darter, had surprising gifts,
if one were to credit travellers' tales. Atta yielded with an ill
grace, and out of his wealth devised an offering to Apollo. So
on this July day he found himself looking across the gulf to
Kallidromos, bound for a Hellenic shrine, but hating all Hellenes
in his soul. A verse of Homer consoled him—the words which
Phocion spoke to Achilles. 'Verily even the gods may be turned,
they whose excellence and honour and strength are greater than
thine; yet even do these men, when they pray, turn from their
purpose with offerings of incense and pleasant vows.' The Far-
Darter must hate the ὕβρις of those Hellenes, and be the more
ready to avenge it since they dared to claim his countenance.
'No race has ownership in the gods,' a Lemnian song-maker had
said when Atta had been questioning the ways of Poseidon.

The following dawn found him coasting past the north end of
Eubœa in the thin fog of a windless summer morn. He steered
by the peak of Othrys and a spur of Œta, as he had learned from
a slave who had travelled the road. Presently he was in the muddy
Malian waters, and the sun was scattering the mist on the landward side. And then he became aware of a greater commotion
than Poseidon's play with the ships off Pelion. A murmur like a
winter's storm came seawards. He lowered the sail, which he had
set to catch a chance breeze, and bade the men rest on their oars.
An earthquake seemed to be tearing at the roots of the hills.

The mist rolled up, and his hawk eyes saw a strange sight. The
water was green and still around him, but shoreward it changed

173

its colour. It was a dirty red, and things bobbed about in it like the Persians in the creek of Sciathos. On the strip of shore, below the sheer wall of Kallidromos, men were fighting—myriads of men, for away towards Locris they stretched in ranks and banners and tents till the eye lost them in the haze. There was no sail on the queer, muddy, red-edged sea; there was no man on the hills: but on that one flat ribbon of sand all the nations of the earth were warring. He remembered about the place: Thermopylæ they called it, the Gate of the Hot Springs. The Hellenes were fighting the Persians in the pass for their fatherland.

Atta was prudent and loved not other men's quarrels. He gave the word to the rowers to row seaward. In twenty strokes they were in the mist again. . . .

Atta was prudent, but he was also stubborn. He spent the day in a creek on the northern shore of the gulf, listening to the weird hum which came over the waters out of the haze. He cursed the delay. Up on Kallidromos would be clear dry air and the path to Delphi among the oak woods. The Hellenes could not be fighting everywhere at once. He might find some spot on the shore, far in their rear, where he could land and gain the hills. There was danger indeed, but once on the ridge he would be safe; and by the time he came back the Great King would have swept the defenders into the sea, and be well on the road for Athens. He asked himself if it were fitting that a Lemnian should be stayed in his holy task by the struggles of Hellene and Barbarian. His thoughts flew to his steading at Larisa, and the dark-eyed wife who was awaiting his home-coming. He could not return without Apollo's favour: his manhood and the memory of his lady's eyes forbade it. So late in the afternoon he pushed off again and steered his galley for the south.

About sunset the mist cleared from the sea; but the dark falls swiftly in the shadow of the high hills, and Atta had no fear. With the night the hum sank to a whisper; it seemed that the invaders were drawing off to camp, for the sound receded to the west. At the last light the Lemnian touched a rock point well to the rear of the defence. He noticed that the spume at the tide's edge was reddish and stuck to his hands like gum. Of a surety much blood was flowing on that coast.

He bade his slaves return to the north shore and lie hidden to await him. When he came back he would light a signal fire on the topmost bluff of Kallidromos. Let them watch for it and come to take him off. Then he seized his bow and quiver, and his short hunting-spear, buckled his cloak about him, saw that the gift to Apollo was safe in the folds of it, and marched sturdily up the hillside.

The moon was in her first quarter, a slim horn which at her rise showed only the faint outline of the hill. Atta plodded steadfastly on, but he found the way hard. This was not like the crisp sea-turf of Lemnos, where among the barrows of the ancient dead sheep and kine could find sweet fodder. Kallidromos ran up as steep as the roof of a barn. Cytisus and thyme and juniper grew rank, but above all the place was strewn with rocks, leg-twisting boulders, and great cliffs where eagles dwelt. Being a seaman, Atta had his bearings. The path to Delphi left the shore road near the Hot Springs, and went south by a rift of the mountain. If he went up the slope in a bee-line he must strike it in time and find better going. Still it was an eerie place to be tramping after dark. The Hellenes had strange gods of the thicket and hillside, and he had no wish to intrude upon their sanctuaries. He told himself that next to the Hellenes he hated this country of theirs, where a man sweltered in hot jungles or tripped among hidden crags. He sighed for the cool beeches below Larisa, where the surf was white as the snows of Samothrace, and the fisher-boys sang round their smoking broth-pots.

Presently he found a path. It was not the mule road, worn by many feet, that he had looked for, but a little track which twined among the boulders. Still it eased his feet, so he cleared the thorns from his sandals, strapped his belt tighter, and stepped out more confidently. Up and up he went, making odd detours among the crags. Once he came to a promontory, and, looking down, saw lights twinkling from the Hot Springs. He had thought the course lay more southerly, but consoled himself by remembering that a mountain path must have many windings. The great matter was that he was ascending, for he knew that he must cross the ridge of Œta before he struck the Locrian glens that led to the Far-Darter's shrine.

At what seemed the summit of the first ridge he halted for breath, and, prone on the thyme, looked back to sea. The Hot

Springs were hidden, but across the gulf a single light shone from the far shore. He guessed that by this time his galley had been beached and his slaves were cooking supper. The thought made him homesick. He had beaten and cursed these slaves of his times without number, but now in this strange land he felt them kinsfolk, men of his own household. Then he told himself he was no better than a woman. Had he not gone sailing to Chalcedon and distant Pontus, many months' journey from home, while this was but a trip of days? In a week he would be welcomed by a smiling wife, with a friendly god behind him.

The track still bore west, though Delphi lay in the south. Moreover, he had come to a broader road running through a little tableland. The highest peaks of Œta were dark against the sky, and around him was a flat glade where oaks whispered in the night breezes. By this time he judged from the stars that midnight had passed, and he began to consider whether, now that he was beyond the fighting, he should not sleep and wait for dawn. He made up his mind to find a shelter, and, in the aimless way of the night traveller, pushed on and on in the quest of it. The truth is his mind was on Lemnos, and a dark-eyed, white-armed dame spinning in the evening by the threshold. His eyes roamed among the oak trees, but vacantly and idly, and many a mossy corner was passed unheeded. He forgot his ill-temper, and hummed cheerfully the song his reapers sang in the barley-fields below his orchard. It was a song of seamen turned husbandmen, for the gods it called on were the gods of the sea. . . .

Suddenly he found himself crouching among the young oaks, peering and listening. There was something coming from the west. It was like the first mutterings of a storm in a narrow harbour, a steady rustling and whispering. It was not wind; he knew winds too well to be deceived. It was the tramp of light-shod feet among the twigs—many feet, for the sound remained steady, while the noise of a few men will rise and fall. They were coming fast and coming silently. The war had reached far up Kallidromos.

Atta had played this game often in the little island wars. Very swiftly he ran back and away from the path up the slope which he knew to be the first ridge of Kallidromos. The army, whatever it might be, was on the Delphian road. Were the Hellenes about to turn the flank of the Great King?

A moment later he laughed at his folly. For the men began to appear, and they were crossing to meet him, coming from the west. Lying close in the brushwood he could see them clearly. It was well he had left the road, for they stuck to it, following every winding—crouching, too, like hunters after deer. The first man he saw was a Hellene, but the ranks behind were no Hellenes. There was no glint of bronze or gleam of fair skin. They were dark, long-haired fellows, with spears like his own, and round Eastern caps, and egg-shaped bucklers. Then Atta rejoiced. It was the Great King who was turning the flank of the Hellenes. They guarded the gate, the fools, while the enemy slipped through the roof.

He did not rejoice long. The van of the army was narrow and kept to the path, but the men behind were straggling all over the hillside. Another minute and he would be discovered. The thought was cheerless. It was true that he was an islander and friendly to the Persian, but up on the heights who would listen to his tale? He would be taken for a spy, and one of those thirsty spears would drink his blood. It must be farewell to Delphi for the moment, he thought, or farewell to Lemnos for ever. Crouching low, he ran back and away from the path to the crest of the sea-ridge of Kallidromos.

The men came no nearer him. They were keeping roughly to the line of the path, and drifted through the oak wood before him, an army without end. He had scarcely thought there were so many fighting men in the world. He resolved to lie there on the crest, in the hope that ere the first light they would be gone. Then he would push on to Delphi, leaving them to settle their quarrels behind him. These were the hard times for a pious pilgrim.

But another noise caught his ear from the right. The army had flanking squadrons, and men were coming along the ridge. Very bitter anger rose in Atta's heart. He had cursed the Hellenes, and now he cursed the Barbarians no less. Nay, he cursed all war, that spoiled the errands of peaceful folk. And then, seeking safety, he dropped over the crest on to the steep shoreward face of the mountain.

In an instant his breath had gone from him. He slid down a long slope of screes, and then with a gasp found himself falling sheer into space. Another second and he was caught in a tangle of bush, and then dropped once more upon screes, where he clutched desperately for handhold. Breathless and bleeding he came to anchor on a shelf of greensward and found himself blinking up at the crest which seemed to tower a thousand feet above. There were men on the crest now. He heard them speak and felt that they were looking down.

The shock kept him still till the men had passed. Then the terror of the place gripped him, and he tried feverishly to retrace his steps. A dweller all his days among gentle downs, he grew dizzy with the sense of being hung in space. But the only fruit of his efforts was to set him slipping again. This time he pulled up at a root of gnarled oak which overhung the sheerest cliff on Kallidromos. The danger brought his wits back. He sullenly reviewed his case, and found it desperate.

He could not go back, and, even if he did, he would meet the Persians. If he went on he would break his neck, or at the best fall into the Hellenes' hands. Oddly enough he feared his old enemies less than his friends. He did not think that the Hellenes would butcher him. Again, he might sit perched in his eyrie till they settled their quarrel, or he fell off. He rejected this last way. Fall off he should for certain, unless he kept moving. Already he was retching with the vertigo of the heights. It was growing lighter. Suddenly he was looking not into a black world, but to a pearl-grey floor far beneath him. It was the sea, the thing he knew and loved. The sight screwed up his courage. He remembered that he was a Lemnian and a seafarer. He would be conquered neither by rock, nor by Hellene, nor by the Great King. Least of all by the last, who was a barbarian. Slowly, with clenched teeth and narrowed eyes, he began to clamber down a ridge which flanked the great cliff of Kallidromos. His plan was to reach the shore and take the road to the east before the Persians completed their circuit. Some instinct told him that a great army would not take the track he had mounted by. There must be some longer and easier way debouching farther down the coast. He might yet have the good luck to slip between them and the sea.

The two hours which followed tried his courage hard. Thrice he fell, and only a juniper root stood between him and death. His hands grew ragged, and his nails were worn to the quick. He had long ago lost his weapons; his cloak was in shreds, all save the breast-fold which held the gift to Apollo. The heavens brightened, but he dared not look around. He knew he was traversing awesome places, where a goat could scarcely tread. Many times he gave up hope of life. His head was swimming, and he was so deadly sick that often he had to lie gasping on some shoulder of rock less steep than the rest. But his anger kept him to his purpose. He was filled with fury at the Hellenes. It was they and their folly that had brought him these mischances. Some day . . .

He found himself sitting blinking on the shore of the sea. A furlong off the water was lapping on the reefs. A man, larger than human in the morning mist, was standing above him.

'Greeting, stranger,' said the voice. 'By Hermes, you choose the difficult roads to travel.'

Atta felt for broken bones, and, reassured, struggled to his feet.

'God's curse upon all mountains,' he said. He staggered to the edge of the tide and laved his brow. The savour of salt revived him. He turned to find the tall man at his elbow, and noted how worn and ragged he was, and yet how upright.

'When a pigeon is flushed from the rocks there is a hawk near,' said the voice.

Atta was angry. 'A hawk!' he cried. 'Nay, an army of eagles. There will be some rare flushing of Hellenes before evening.'

'What frightened you, Islander?' the stranger asked. 'Did a wolf bark up on the hillside?'

'Ay, a wolf. The wolf from the East with a multitude of wolflings. There will be fine eating soon in the pass.'

The man's face grew dark. He put his hand to his mouth and called. Half a dozen sentries ran to join him. He spoke to them in the harsh Lacedæmonian speech which made Atta sick to hear. They talked with the back of the throat, and there was not an 's' in their words.

'There is mischief in the hills,' the first man said. 'This islander has been frightened down over the rocks. The Persian is stealing a march on us.'

The sentries laughed. One quoted a proverb about island courage. Atta's wrath flared and he forgot himself. He had no wish to
warn the Hellenes, but it irked his pride to be thought a liar. He
began to tell his story hastily, angrily, confusedly; and the men
still laughed.

Then he turned eastward and saw the proof before him. The
light had grown and the sun was coming up over Pelion. The
first beam fell on the eastern ridge of Kallidromos, and there,
clear on the sky-line, was the proof. The Persian was making a
wide circuit, but moving shoreward. In a little he would be at
the coast, and by noon at the Hellenes' rear.

His hearers doubted no more. Atta was hurried forward through
the lines of the Greeks to the narrow throat of the pass, where
behind a rough rampart of stones lay the Lacedæmonian headquarters. He was still giddy from the heights, and it was in a
giddy dream that he traversed the misty shingles of the beach
amid ranks of sleeping warriors. It was a grim place, for there
were dead and dying in it, and blood on every stone. But in the
lee of the wall little fires were burning and slaves were cooking
breakfast. The smell of roasting flesh came pleasantly to his
nostrils, and he remembered that he had had no meal since he
crossed the gulf.

Then he found himself the centre of a group who had the air of
kings. They looked as if they had been years in war. Never had
he seen faces so worn and so terribly scarred. The hollows in their
cheeks gave them the air of smiling, and yet they were grave. Their
scarlet vests were torn and muddied, and the armour which lay
near was dinted like the scrap iron before a smithy door. But what
caught his attention were the eyes of the men. They glittered as
no eyes he had ever seen before glittered. The sight cleared his
bewilderment and took the pride out of his heart. He could not
pretend to despise a folk who looked like Ares fresh from the wars
of the Immortals.

They spoke among themselves in quiet voices. Scouts came and
went, and once or twice one of the men, taller than the rest, asked
Atta a question. The Lemnian sat in the heart of the group,
sniffing the smell of cooking, and looking at the rents in his cloak
and the long scratches on his legs. Something was pressing on
his breast, and he found that it was Apollo's gift. He had forgotten

all about it. Delphi seemed beyond the moon, and his errand a child's dream.

Then the King, for so he thought of the tall man, spoke—

'You have done us a service, Islander. The Persian is at our back and front, and there will be no escape for those who stay. Our allies are going home, for they do not share our vows. We of Lacedæmon wait in the pass. If you go with the men of Corinth you will find a place of safety before noon. No doubt in the Euripus, there is some boat to take you to your own land.'

He spoke courteously, not in the rude Athenian way; and somehow the quietness of his voice and his glittering eyes roused wild longings in Atta's heart. His island pride was face to face with a greater—greater than he had ever dreamed of.

'Bid yon cooks give me some broth,' he said gruffly. 'I am faint. After I have eaten I will speak with you.'

He was given food, and as he ate he thought. He was on trial before these men of Lacedæmon. More, the old faith of the islands, the pride of the first masters, was at stake in his hands. He had boasted that he and his kind were the last of the men; now these Hellenes of Lacedæmon were preparing a great deed, and they deemed him unworthy to share in it. They offered him safety. Could he brook the insult? He had forgotten that the cause of the Persian was his; that the Hellenes were the foes of his race. He saw only that the last test of manhood was preparing, and the manhood in him rose to greet the trial. An odd wild ecstasy surged in his veins. It was not the lust of battle, for he had no love of slaying, or hate of the Persian, for he was his friend. It was the joy of proving that the Lemnian stock had a starker pride than these men of Lacedæmon. They would die for their fatherland, and their vows; but he, for a whim, a scruple, a delicacy of honour. His mind was so clear that no other course occurred to him. There was only one way for a man. He, too, would be dying for his fatherland, for through him the island race would be ennobled in the eyes of gods and men.

Troops were filing fast to the east—Thebans, Corinthians.

'Time flies, Islander,' said the King's voice. 'The hours of safety are slipping past.'

Atta looked up carelessly. 'I will stay,' he said. 'God's curse on all Hellenes! Little I care for your quarrels. It is nothing to me if your Hellas is under the heel of the East. But I care much for brave men. It shall never be said that a man of Lemnos, a son of the old race, fell back when Death threatened. I stay with you, men of Lacedæmon.'

The King's eyes glittered; they seemed to peer into his heart. 'It appears they breed men in the islands,' he said. 'But you err. Death does not threaten. Death awaits us.'

'It is all one,' said Atta. 'But I crave a boon. Let me fight my last fight by your side. I am of older stock than you, and a king in my own country. I would strike my last blow among kings.'

There was an hour of respite before battle was joined, and Atta spent it by the edge of the sea. He had been given arms, and in girding himself for the fight he had found Apollo's offering in his breastfold. He was done with the gods of the Hellenes. His offering should go to the gods of his own people. So, calling upon Poseidon, he flung the little gold cup far out to sea. It flashed in the sunlight, and then sank in the soft green tides so noiselessly that it seemed as if the hand of the Sea-god had been stretched to take it. 'Hail, Poseidon!' the Lemnian cried. 'I am bound this day for the Ferryman. To you only I make prayer, and to the little Hermes of Larisa. Be kind to my kin when they travel the sea, and keep them islanders and seafarers for ever. Hail and farewell, God of my own folk!'

Then, while the little waves lapped on the white sand, Atta made a song. He was thinking of the homestead far up in the green downs, looking over to the snows of Samothrace. At this hour in the morning there would be a tinkle of sheep-bells as the flocks went down to the low pastures. Cool wind would be blowing, and the noise of the surf below the cliffs would come faint to the ear. In the hall the maids would be spinning, while their dark-haired mistress would be casting swift glances to the doorway, lest it might be filled any moment by the form of her returning lord. Outside in the chequered sunlight of the orchard the child would be playing with his nurse, crooning in childish syllables the chanty his father had taught him And at the thought of his home a great passion welled up in Atta's heart. It was not regret, but joy and pride and aching love. In his antique island creed the death he was awaiting was not other than a bridal. He was dying for the things he loved, and by his death they would be blessed eternally. He would not have long to wait before bright eyes came to greet him in the House of Shadows.

So Atta made the Song of Atta, and sang it then, and later in the press of battle. It was a simple song, like the lays of seafarers. It put into rough verse the thought which cheers the heart of all adventurers—nay which makes adventure possible for those who have much to leave. It spoke of the shining pathway of the sea which is the Great Uniter. A man may lie dead in Pontus or beyond the Pillars of Herakles, but if he dies on the shore there is nothing between him and his fatherland. It spoke of a battle all the long dark night in a strange place—a place of marshes and black cliffs and shadowy terrors.

'*In the dawn the sweet light comes,*' said the song, '*and the salt winds and the tides will bear me home. . . .*'

When in the evening the Persians took toll of the dead, they found one man who puzzled them. He lay among the tall Lacedæmonians, on the very lip of the sea, and around him were swathes of their countrymen. It looked as if he had been fighting his way to the water, and had been overtaken by death as his feet reached the edge. Nowhere in the pass did the dead lie so thick, and yet he was no Hellene. He was torn like a deer that the dogs have worried, but the little left of his garments and his features spoke of Eastern race. The survivors could tell nothing except that he had fought like a god and had been singing all the while.

The matter came to the ear of the Great King, who was sore enough at the issue of the day. That one of his men had performed feats of valour beyond the Hellenes was a pleasant tale to tell. And so his captains reported it. Accordingly when the fleet from Artemision arrived next morning, and all but a few score Persians were shovelled into holes, that the Hellenes might seem to have been conquered by a lesser force, Atta's body was laid out with pomp in the midst of the Lacedæmonians. And the seamen rubbed their eyes and thanked their strange gods that one man of the East had been found to match those terrible warriors whose name was a nightmare. Further, the Great King gave orders that the body of Atta should be embalmed and carried with the army,

So Atta made the Song of Atta, and sang it then and later in the press of battle

and that his name and kin should be sought out and duly honoured. This latter was a task too hard for the staff, and no more was heard of it till months later, when the King, in full flight after Salamis, bethought him of the one man who had not played him false. Finding that his lieutenants had nothing to tell him, he eased five of them of their heads.

As it happened, the deed was not quite forgotten. An islander, a Lesbian and a cautious man, had fought at Thermopylæ in the Persian ranks, and had heard Atta's singing and seen how he fell. Long afterwards some errand took this man to Lemnos, and in the evening, speaking with the Elders, he told his tale and repeated something of the song. There was that in the words which gave the Lemnians a clue, the mention, I think, of the olive-wood Hermes and the snows of Samothrace. So Atta came to great honour among his own people, and his memory and his words were handed down to the generations. The song became a favourite island lay, and for centuries throughout the Ægean seafaring men sang it when they turned their prows to wild seas. Nay, it travelled farther, for you will find part of it stolen by Euripides and put in a chorus of the *Andromache*. There are echoes of it in some of the epigrams of the *Anthology*; and, though the old days have gone, the simple fisher-folk still sing snatches in their barbarous dialect. The Klephts used to make a catch of it at night round their fires in the hills, and only the other day I met a man in Scyros who had collected a dozen variants, and was publishing them in a dull book on island folklore.

In the centuries which followed the great fight, the sea fell away from the roots of the cliffs and left a mile of marshland. About fifty years ago a peasant, digging in a rice-field, found the cup which Atta had given to Poseidon. There was much talk about the discovery, and scholars debated hotly about its origin. Today it is in the Berlin Museum, and according to the new fashion in archæology it is labelled 'Minoan', and kept in the Cretan Section. But any one who looks carefully will see behind the rim a neat little carving of a dolphin; and I happen to know that that was the private badge of Atta's house.

1910

ATTA'S SONG

(Roughly translated)

I will sing of thee,
Great Sea-Mother,
Whose white arms gather
Thy sons in the ending:
And draw them homeward
From far sad marches——
Wild lands in the sunset,
Bitter shores of the morning——
Soothe them and guide them
By shining pathways
Homeward to thee.

All day I have striven in dark glens
With parched throat and dim eyes,
Where the red crags choke the stream
And dank thickets hide the spear.
I have spilled the blood of my foes,
But their wolves have torn my flanks.
I am faint, O Mother,
Faint and aweary.
I have longed for thy cool winds
And thy kind grey eyes
And thy lover's arms.

The Lemnian

At the even I came
To a land of terrors,
Of hot swamps where the feet mired
And streams that flowered red with blood.
There I strove with thousands,
Wild-eyed and lost,
As a lion among serpents.
——But sudden before me
I saw the flash
Of the sweet wide waters
That wash my homeland
And mirror the stars of home.
Then sang I for joy,
For I knew the Preserver,
Thee, the Uniter,
The great Sea-Mother.
Soon will the sweet light come,
And the salt winds and the tides
Will bear me home.

Far in the sunrise,
Nestled in thy bosom,
Lies my own green isle.
Thither wilt thou bear me
To where, above the sea-cliffs,
Stretch mild meadows, flower-decked, thyme-scented,
Crisp with sea breezes.
There my flocks feed
On sunny uplands,
Looking over the waters
To where the mount Saos
Raises pure snows to God.

Hermes, guide of souls,
I made thee a shrine in my orchard,
And round thy olive-wood limbs
The maidens twined Spring blossoms——
Violet and helichryse

And the pale wind flowers.
Keep thou watch for me,
For I am coming
Tell to my lady
And to all my kinsfolk
That I who have gone from them
Tarry not long, but come swift o'er the sea-path.
My feet light with joy,
My eyes bright with longing.
For little it matters
Where a man may fall,
If he fall by the sea-shore;
The kind waters await him,
The white arms are around him,
And the wise Mother of Men
Will carry him home.

I who sing
Wait joyfully on the morning.
Ten thousand beset me
And their spears ache for my heart.
They will crush me and grind me to mire,
So that none will know the man that once was me.
But at the first light I shall be gone,
Singing, flitting, o'er the grey waters,
Outward, homeward,
To thee, the Preserver,
Thee, the Uniter,
Mother the Sea.

1910

Titles in this Series of Illustrated Classics

CHILDREN'S ILLUSTRATED CLASSICS

(Illustrated Classics for Older Readers are listed on fourth page)

R. M. Ballantyne's THE DOG CRUSOE. Illustrated by VICTOR AMBRUS.

E. Nesbit's THE ENCHANTED CASTLE. Illustrated by CECIL LESLIE.

FAIRY TALES FROM THE ARABIAN NIGHTS. Illustrated by KIDDELL-MONROE.

FAIRY TALES OF LONG AGO. Edited by M. C. CAREY. Illustrated by D. J. WATKINS-PITCHFORD.

Louisa M. Alcott's GOOD WIVES. Illustrated by S. VAN ABBÉ.

Frances Browne's GRANNY'S WONDERFUL CHAIR. Illustrated by D. J. WATKINS-PITCHFORD.

GRIMMS' FAIRY TALES. Illustrated by CHARLES FOLKARD.

HANS ANDERSEN'S FAIRY TALES. Illustrated by HANS BAUMHAUER.

Mary Mapes Dodge's HANS BRINKER. Illustrated by HANS BAUMHAUER.

Oscar Wilde's THE HAPPY PRINCE AND OTHER STORIES. Illustrated by PEGGY FORTNUM.

Johanna Spyri's HEIDI. Illustrated by VINCENT O. COHEN.

Charles Kingsley's THE HEROES. Illustrated by KIDDELL-MONROE.

Edith Nesbit's THE HOUSE OF ARDEN. Illustrated by CLARKE HUTTON.

Mark Twain's HUCKLEBERRY FINN

TOM SAWYER
Both illustrated by C. WALTER HODGES.

Louisa M. Alcott's JO'S BOYS. Illustrated by HARRY TOOTHILL.

A. M. Hadfield's KING ARTHUR AND THE ROUND TABLE. Illustrated by DONALD SETON CAMMELL.

Charlotte M. Yonge's THE LITTLE DUKE. Illustrated by MICHAEL GODFREY.

Frances Hodgson Burnett's LITTLE LORD FAUNTLEROY.

Louisa M. Alcott's LITTLE MEN. Illustrated by HARRY TOOTHILL.

LITTLE WOMEN. Illustrated by S. VAN ABBÉ.

Mrs Ewing's LOB LIE-BY-THE-FIRE and THE STORY OF A SHORT LIFE. Illustrated by RANDOLPH CALDECOTT ('Lob') and H. M. BROCK ('Short Life').

MODERN FAIRY STORIES. Edited by ROGER LANCELYN GREEN. Illustrated by E. H. SHEPARD.

Jean Ingelow's **MOPSA THE FAIRY**. Illustrated by DORA CURTIS.

NURSERY RHYMES. Collected and illustrated in two-colour line by A. H. WATSON.

Carlo Collodi's **PINOCCHIO. The Story of a Puppet.** Illustrated by CHARLES FOLKARD.

Mark Twain's **THE PRINCE AND THE PAUPER.** Illustrated by ROBERT HODGSON.

Andrew Lang's **PRINCE PRIGIO and PRINCE RICARDO.** Illustrated by D. J. WATKINS-PITCHFORD.

George MacDonald's **THE LOST PRINCESS**

THE PRINCESS AND CURDIE

THE PRINCESS AND THE GOBLIN

The first two volumes illustrated by CHARLES FOLKARD, the third by D. J. WATKINS-PITCHFORD.

Stephen Crane's **THE RED BADGE OF COURAGE.** Illustrated by CHARLES MOZLEY.

Carola Oman's **ROBIN HOOD.** Illustrated by S. VAN ABBÉ.

W. M. Thackeray's **THE ROSE AND THE RING** and Charles Dickens's **THE MAGIC FISH-BONE.**

Two children's stories, the first containing the author's illustrations, the latter containing PAUL HOGARTH'S work.

H. W. Longfellow's **THE SONG OF HIAWATHA** Illustrated by KIDDELL-MONROE.

J. R. Wyss's **THE SWISS FAMILY ROBINSON.** Illustrated by CHARLES FOLKARD.

Charles and Mary Lamb's **TALES FROM SHAKESPEARE.** Illustrated by ARTHUR RACKHAM.

TALES OF MAKE-BELIEVE. Edited by ROGER LANCELYN GREEN. Illustrated by HARRY TOOTHILL.

Charles Dickens, Rudyard Kipling, E. Nesbit, Thomas Hardy, E. V. Lucas, etc.

Nathaniel Hawthorne's **TANGLEWOOD TALES.** Illustrated by S. VAN ABBÉ.

Thomas Hughes's **TOM BROWN'S SCHOOLDAYS.** Illustrated by S. VAN ABBÉ.

Charles Kingsley's **THE WATER-BABIES.** Illustrated by ROSALIE K. FRY.

Susan Coolidge's **WHAT KATY DID.** Illustrated by MARGERY GILL.

Nathaniel Hawthorne's **A WONDER BOOK.** Illustrated by S. VAN ABBÉ.

Selma Lagerlöf's **THE WONDERFUL ADVENTURES OF NILS**

THE FURTHER ADVENTURES OF NILS

Both illustrated by HANS BAUMHAUER.

Illustrated Classics for Older Readers

Jack London's **THE CALL OF THE WILD.** Illustrated by CHARLES PICKARD.

Cervantes's **DON QUIXOTE.** (Edited) Illustrated by W. HEATH ROBINSON.

Jonathan Swift's **GULLIVER'S TRAVELS.** (Edited) Illustrated by ARTHUR RACKHAM.

Robert Louis Stevenson's **KIDNAPPED.** Illustrated by G. OAKLEY.

H. Rider Haggard **KING SOLOMON'S MINES.** Illustrated by A. R. WHITEAR.

R. D. Blackmore's **LORNA DOONE.** Illustrated by LIONEL EDWARDS.

Frank L. Baum's **THE MARVELLOUS LAND OF OZ**

> **THE WONDERFUL WIZARD OF OZ**
Both illustrated by B. S. BIRO.

John Bunyan's **THE PILGRIM'S PROGRESS.** Illustrated by FRANK C. PAPÉ.

Anthony Hope's **THE PRISONER OF ZENDA.** Illustrated by MICHAEL GODFREY.

Erskine Childers's **THE RIDDLE OF THE SANDS.** Illustrated by CHARLES MOZLEY.

Daniel Defoe's **ROBINSON CRUSOE.** (Edited) Illustrated by J. AYTON SYMINGTON.

Anthony Hope's **RUPERT OF HENTZAU.** Illustrated by MICHAEL GODFREY.

TEN TALES OF DETECTION. Edited by ROGER LANCELYN GREEN. Illustrated by IAN RIBBONS.

Roger Lancelyn Green's **THE TALE OF ANCIENT ISRAEL.** Illustrated by CHARLES KEEPING.

THIRTEEN UNCANNY TALES. Illustrated by RAY OGDEN.
F. Anstey, M. R. James, Sir Arthur Conan Doyle, H. G. Wells and others.

John Buchan **THE THIRTY-NINE STEPS.** Illustrated by EDWARD ARDIZZONE.

Ernest Thompson Seton's **THE TRAIL OF THE SANDHILL STAG** and Other Lives of the Hunted. Illustrated with drawings by the author and coloured frontispiece by RITA PARSONS.

Robert Louis Stevenson's **TREASURE ISLAND.** Illustrated by S. VAN ABBÉ.

Jules Verne's **AROUND THE MOON**

> **AROUND THE WORLD IN EIGHTY DAYS**

> **FROM THE EARTH TO THE MOON**

> **JOURNEY TO THE CENTRE OF THE EARTH**
All illustrated by W. F. PHILLIPPS.

> **TWENTY THOUSAND LEAGUES UNDER THE SEA**
Illustrated by WILLIAM MCLAREN.

Jack London's **WHITE FANG.** Illustrated by CHARLES PICKARD.

Further volumes in preparation